THE SEARCH FOR
JUDD McCARTHY

DENNIS M. CLAUSEN

BROWN POSEY PRESS

an imprint of Sunbury Press, Inc.
Mechanicsburg, PA USA

an imprint of Sunbury Press, Inc.
Mechanicsburg, PA USA

For information about special discounts for bulk purchases, please contact Sunbury Press Orders Dept. at (855) 338-8359 or orders@sunburypress.com.

To request one of our authors for speaking engagements or book signings, please contact Sunbury Press Publicity Dept. at publicity@sunburypress.com.

ISBN: 978-1-62006-757-4 (Trade paperback)

Library of Congress Control Number: 2018942416

FIRST BROWN POSEY PRESS EDITION: May 2018

Product of the United States of America
0 1 1 2 3 5 8 13 21 34 55

Set in Bookman Old Style
Designed by Crystal Devine
Cover by Lawrence Knorr
Edited by Lawrence Knorr

Continue the Enlightenment!

PREFACE

The human spirit, confined for any period of time, grows inwards in strength. Like the river diverted from its natural course, it will overflow all boundaries. For the river's relentless, unyielding search for the sea is eternal. The things that are meant to be—will be . . .

CHAPTER ONE

October 1926

Judd McCarthy tugged at the straps of the canvas bag he carried across his shoulders and looked down at his dirty leather shoes as they crunched through the gravel and small rocks on the railroad embankment. A leather holster and a large hunting knife were strapped around his waist, and the brim of a floppy black hat tilted awkwardly over his forehead. His right hand moved back and forth between the straps of the canvas bag and the .45-caliber Smith & Wesson revolver that protruded from the holster. His eyes constantly scanned the surrounding terrain, searching for any movement in the brush and clumps of trees on both sides of the railroad tracks.

Earlier in the day, he had been sent to Carson to bring the Hanley Brothers Construction Company payroll back to Danvers. He was now within a few miles of the construction camp, but the sun was bending into the western horizon, and he knew if an attempt were to be made on his life, it would probably be at dusk in the marsh he would soon enter.

It had occurred to McCarthy that there was something strange in Fred Hanley's decision to send him for the company payroll on a day when the trains were not running. Normally two or three heavily armed men went to Carson to accompany the payroll back by railroad car.

"The men are getting nervous about not being paid," Fred Hanley had said. "We can't wait for a day when the trains be runnin'. Besides, Mac, with your reputation, no one'll mess with ya."

Judd McCarthy had the reputation of being one of the most violent men in Carver County, a reputation he had earned in numerous bar fights and wrestling matches during his two years as a laborer for the Hanley Brothers.

He was a huge man, well over six feet tall, and his wide, muscular shoulders easily bore the weight of the canvas payroll bag.

His large hands were callused from years of hard labor in heavy construction projects. Only his eyes betrayed a gentleness and sensitivity that contradicted his otherwise menacing appearance. There was a twinkle of life and good humor in his brown eyes, even as they moved apprehensively over the terrain.

Signs of Indian summer were all around him. The stubble of recently harvested wheat fields poked out of the parched earth. Dead leaves, propelled by steady autumn breezes, skipped across newly plowed fields. Hen pheasants clucked in the nearby brush, while an occasional rooster pheasant emitted a shrill mating call that echoed across the desolate Midwestern landscape. In sloughs and ponds, muskrats busily stockpiled reeds and fallen branches, and overhead a V-shaped formation of Canadian geese flew gracefully south.

McCarthy paused briefly to watch the geese as the formation slowly opened and closed high overhead. Their loud honking also echoed across the prairie.

"Damn, if me soul don't feel like going south like that," McCarthy blurted out in a thick Irish accent. "But Kate said it's time to do somethin' else with me life. An' she's right."

The thought of Kate reminded him of the present he had brought back from Carson, and he reached into the front pocket of his canvas overalls and pulled out a gold locket. The tiny piece of jewelry almost disappeared in his huge palm.

As he admired the locket, he remembered the wrestling match in Carson. While he was waiting for the payroll to arrive, Farmer Tobin had challenged him to a wrestling match, winner take all. Tobin was the strongest man in Carver County, stronger and bigger even than McCarthy. But McCarthy had managed to avoid Tobin's hammerlock long enough to wear him out. When it was over, Tobin was flat on his back, exhausted and unable to move.

"Ah, Tobin," McCarthy laughed to himself as he admired the locket. "Ya ugly Norwegian. Ya jus' ain't no match for an Irishman, lad. But I thank ya for the money to buy a locket for me Lady Kate." The thought of Kate brought the gentleness back into McCarthy's brown eyes. "I made a promise to ya, Kate, an' I mean to keep it. Above all else, Judd McCarthy means ta keep that promise. I loves ya, lass, more'n anything else in the world."

He carefully placed the locket back into his pants pocket, and again his dirty leather shoes crunched through the gravel and small rocks. Just ahead of him was the last marsh he would have to pass through before reaching the wheat fields just outside of Danvers. He was almost home. He knew that Kate was waiting for him farther south, by the banks of the Little Sioux River, but first he would have to leave the payroll with the company paymaster and collect his wages. Then he was free.

"Got a locket for me darlin', for me darlin' Lady Kate." He sang the chorus of an old Irish folk ballad and then stopped singing as he entered the fringes of the marsh. The railroad company had been negligent in caring for the Little Sioux line, and the weeds and brush grew almost to the edge of the trestles. McCarthy proceeded cautiously, his hand never more than a few inches from the revolver.

Suddenly there was a movement in the brush near the embankment. McCarthy came to an abrupt halt, his right hand drawing the revolver out of the leather holster.

"Who be it there?" he yelled into the reeds and brush. "If ya be waitin' for me, ya best come out or get yur head blown off."

The dried reeds swayed slowly on the fringe of the marsh, but there was no response to McCarthy's challenge. Slowly he knelt on the edge of the railroad embankment, his eyes never leaving the brush where he had spotted the movement. He picked up a large rock and stood back up to his full height.

"I be warnin' ya! If ya don't come out, ya'll be a mighty sore lad!" he yelled into the marsh.

Still there was no response. McCarthy fired the rock into the brush, and a shrill screech pierced the autumn air. There was a brief flurry of movement where the rock had entered the brush. Then there was stillness and silence.

McCarthy crept to the edge of the marsh and slowly, cautiously parted the reeds. In the middle of the dried vegetation, a rooster pheasant lay prone on the ground, its neck broken from the impact of the rock. The pheasant's eyes blinked twice, then remained open.

"Ah, no, me beauty. I only meant ta scare ya, not ta kill ya." McCarthy placed the revolver on the ground and gently stroked the beautiful red and brown feathers of the rooster pheasant. Beneath his hand, he felt a convulsive movement in the animal's chest.

"I only meant ta scare ya, lad," McCarthy repeated softly and sadly as he felt the bird stiffen and die beneath the stroke of his hand.

A few yards away, in the waters of the marsh, the early evening crickets began to chirp, and a frog leaped off a fallen log and splashed into the shallow slough.

McCarthy listened to these sounds as he stroked the dead body of the rooster pheasant. Then he dug a hole in the black soil with his hunting knife and placed the bird in it. He piled dirt and weeds over the pheasant, picked up the revolver and canvas bag, and walked back to the embankment.

The sun was dipping into the western horizon when McCarthy stepped out of the marsh and entered the wheat fields a few miles outside of Danvers. He paused briefly to watch the sun cast its shadows across the stubble of the wheat fields. In the distance, the Little Sioux River was curling south across the prairie. He remembered that Kate was waiting for him down by the river, as they had planned, and he walked faster in the direction of Danvers.

Suddenly he saw something in the shadows of a small clump of trees a few hundred feet to the east of the railroad embankment. As he looked in that direction, a gust of wind caused the dead autumn leaves to wave wildly in the thicket and tumble out into the prairie.

McCarthy reached instinctively for the revolver. He realized something was hiding in the shadows of the trees. As he drew the revolver out of the holster and pointed it at the clump of trees, a human figure stepped out of the shadows and waved to him. McCarthy recognized who it was immediately, and he placed the pistol back in the holster.

He walked down the railroad embankment, entered the wheat field, and approached the figure . . .

But it did not end there. It was days later, maybe weeks. Maybe even months. It did not matter. Surrounded by the impenetrable darkness, time ceased to exist. Except as measured by his failing strength, his dying will.

At first he lashed out frantically, until the blade of the hunting knife shattered. When that failed, he fired the revolver into the darkness. He watched the orange flames spit out of the barrel as the muffled gunshots echoed harmlessly all around him. Still it did not end.

And each time he fell, the rats would scurry over to sniff at his mildewed clothing. Bolder they became with the passage of time, until he would lash out with the butt end of the knife, sending them scurrying away. But always they came back. And he grew weaker.

Sometime, near the end, he heard the scream. Loud and shrill, it echoed in the darkness. First in anger, then in agony. Growing weaker as his strength deserted him. When it too failed, he again heard the rats' tiny feet moving ceaselessly, relentlessly.

When the end came, he was lying face down. The rats sensed that he had lost his will to fight. He heard them padding softly across the ground to where he lay. They sniffed at his clothing and brushed against his cheek. Then a sharp pain tore through his arm like a thousand needles penetrating his flesh. But he was too weak to care. He lay there, enduring the pain until it turned into a moist numbness.

As the life poured out of his body, he was filled with rage at the horror of how he had been duped. And even as he yielded to the darkness, his soul held firm against the night and refused to accept what had been left undone.

It was then that he thought of the locket. He reached for his pocket to see if it was still there. But the numbness had spread over his entire body, and his arm would not move . . .

When Judd McCarthy failed to return to Danvers with the payroll, the Hanley Brothers sent a search team out after him. At first they assumed McCarthy was the victim of foul play, but when no body was found alongside the Little Sioux Railroad, they concluded he had fled into the Dakotas with the money. A reward of five thousand dollars was posted, and McCarthy became a wanted man.

To the men who worked for Fred Hanley, McCarthy's disappearance was not exactly unexpected. He was a drifter, a man who lived for the moment, and it was not surprising that he would seize an opportunity to become wealthy beyond their wildest dreams. The men on the construction crew cursed him because his disappearance with the company payroll meant they would not be paid for three months of work. But they also felt that Fred Hanley should have known better than to send a man with McCarthy's reputation to pick up the payroll.

Within weeks after McCarthy's disappearance, the Hanley Brothers Construction Company abandoned the Little Sioux Water Reclamation Project. Fred Hanley moved to the East Coast, where he retired and lived until his death in 1936. Ben Hanley disappeared somewhere in Florida. Some of the construction workers stayed in the area for weeks after the company folded, hoping that McCarthy might yet return with the long overdue payroll. Then they too drifted away.

The Little Sioux Railroad that connected Danvers and Carson was abandoned in 1927. As the seasons changed and the years passed, the vegetation crept steadily toward the tracks, completely burying them.

For thirty-three years the seasons passed with monotonous regularity. In winter the prairie was buried beneath the glistening snow. In spring the waters of the Little Sioux River would break free from the ice-covered lakes farther north and drift slowly south toward the Mississippi River and the Great Sea beyond. In summer the tiny heads of grain would dance playfully above the wheat fields that now grew almost to the very edge of the abandoned railroad. In late fall, Indian summer would settle over the marshes and newly harvested fields of wheat and corn, and the Canadian geese would fly high overhead in V-formation on their annual pilgrimages south.

The Great Depression wiped out most of the farmers along the Little Sioux River, forcing entire families to abandon their farms to follow their shattered dreams west to California and Oregon. World War II and the Korean War came and went. By October of 1959, so much history had passed through Carver County that the name Judd McCarthy was buried in the memories of all but a few of the oldtimers. Like the thousands upon thousands of itinerant laborers who had passed through the Midwest in the 1920s and 1930s, McCarthy and his mysterious disappearance became a forgotten issue, another of the eternal secrets buried beneath the prairie soil. Certainly his life carried no special significance for most of those who continued to live in Carver County into the middle of the twentieth century.

But Judd McCarthy had made a promise in October of 1926 before he journeyed from Danvers to Carson. And, more than anything else, he meant to keep that promise.

CHAPTER TWO

October 1959

When Joel Hampton awoke, his body was drenched in a feverish sweat, and his wife, looking puzzled and frightened, was staring down at him. She was shaking him by his shoulder.

"Huh?" he managed to whisper through dried lips. His eyelids were heavy. They opened, then slowly closed again.

"Joel, wake up!" Susan insisted. She seemed to be calling to him from far away, pulling him out of the darkness. "You're having that nightmare again."

"Nightmare?" He only faintly recognized the word.

"You're talking in your sleep."

Slowly he pushed himself up to a sitting position. His eyelids blinked twice, then remained open. He was beginning to remember.

"Did I do it again?"

"Yes, Joel. God, you scared me half to death," Susan said, the concern evident in her voice.

He knew then why she was afraid. He had been having the same nightmare ever since he was a boy. It had gone away while he was in high school and college, but as soon as he became a junior partner in the law firm, it came back.

It was always the same. He was walking alone, somewhere out in the country. It was autumn and colorful leaves waved in the wind and blew out into the empty fields. He was happy, but also apprehensive about something. Something that was lurking in the shadows of a cluster of trees. He took a step into an empty wheat field and was suddenly surrounded by darkness. There were strange and threatening noises that he did not understand. Then he felt pain and fear, and he heard the scream as his body grew numb. The scream grew louder and louder and . . .

As a boy he would awaken to look up into the eyes of his mother. She would be staring down at him, struggling to help him wake up. Now it was his wife who had pulled him out of the darkness.

"I'm sorry," he said gently as he looked into his wife's dark eyes. "What did I say?"

"Nothing I could understand. Then you just started to sweat and scream. Joel . . ." Susan paused to sit up on the edge of the bed.

"Yes, honey?"

"You've got to stop working so hard," she said wearily. "I know it's your first year at the firm, and you feel you have to prove something to the others, but you can't kill yourself in the process. You're just trying to do too much."

"It isn't the firm, Susan. I've been having that nightmare for years, ever since I was a boy. Sometimes I would walk in my sleep when I was having it. My mother would find me in different parts of the house."

"I think it's time you see someone about it. Someone who can help you figure out what it means and why it keeps coming back."

"What are you suggesting?"

"I don't know . . ."

"Mommy!" The voice of a child drifted into the bedroom, and Susan and Joel glanced toward the open doorway.

"Just a minute, Aggy," Susan yelled out to the hallway. "I'm coming."

Before she could push herself away from the bed, Joel reached over and gently grabbed her forearm. "Wait. Why have you started to call her Aggy?"

"It's just a nickname. The kids in the neighborhood couldn't pronounce Seneca or Angela, so they scrambled the two together and somehow came up with Aggy. She seems to like it."

"Mommy," the little girl's voice implored again.

"I don't like it," Joel said firmly. "I think it's wrong to saddle her with a nickname when she's only four years old."

"Mommy, I'm hungry," the little girl pleaded.

"I'm coming, honey," Susan yelled again. Then she looked at her husband. "It's harmless. Besides, she'll outgrow it. But, Joel, please do me one favor."

"What's that?"

"See someone about that nightmare. There must be some reason why you've been having it all these years." She kissed him gently on the cheek.

Joel watched the white linen nightgown and the flowing black hair disappear through the doorway. After six years of marriage, he was still proud of his wife's radiant beauty.

He kicked back the covers with one foot and looked toward the window. It had been left open an inch or two, and a slight breeze drifted lazily into the room, lifting the blue curtains as it passed over the windowsill.

He walked over and pulled down hard on the cord attached to the shade. As the shade clattered upwards, light streamed into the room. He stretched as he looked out at the autumn landscape and felt the cool breeze against his bare skin.

In the east the sun was rising slowly, pouring light through the leaves that hung from the trees surrounding the house. He thought of how very much he loved the fall. He loved the colors and the sense of passing that he felt in the breezes. Sometimes he thought of moving west to Arizona or California, where he wouldn't have to face another winter. But he knew he would miss the autumns in the Midwest. More than that, he would miss the small towns. The thought of living in a large city made him claustrophobic.

He heard sounds of activity in the kitchen below. The clinking dishes, mixed with the quiet chatter of mother and daughter, floated up to him. The noises gave him a pleasant domestic feeling, and he knew that he was happy to be married.

As he walked to the bathroom, he checked the clock on the nightstand. It was seven-thirty. He had to be in court by nine to argue the Thomas Mallory case. Mallory had driven into the back of a police car while drunk, and the county was trying to take away his driver's license. Since Mallory was a salesman, Joel planned to argue that this would be excessive punishment because it would deny Mallory his livelihood and create undue hardships for him and his family. It wasn't exactly Clarence Darrow and William Jennings Bryant arguing the theory of evolution, but it was a start. As the junior partner in the law firm, Joel received the cases no one else wanted to argue.

In the bathroom, he quickly brushed his teeth and washed his face. As he was starting to shave, he heard the sound of footsteps on the carpet outside the door.

"She wants to watch you shave," Susan announced as she stepped into the bathroom carrying Seneca. The little girl had coal black hair and an impish grin on her face.

"Hi, Daddy," she announced as she studied the strange assortment of brushes, colognes, and shaving equipment scattered across the counter.

"Hi, honey," Joel replied. He leaned over to kiss her on the cheek. Then he applied the thick shaving cream to his rough beard.

Susan set the girl on the counter and left.

Seneca studied her father as he moved the safety razor carefully through the shaving cream. "Can I do that, too?" she asked.

"Shave?"

"What you're doing, Daddy."

"Honey, little girls don't shave. They don't have to."

"Why?"

"Because they don't have beards."

"I want a beard."

"Okay." Joel pressed the button on the aerosol can of shaving cream and squirted the foam into his daughter's palm. "Now rub it on your face."

"Like this?" she asked, smearing it over her cheeks and into the long black locks that curled over her ears.

"Yes, just like that," Joel said. He finished the last swipe with the razor and inspected his chin in the mirror. Then he rubbed a green aftershave lotion on his face.

"Me too, Daddy," Seneca insisted.

"You want some of this?" He held out the bottle to her.

"Yes, me too."

He poured the lotion into his palm and rubbed it gently over his daughter's cheeks. Then he stepped back and studied her. Her black hair was matted with shaving cream. "You're a mess, Seneca." He laughed as he reached for a towel to wipe her off.

"My name is Aggy," she said as she leaned over to admire herself in the mirror.

"Seneca," he announced firmly. "I don't want you calling yourself Aggy. Do you understand me?"

"My name is Aggy," she insisted. She turned away from the mirror and looked at her father. Her eyes were wide and teasing.

He had seen that look before. But where? Or was it the name? Something in his daughter's eyes suddenly made him both fearful and angry.

He grasped her tiny shoulders and spoke in a strong, menacing tone. "Don't you ever call yourself by that name again! Do you understand me, Seneca?"

"You're hurting me, Daddy," she said, beginning to cry.

"Your name is Seneca! Repeat it!" He was breathing heavily now.

"Daddy!" she moaned and sobbed.

"Repeat it!" he insisted fiercely.

"Aggy, come down here and finish your breakfast!" Susan's voice suddenly drifted into the bathroom from the parlor below.

His wife's voice made Joel realize how hard he had been squeezing his daughter's shoulders. She was now sobbing hysterically.

"Oh, honey, I'm sorry!" He pulled her close to his naked chest and tried to comfort her, but she wiggled out of his grasp and ran quickly out of the bathroom, still crying quietly.

Within seconds, Susan stepped into the doorway. "What happened?" she asked, puzzled.

"She . . . she got into the shaving cream," Joel stammered. "I punished her. I was probably too hard on her. I guess she's upset with me."

"Oh," Susan said complacently. She was accustomed to many such tear-filled experiences with her daughter. "Hurry down. Your breakfast is ready," she said as she walked away.

As Joel studied his features in the mirror, he took a deep breath and sighed nervously.

What was wrong with him? Was he going crazy?

He shuddered as he looked away from the mirror. For a few seconds a moment earlier, he had felt as though he could actually strangle his own daughter. The thought terrified him, and he shuddered again.

As Joel drove to the county courthouse, he decided that maybe Susan was right. He had been working too hard. He would have to speak with Jim Morris about taking a couple weeks off. Perhaps he could go up north with Susan and Seneca. Rent a cabin, do some fishing, just be with them. He hadn't taken a day off since he joined the firm almost a year earlier. Surely he was entitled to a vacation after all that time.

The courthouse was on the other side of Kenyon. Large oak and willow trees hovered over the streets that twisted through the Midwestern community. The red and yellow leaves flashed past his windows as he drove through town. He tried to concentrate on what he planned to tell the judge about the Mallory case, but he found his mind drifting back to Seneca and the scene in the bathroom earlier that morning. He felt terribly guilty about what he had done. Seneca had kissed him good-bye, but not with her usual wet-lipped love and exuberance.

As the leaves continued to fly by the car windows, he forgot completely about the Mallory case. There were things of much greater importance than defending a drunken salesman. The leaves mesmerized him, sent his mind reeling back to a time long, long ago.

Who was he then? What was he doing? The answers were all out there, somewhere, but he could not grasp them. They constantly eluded him. They were just beyond his reach.

He drove past the county courthouse and continued down the two-lane road toward the surrounding countryside. He parked on a narrow shoulder next to an empty wheat field, climbed out of the car, and looked out over the area.

It was out there, somewhere.

He stepped off the gravel road and walked into the field . . .

It had started in a place like this. Autumn. An empty wheat field. And a thicket of trees colored with red and yellow leaves. Where was he going? What had happened to him? He was singing and he was happy. Someone was waiting for him. That's why he was happy. But who?

It was almost night, and something else was waiting for him in the thicket. He felt apprehension, but not fear. But then there was darkness, and he felt real fear—and terror. And there were mysterious sounds in the darkness. And screams. Oh God, the screams! It had started among the trees. And he was someone else . . .

Joel looked at his watch. It was four o'clock. In the distance the sun was falling into the prairie. He knew, then, that he had been wandering all day through the fields, looking for something he only vaguely remembered from somewhere in his past.

He had never made it to the courthouse. Mallory had probably lost his driver's license, and Joel knew he was probably going to lose his job in the law firm.

He was going insane. Now he was certain of it.

When he returned home, Susan was already cleaning up in the kitchen. A bowl of peaches and an untouched plate of pot roast and potatoes were on the table.

"Hi, honey," Susan greeted him. "Did Jim Morris get ahold of you?"

"Morris?"

"He called right after you left. He told me to tell you the Mallory case was postponed until Friday. He said there was no need for you to hurry into the office."

"Did he call back?"

"No," Susan replied, somewhat puzzled. "Didn't you talk to him?"

"Yes," he lied, not wanting to explain to her what had happened to him that afternoon. "I just didn't know if he had called back. I spent the day at the law library." He looked around the kitchen and the adjacent living room. "Where's Seneca?"

"I put her down early," Susan said as she placed a plate of food in front of him. "She hasn't been feeling too well. She didn't want to go outside all day. She spent the afternoon upstairs in the attic, playing in her dollhouse. I think she's coming down with something."

"Did you call the doctor?" Joel inquired. He toyed with his food and looked out the window at the oak trees. The departing rays of sunlight were flashing through the branches.

"No. I thought I'd wait until tomorrow morning to see if it's anything serious. One of these days those tonsils will have to go. But I don't know if now is the right time, even though Dr. Lawler thinks we should do it as soon as possible."

He remembered the leaves waving in the wind. Orange and red and yellow and brown leaves in the trees next to a small road. Or was it a road? No, it was more of a . . . hill of some kind. And he was walking. Walking beneath a clear blue sky . . .

"Did you hear me?" Susan looked away from the dishes she was washing. Joel was staring out the window, seemingly mesmerized by the autumn leaves swaying listlessly in the trees. "Joel?"

"What?" he replied without taking his eyes off the trees.

"I asked if you thought we should let Dr. Lawler take Aggy's tonsils out. He's been after us to do it for a couple of months now."

It was an oak tree and it was early morning. She was swinging under the branches of the tree as the sun caught her golden hair, and her laughter rang out . . .

"Are you all right?" Susan walked over to the table and studied her husband's face as he continued to stare out the window.

She wore a white dress, but her back was turned toward him and he could not see her face. She giggled as she threw herself into the blue autumn sky, and the ropes creaked against the overhanging branch of the tree.

"Joel, what are you talking about?"

He remembered it now. How could he forget that name? It was burned into his soul . . .

"Joel?" Susan shook him by the shoulders.

"What?"

"Who is Katharine?"

He slowly turned and looked into his wife's eyes. "Katharine?" he asked, confused.

"You were just talking about someone named Katharine."

Joel glanced in the direction of the trees, then quickly looked back at his wife. "I don't know anyone by that name."

"You repeated her name three times."

"I don't remember . . ."

"Are you seeing another woman? Is that what's been wrong with you?"

"Of course not. Why do you ask?"

"You just haven't been yourself lately. Your attitude toward Aggy and me . . . well, it just isn't the same."

He stood and pulled her close to him. "There's no one else, honey. I must have been daydreaming."

"I still think you should see a therapist. Sometimes I feel like I don't even know who you are anymore. You seem different from the person I married."

"In what way?"

"In little ways. You seem so frustrated. And when you start repeating another woman's name, what am I to think?"

"You're right about one thing, Susan, but it doesn't involve another woman. We need a vacation. Today I decided that we'll go up north and get a cabin. Just you and me and Seneca. It'll be beautiful up there this time of year."

"Is that a promise?"

"Yes."

"I'd like that," she whispered to him as she leaned against his shoulder.

Joel glanced out the window as the last rays of sunlight streaked through the leaves. Then there was darkness.

He remembered the darkness and the screams and the soft, threatening footsteps that came closer and retreated, came closer again and retreated. But most of all he remembered the promise . . .

Susan knew there was something terribly wrong as soon as she opened her eyes and reached over to where her husband should have been sleeping. The warmth of his body still clung to the sheets, and she could smell his aftershave lotion on the crumpled pillow next to her. But as the moonlight filtered through the half-open window, she could see that Joel was not in the semi-darkened bedroom or adjacent bathroom.

She sat up, leaning on one elbow as she looked around. She felt her stomach tighten as she slowly pushed herself out of bed and crept toward the open doorway leading into the hall. Below her there was an eerie silence.

She paused briefly in Aggy's room. A small battery-powered nightlight glowed weakly in the far corner of the room, illuminating three rag dolls propped up against the wall. Susan paused beside the bed and placed her hand gently on the sleeping child's chest. The little girl was breathing strongly beneath her gentle touch.

Susan carefully placed another blanket over Aggy. Then she walked back to the hallway. She felt along the wall for the light switch and flicked it up and down, but the overhead light failed to go on.

Did a fuse blow?

She walked over to the staircase that circled into the parlor and looked down. A weak light filtered out of the living room and spread across the wooden floor.

"Joel, are you there?" she whispered. She waited and then said more loudly, "Are you all right?"

When there was no response, she walked down the stairs, peering constantly into the shadows. At the bottom, she paused and looked apprehensively around her.

Then she walked toward the open archway of the living room. Joel was sitting in an easy chair with his back toward her. A flashlight glowing on the coffee table illuminated several electrical fuses lying in a pile.

"Joel, what are you doing? Why are all the lights out?"

As Susan entered the room, Joel lifted himself slowly out of the chair and turned to face her. She stopped abruptly, horrified as he raised a large butcher knife in his right hand. As the light from the flashlight gleamed off the blade, she bolted back into the parlor and raced up the stairs. She swept Aggy out of her bed, ran back to the hallway, and climbed another flight of stairs into the attic. She slammed the door behind her and quickly threw the bolt into position. She leaned against the door for a moment, panting.

"Mommy," Aggy whispered sleepily as she rubbed her eyes and stared into the darkness of the attic. "Where are we?"

"Shh, honey, just be quiet," Susan admonished. She tried to control her own breathing so she could hear any movement on the other side of the door. But she heard nothing.

The moonlight filtered gently through a gable window at the other end of the attic, illuminating children's toys that were strewn across the floor. A large dollhouse, big enough for a child to play inside, was hidden in the shadows between two rafters.

Susan leaned closer to the door and listened to the sounds on the stairway below. Suddenly the silver blade of the butcher knife splintered through the thin wooden panels of the door. The knife quickly retreated, then slashed again through the door.

Susan heard her husband's heavy breathing on the other side.

"Mommy, I'm scared," Aggy whimpered as she pressed her face into her mother's neck.

Susan ran to the dollhouse and pushed her daughter through the open doorway. Then she crawled in after her.

"Mommy!"

"Hush, honey, you mustn't cry."

"What's wrong with Daddy?"

Susan held Aggy close to her as the sound of the butcher knife slicing into the door grew louder and more frenzied. Then, suddenly, the sounds ceased.

As Susan peered through one of the windows of the dollhouse, she expected the attic door to come crashing down at any minute. But the heavy breathing was gone, and the only sound was the wind whistling gently around the chimney.

"Go to sleep, honey," Susan said, trying to steady her voice as she placed Aggy's head in her lap. "Pretend this is all a game. Won't it be fun to sleep in a dollhouse?"

As the little girl cried herself to sleep, Susan kept her eyes focused on the door at the other end of the attic.

Susan awoke as the first rays of sunshine filtered through the attic windows. Aggy was asleep beside her. The little girl had found a doll and was cuddled up to it on the floor.

Being careful not to wake Aggy, Susan crawled out of the dollhouse and walked over to the attic door. The wooden panels had been destroyed by knife slashes. Susan cautiously unlocked the door and stepped onto the attic stairway.

She knew she couldn't hide in the attic forever. Sooner or later she'd have to face Joel.

She walked silently down the steps to the first floor of the house. As she peered around the corner into the living room, she saw Joel sprawled out next to the brick fireplace. The knife blade had shattered against the hard stone surface of the hearth, but he still clenched the handle firmly in his hand.

One of Aggy's rag dolls lay crumpled in a heap next to him. Its stomach had been cut open and the stuffing was strewn across the floor.

CHAPTER THREE

"Joel," Susan called cautiously across the living room. "Are you all right?"

Joel stiffened, then sat up slowly and looked around the room. There was fear and confusion in his eyes. "What happened?" he asked, looking first at the knife handle and then at Susan. "What am I doing down here?"

"You had a nightmare again last night." Susan sat down on the couch and nervously clenched and unclenched her hands, trying to remember that this was the man she loved, a kind and gentle man. "You came down here, removed the fuses from the fuse box, and did this in your sleep," she said, gesturing around the room.

Joel surveyed the damaged furniture and the chunks of mortar and rock that had been chipped out of the fireplace. He looked again at the knife handle. "Did anyone get hurt?" he asked, his voice hollow with fear.

Susan shook her head slowly. "Joel, you have to see someone about those nightmares." She started to sob. "We just can't go on like this, not knowing what . . ."

"Mommy," a voice suddenly called from the staircase. "Are you okay?"

Susan quickly composed herself and looked up. Aggy was staring at her from between the wooden banisters. "Yes, honey, I'm okay," Susan said reassuringly. "You go back to your room. Mommy will be right up."

The little girl's eyes grew wide as she spotted the mutilated remains of her rag doll on the floor. "Mommy, what happened to Tina?" she shrieked as she raced down the stairway into the room. She stared in horror at the doll, then gently picked it up. "Tina, Tina!" she cried hysterically, clutching it.

"It's okay, honey," Susan said, picking up Aggy and hugging her. "It was an accident," she stammered unconvincingly. "Mommy will get you a new doll."

"Tina's dead, Mommy," Aggy cried as Susan carried her back up the staircase.

Susan tried to comfort her daughter, but each time Aggy looked down at the crumpled remains of the doll, she would start sobbing hysterically. "Tina's dead and Daddy did it."

Outside Ned Finley's office, a storm was whipping the trees into a frenzy of activity. A light mist had settled over the dead grass and fallen leaves in the park next to the county health center. As the mist fell, it collected on the rear window of Finley's office, and tiny rivulets of water streamed down the glass pane, dissolving the autumn scene in the park. A poor caulking job enabled the water to seep through the sash.

Doctor Finley was seated at his desk. He could hear the steady dripping of water behind him as it collected in puddles on the ledge and either fell to the floor or rolled down the plaster wall. Finley had long ago given up on trying to patch the leak in the window. He was content to mop up the puddle on the floor whenever it rained.

Light and shadows intermingled across the comfortable clutter of the room. Finley was a collector of things, not in the traditional sense of those enthusiasts who have a disciplined need to collect stamps or coins or rocks. Finley collected junk. Even he wouldn't be able to find a pattern to the many objects that littered his office walls and floor. Small stuffed birds and other animals, ancient muskets and ammunition pouches, old books and magazines, a turn-of-the-century Thermos jug—these and other worthless objects were scattered randomly throughout the room.

Finley lived by the axiom that "an organized man is a dull man." He preferred his surroundings to be cluttered, full of surprises and mysteries. He liked to think his office reflected the human psyches he worked with every day. They too were full of hidden surprises and mysteries, possessing depths unfathomed by even the most skilled psychologist or psychiatrist. But this was a rationalization. The truth of the matter was that Finley was a bit of a slob, and he just liked junk.

Finley's appearance was equally unconventional. He was an exceptionally tall man, well over six feet, with prematurely snow-white hair. He refused to wear suits, preferring instead comfortable old sweaters and tan cotton pants, complemented by an ancient brown beret he had won from a drifter in a buck euchre game. Finley was convinced the beret gave him a rakish look, so he wore it constantly. In moments of candor, his friends informed him that it made him look like a lost seaman in search of his ship. Finley liked that image of himself even better, and he continued to wear the beret at all times, even indoors.

He carefully studied the face of Susan Hampton, who was sitting on the other side of the desk. In two decades as a clinical psychologist, Finley had become a keen student of human nature. At the nearby Farmington State Mental Hospital, he had worked with all forms of deviant behavior, ranging from mild paranoia to criminal insanity. He prided himself on his ability to size people up quickly. Normally his first impressions were accurate.

He decided the beautiful young woman before him had considerable poise and stability, but she had probably never before been exposed to the darker side of life. Perhaps that was for the best, he thought. God chooses to spare some people the real agony of human existence so their innocence can serve as a beacon to others who have been hardened by time and circumstances. As one who had spent a good part of his life working with the mentally ill, Finley found it occasionally refreshing to share the company of those who remained relatively unscathed by the traumas less fortunate human beings have to endure.

"Does your husband have any previous history of mental illness?" Finley asked Susan after they had exchanged small talk, and he was certain she was comfortable in his presence.

"No."

"Is there anything in his family history that reflects abnormal behavior?"

"Not that we know of."

"Anything . . ."

"Dr. Finley, I should explain that Joel was adopted. We know nothing about his real mother or father. His adoptive parents were very secretive about his past."

"Where are they now?"

"Joel's adoptive parents?"

"Yes."

"They're both dead."

Finley glanced at the storm that was rattling the window casing behind him. Then he looked again at Susan. "Tell me precisely what your husband has been doing that makes you think he needs psychiatric help."

Susan sighed deeply and looked down at her hands as she struggled to collect her thoughts. "Well, first of all there are the nightmares," she said, looking up at Finley. "He had them as a boy and he's starting to have them again."

"What kind of nightmares?" Finley asked.

"It's always the same one."

"Has he described it to you?"

Susan nodded. "He says he's walking out in the country. It's autumn and he's surrounded by empty fields and groves of trees. He's happy. Then he starts to feel apprehensive about something. He goes into one of the fields, and it gets really dark and there are strange noises. He's scared and he's hurt. Then he starts to scream. That's when he wakes up, or I wake him up."

Finley made several notations in a small, blue notebook. "You say he had this nightmare as a boy?"

"Yes. When he joined the law firm about a year ago, the nightmare started again."

"Has your husband been under a lot of pressure at his job?"

"Yes."

"That could account for part of it," Finley mused. "You indicated in your phone call that there are other things your husband has been doing that concern you. What are they?"

"Joel came home later than usual last night. I had already put Aggy to bed . . ."

"Aggy?"

"Our daughter."

Finley nodded. "Go ahead."

"When he left for work in the morning, he was kind of strange. He was still acting strange when he came home."

"Strange, in what way?"

"Like he was locked up inside of himself," Susan said, struggling to find the right words. "He just wasn't the same toward Aggy or me."

"Was he angry or frustrated? Did he display any outward signs of resentment or aggression?"

"No. It was more like he was in a trance. Almost . . . like he didn't know what he was doing or who he was. I was washing the dishes and Joel was sitting by the kitchen table toying with his supper. He was staring out the window at the trees. Then he mumbled something like, 'Katharine, what happened?' I couldn't hear the rest of it. He mumbled the name two more times. When I asked him what he had said, he looked dazed. I asked him who Katharine was, and he said he didn't know anyone by that name."

"Maybe he was daydreaming?"

"At first I thought that might be the case, but it happened again this morning. He was looking out the living room window at the trees—something in the leaves seems to trigger it. He had his back to me when I came down the stairs, but I distinctly heard him ask the same question, 'Katharine, what happened?' He denied it, but I know I heard him say that."

"Does your husband know anyone by that name?"

"You mean, does he have a girlfriend?"

The question surprised Finley. His first impression of her was that she was perhaps too naive and innocent to want to admit that possibility to herself. Yet she had not hesitated at all to confront the unthinkable. "Yes," he said gently. "Do you think your husband has another woman?"

"No, I'm almost positive he doesn't."

"Was there anything else?"

"Only that last night I awoke to find Joel missing. I found him in the living room. He had destroyed some of the furniture and was passed out on the floor."

"Has he ever threatened to harm you or your daughter?"

Susan toyed with the idea of telling Finley what had happened in the attic, but decided against it. She still found it hard to accept that her husband could have done that. "No, he's never threatened to harm either of us," she stammered.

Finley thought for a moment. "Your husband is not epileptic or subject to convulsions, is he?" he asked.

"No, he's in perfect health."

"Would he be willing to come in to see me?"

"Yes, I think so. He promised me this morning he would come in if I arranged an appointment."

"Bring him by tomorrow. About four o'clock, if you can. In the meantime, see if you can find out anything more about Joel's adoption in any papers or pictures that he might have in the house."

Susan promised she would and left the room. Afterward, Finley sat at his desk, toying with a ballpoint pen and pondering his conversation with her. He dropped the pen, and it rolled over to a plastic paperweight next to a notepad. Inside the paperweight, imprisoned in a cube, an eagle raised its wings in a futile effort to launch itself into the sky. Finley studied the paperweight briefly, then walked over to the window.

The mist had stopped falling from the gray sky, but the wind still rattled the window casing. Outside, dead leaves were swirling across the park. Finley watched them as they skimmed over the dead grass and were trapped against a concrete retaining wall.

As Joel drove home from work that afternoon, he thought of his upcoming vacation. Jim Morris had told him he could take some time off, so long as he waited until later in the month when the Mallory case and several other smaller lawsuits had been settled. Morris had even suggested that they use his cabin on Lake Salizar, about 120 miles north of Kenyon. Lake Salizar would be beautiful in late autumn. It would be quiet and peaceful, a perfect place for the three of them to take long walks and go on picnics.

Joel knew Susan would be pleased. In the meantime, he decided he would stop the nightmares by taking sleeping pills. He knew that Seneca and Susan had been terrified by whatever had happened the previous night. His own memories were vague. He remembered moving around in the darkness, and he remembered lashing out at something hard. But suddenly it was morning, and Susan was calling to him from across the living room. She wouldn't tell him exactly what had occurred, but she was still frightened. That was obvious.

Joel parked his car next to a drugstore and bought some nonprescription sleeping tablets that were guaranteed to produce "eight hours of comfortable sleep in any adult male or female." He also picked up a big box of gumdrops for Seneca. They were her favorite. Susan wouldn't let her have them very often because of her teeth, but this was kind of a special occasion. He wanted Seneca to forgive him. Hopefully the candy would be an effective bribe. He loved his daughter so much that he couldn't bear the thought of her being mad at him.

As he walked to his car, Joel remembered that Susan also needed some reassurance from him. If he had some small present to give her when he told her about the vacation, perhaps that would make her feel better.

There was a jewelry store several shops down from the drugstore. He knew Susan wasn't much for fancy trinkets, but maybe a small charm or ring would please her. At the very least, it would show her that he still cared, that there was no one else in his life.

He studied the watches, charms, necklaces, and earrings in the front window. Maybe a pair of earrings would be the best present. She already had a beautiful watch. He had given it to her as a wedding present, inscribed, "With love always."

Or what about a charm? Or a locket?

A locket? Once before . . . he had bought a locket. No, he had won it. Somehow he had won a locket and was bringing it back with him as a present. And he was singing a song. A locket for . . . He could almost hear the song. It had been a long time ago, but he still remembered the melody . . .

"Mommy," a voice behind him said, "who's that man talking to?"

Joel turned to find a small boy pointing at him. "Now, Peter," the boy's mother admonished him, "you mustn't point at people. It's very impolite. Come along now." The woman grabbed her son by the hand and pulled him down the sidewalk. The boy's head turned, and he looked curiously back at Joel as his mother dragged him away.

Joel turned again to the window.

So he had been talking to himself. About what this time?

His mind made up, he entered the jewelry store. A short, elderly man was standing behind the glass-enclosed counter next to a cash register. He was tinkering with the mechanism of a large, pendulum-operated clock. "Yes?" he asked, smiling cheerfully at Joel. "What can I do for you today?"

"That gold locket in the display window," Joel explained nervously, pointing toward the front of the store. "How much is it?"

The clerk walked quickly over to the window and removed the locket from its black felt pad. "This one?" he asked, holding it up as he walked behind the counter. "This one retails at $170, but, for you, $130."

One hundred thirty dollars? Had it cost him that much? He had never made that much money in his life, except maybe once or twice gambling. He worked with his hands then. He was strong, very strong. He had won the locket with his strength. But who was he then?

"Say, are you all right?" the clerk asked suspiciously.

"What?" Joel asked as he reached for the locket. He held it gently in his hands.

"Nothing. You looked very pale there for a moment. I thought maybe you were going to pass out."

"How much did you say this was?" Joel asked, still admiring the locket as the chain dangled from his palm.

"One thirty. It's genuine fourteen-karat gold. See, on the back." The clerk reached for the locket to turn it over.

What happened to the locket? He had won it and he was going to give it to someone. He knew the name, but something happened. Something terrible. And he was never to get there . . .

Joel stepped back from the counter. His huge, sweaty palm encircled the tiny piece of jewelry protectively as he glared at the clerk.

There was always someone, every time he tried to . . . Not this time. This time he would do it. No one would stop him . . .

"Hey, where are you going with that?" the clerk asked. He scrambled around the counter and positioned himself between Joel and the front door. "You can't take that out of here without paying for it. There are laws. The police will arrest you."

He had a knife and a gun. So why was he afraid? There was nothing to be afraid of . . . What was that? The loud ticking of a pocket watch. It didn't work too well and . . . she was going to buy him a new one. She said his made too much noise. And he was going to get her the locket.

But then there was the darkness. He heard the watch ticking away. Tick. Tick. Tick. Tick. It was driving him insane. He could not stand the loud noise. He had to stop it. He put the watch on the ground and stomped on it with his boot. Still it did not stop. Tick. Tick. Tick. Tick. He held his hands up to his ears to shut out the relentless sound of the pocket watch . . .

"You're drunk, right? You're drunk! Or are you crazy?" the jeweler asked excitedly as Joel stood with both hands covering his ears. On the counter, the large clock chimed merrily away. "Either you give me back that locket and get out of here, or I call the police."

Joel slowly lowered his arms and unclenched both fists. He held his hands out, palms upward. The clerk quickly snatched the locket and retreated behind the counter.

Joel paused to study the lines in his hand. He had clenched the small piece of jewelry so hard that the imprint of the locket was sharply outlined in his sweaty palm.

"Now get out of here, or I call the police!" the clerk shouted. "Out! Out!"

Joel's eyes moved slowly around the store. Then he turned and walked toward the front door.

This wasn't the place. The other store had the smell of tobacco hanging heavily in the air. And there was a card game in the back. At first, he had thought of joining the game, but he knew he would not leave until the money was gone. And he had made a promise to buy the locket. That much, he knew for sure. The rest was confusion and pain and an impenetrable, lonely darkness . . .

The next afternoon Susan escorted Joel into Dr. Finley's office. Finley exchanged small talk with them until he felt Joel had relaxed enough to discuss his problems. On the surface, Joel appeared to be in control of his moods and emotions. But Finley knew from his experiences with other patients that appearances could be deceptive.

"Joel," Finley said, "your wife tells me you've been under some stress lately. She also says you've had temporary blackouts and losses of memory."

Joel looked at his wife, then back at Finley. "Well, I have felt some stress, yes," he replied. "But I suspect it's the same with every young lawyer who is first starting out."

"Do you remember having temporary blackouts?"

Joel looked again at his wife. "Yes," he admitted. "But I don't know what importance to place on them. I think they're more daydreams than blackouts."

"Your wife tells me you've had the same nightmare ever since you were a small boy. Tell me, does it ever intrude on your waking hours?"

"In what way?"

"Are you ever just walking along, and suddenly visual impressions from this nightmare flood into your mind? In other words, do you have the nightmare when you are awake as well as when you're asleep?"

"I don't know," Joel said sheepishly.

"What do you mean?"

"I daydream a lot. And sometimes I can't seem to control them. But I don't know if they're connected to the nightmare. I don't remember my daydreams, but I remember the nightmare vividly."

Finley made several notations in his blue notebook. "Joel, does the name Katharine mean anything to you?"

"No," Joel answered emphatically.

"Your wife tells me you've mentioned that name while you were daydreaming. Do you remember any of those times?"

"No," Joel said, looking reassuringly at his wife. "I know absolutely no one by the name of Katharine. I never have."

Finley made more notations in the notebook. As he did so, Joel patted his wife's hand comfortingly. Then the movements of the dead leaves in the trees outside the window caught his attention, and he stared wistfully in that direction.

"Joel," Finley said quietly, looking up from his notebook, "how would you feel about seeing me on a regular basis? At least until we can get to the source of these nightmares and daydreams you've been having. We might even try regressive hypnosis . . ."

As Finley spoke, Joel's gaze fixed on the dead leaves waving in the wind and tumbling across the park.

It was a long, long time ago, next to an oak tree like the one outside the window. A young woman in a swing glided gracefully back and forth, propelled by some unseen force behind her. She wore an old-fashioned white dress. He could not see her face because her back was turned toward him. She laughed as the sunshine sparkled off her golden blond hair and she soared gracefully into the clear blue sky, propelled higher and higher by some unseen force . . .

"Come, Katharine, we must go!" There was a note of urgency, almost panic in Joel's voice as he reached for his wife's hand.

"What did you just call her?" Finley quickly asked.

"I told Katharine it was time for us to go!" Joel's response was firm, almost menacing.

"Joel, you just called your wife Katharine," Finley replied softly.

Joel glanced in disbelief, first at Finley, then at his wife. Then he stood and stalked out of the room.

><><><

Joel took one of the sleeping tablets that night, but he was still unable to sleep. He tossed and turned until the sheet was wet beneath his body. The sun was already filtering through the eastern window of the bedroom when he finally fell asleep.

As his eyelids closed, he felt the same frustration. It was out there, just beyond his reach. If only he could . . .

He remembered it again. The girl in the swing with the golden hair and the white linen dress soared higher and higher into a blue sky. Then the swing turned into a piece of jewelry, swaying back and forth on the end of a large gold chain, like a huge pendulum, while a clock ticked loudly in the background. Two large hands reached through the chain as though to strangle someone. Then a door slammed and there was total darkness. A scream pierced the darkness and grew louder and louder . . .

After another night interrupted repeatedly by more strange nightmares, Joel was frightened and exhausted when he walked into Finley's office. Finley made him comfortable in a reclining chair and listened carefully while Joel related the details of his latest nightmares.

Afterward, Finley asked him gently, "Have you ever heard of regressive hypnosis?"

"Isn't that when you take someone back through the various stages in their life?"

"Yes. If these things you've been seeing in your dreams are a part of your past, maybe we can find them. Maybe we can also find out who Katharine is."

"How does it work?"

"Through the powers of suggestion and concentration. You must allow your mind to be totally relaxed while I create an image of time. You must concentrate completely on that image as I describe it to you."

"Okay."

"Your wife tells me that something in the dead and dying leaves seems to trigger these nightmares you're having in your subconscious mind. So I want you to relax completely while I describe for you the seasonal changes in a single tree. Do you understand me?"

"Yes."

"I want you to picture this tree in the fall. I want your imagination to provide color and detail while I describe the tree to you. I want you to create the strongest visual impression possible. Do you understand me?"

"Yes," Joel answered softly.

"It is autumn and this tree is filled with leaves of all different colors. There are orange, brown, red, and yellow leaves waving in the breeze. Some of them tear loose from the tree and blow away with the wind, but most are still swaying in the breeze. Orange, brown, red, and yellow leaves swaying against a blue sky. Can you see them?"

"Yes," Joel whispered.

"Concentrate on the leaves," Finley said soothingly. He repeated the instructions softly as he leaned over to switch on a tape recorder. "Allow yourself to relax completely, Joel."

Joel sighed but did not speak.

"Now, Joel, we are going backward in time. I want you to visualize the seasonal changes in the leaves, only in reverse order from fall to summer to spring to winter to fall again. Do you understand me?"

Again Joel did not speak.

"The oranges and reds and browns and yellows are now changing and blending together. They are gradually turning into a deep green as the white clouds drift faster and faster across the blue sky. The leaves are turning the deepest, darkest green against the blue sky, and they are filling the tree, covering the branches and swaying in the breeze. Huge summer leaves turning a dark green beneath a blue sky. Do you see them?"

Finley looked closely at Joel's face. "Yes, I see them," Joel whispered.

"Now the leaves are turning a lighter green as the clouds move rapidly overhead, and the sun moves backward across the sky from west to east. As the sun moves more and more rapidly in this direction, the leaves shrink in size and turn an even lighter green. Then they fold into the branches and disappear. Now it is winter and the tree has no leaves. It stands alone in an empty field. Can you see the tree standing alone in an empty field in winter?"

"Yes," Joel whispered.

"Good," Finley said gently. He quickly took Joel's pulse, then placed his arm back on the side of the black reclining chair. "Now, I want you to see how fast you can put leaves back on that tree and make them change colors as the seasons move in reverse order from autumn to summer to spring to winter to autumn again. Make your mind work to change the colors of those leaves as the clouds float rapidly by overhead, and the sun swirls around the earth from west to east. Make them go faster and faster, Joel. Red and orange and brown and yellow leaves turning dark green, then light green, then disappearing into the branches and reappearing as red and orange and brown and yellow leaves . . ."

Finley reached for the microphone on the tape recorder and placed it on top of the reclining chair within inches of Joel's head.

"The sun is moving across the sky, and the changes in the leaves are taking place so fast that the colors are becoming a blur, a spinning whirlpool of color that blends together as it sucks you into its depths. Do you see the spinning whirlpool of colors on all sides of you, Joel?"

"Yes," Joel whispered sleepily.

"Now, I want you to reach out to stop the whirlpool. Stop it momentarily while I ask you some questions. Just place your hand against the spinning wall of colors."

"Yes."

"What year is it, Joel?"

Joel paused for a moment. "1950," he finally said.

"Where are you in 1950?"

"College."

"What is your name?"

"Joel Hampton."

"Did you know a Katharine in 1950?"

Joel hesitated. "No."

"Did anything happen to you in 1950 while you watched the autumn leaves blow away in the wind?"

"No."

"Then let's go back further yet. Start the whirlpool of color spinning again. Make it spin faster and faster until the colors blend together and you are sucked deeper and deeper into the swirling tail of the vortex. Make it spin faster and faster, Joel." Finley paused, then peered closely again into Joel's face. "Now, stop the whirlpool. Stop it and tell me what year it is."

"1935," Joel whispered almost incoherently.

"Okay, you are a young boy. Did you know anyone by the name of Katharine in 1935?"

"No."

"Are you standing next to a tree filled with dead leaves?"

"Katharine," Joel whispered sleepily.

"Did you know a Katharine in 1935?" Finley leaned forward, listening closely.

"No."

"Then start the whirlpool spinning again. Make the reds and browns and oranges and yellows of the autumn leaves change to a dark green, then light green, then have them disappear altogether as you're sucked into a prism of color. The reds and browns and oranges and yellows blend with the greens as you move closer and closer toward the center of the vortex . . ."

Finley glanced out the window at the light mist that was settling on the dead grass. Then he turned his attention back to Joel.

"Joel, I want you to stop the whirlpool again. Stop it from sucking you deeper into the vortex. What year is it?" Joel mumbled something and Finley leaned closer to hear him. "What did you say?" Finley asked.

Joel did not respond.

"What year is it?" Finley asked again.

"1926," Joel said softly. "October, 1926."

"October of 1926," Finley said, leaning even closer to the reclining chair. "What is your name in October of 1926?"

"No name. I have no name . . ."

"Who is Katharine, Joel?" Finley asked.

Her blond hair caught the golden rays of sunlight as they filtered through the leaves in the oak tree. She threw her head back and held on tightly to the ropes of the swing as her feet almost touched the dead and dying leaves on the lower branches.

"Who is Katharine?" Finley repeated.

"Kate, Kate, me lass," Joel blurted out cheerfully, his voice taking on a thick Irish accent. "You are such a lady."

Finley was momentarily stunned by the voice and accent Joel had assumed. "Who is Kate?" he asked eagerly.

"Such a lady . . ."

"What is your name?" Finley asked again. "Who are you? What happened to you in October of 1926?"

"Ah, Kate, ya just tamed the toughest man in Carver County," Joel replied tenderly, still with a strong Irish accent. "Have ya no pride, girl?"

"Joel, who are you talking to? Where are you in October of 1926?"

His shoes crunched through the gravel and the rocks while he walked beneath a blue sky. Walking and singing beneath a clear blue sky . . .

"Got a locket for me darlin', for me darlin', Lady Kate," Joel whispered slowly, dreamily. Then he chuckled softly to himself.

"What happened to you in October of 1926?" Finley asked.

"Ah, Kate," Joel whispered dreamily.

"What happened to you in October of 1926, Joel?" Finley repeated the question.

The leaves were blowing off the trees and drifting into the fields, while the crickets chirped contentedly behind him. The sun was drifting into the western horizon and he heard the sound of water. He took one long step and then there was darkness. A deep impenetrable darkness and a scream that grew louder and louder and . . .

That afternoon Finley met Susan in the playground behind the elementary school where she worked as a substitute teacher. Overhead, the first of the Canadian geese were flying south in V-formation. Their honking sounds echoed across the playground and mingled with the sounds of children laughing and playing.

"Did you find out anything at all about Joel's adoption?" Finley inquired as a volleyball bounced across their path.

"Nothing. The Hamptons must have destroyed the adoption records. All I found was this, in a box of old baby clothes that belonged to Joel."

Susan handed Finley a large envelope that had yellowed with age. The return address in the upper left corner had been torn off, though the names "Mr. and Mrs. Tom Hampton" were still legible on the face of the envelope. The Hamptons' address was smeared and illegible.

Finley extracted from the envelope a small lock of hair and an old sepia photograph of a farmhouse. He examined them for a few seconds and placed them back into the envelope.

"When a child is adopted, aren't the permanent records sent to the state capital?" he inquired.

"I would think so, but aren't they sealed?"

"Maybe a court order would release them?" Finley paused to watch the Canadian geese pass overhead. "Susan, what do you know about Carver County?"

"Only that it's some miles northwest of here. Why?"

"I put Joel in a hypnotic trance yesterday and took him back to 1926. He said he lived in Carver County in 1926."

"Joel wasn't born until 1927, Dr. Finley."

Finley stopped watching the geese and looked directly at Susan. "I know," he said softly.

CHAPTER FOUR

The red granite walls and turrets of the Farmington State Mental Hospital rose out of the Midwestern prairie like an ancient Gothic fortress. Built out of granite blocks hauled by horses from the quarries in nearby Archer County, Farmington had served as an asylum for the mentally ill and the criminally insane since the early 1850s. Somehow, in spite of its architectural design, Farmington had managed to blend into the surrounding landscape during its one hundred and ten years of existence.

Nonetheless, residents throughout the adjacent communities eyed the red walls and turrets with suspicion. The lost souls of the insane who were housed there still roamed through its basement catacombs and haunted the nearby farmlands at night, or so it was rumored among the more imaginative members of the local population. Tales of the hideous deeds of these tortured souls were still told around hearths and coal stoves in the surrounding farms and small towns.

Ned Finley pushed hard on the heavy oak doors of the hospital and stepped out into the bright sunshine. He had come to Farmington to seek the advice of an old friend, Aurther Schlepler, but the receptionist had told him Schlepler was somewhere outside on the grounds. Finley paused at the top of the steps to view the beauty of Indian summer as it settled lightly over the countryside. Then he walked down the flight of granite steps and crossed the lawn to a far corner, where a small, elderly man was examining and rearranging the vines that clung to one of the tall walls. Schlepler was totally preoccupied with his work and did not turn to acknowledge the approaching footsteps.

"Your plants look healthy today, Aurther," Finley said after watching the old man inspect the vines.

"They are dying. Any fool can see that they are dying," Schlepler responded impatiently, as though not wanting to be disturbed.

"They look healthy to me," Finley replied.

"That's because you spend too much of your time probing into the depths of the human psyche, Ned," Schlepler admonished him. "You have lost touch with the essential rhythms of nature."

As Schlepler turned to face him, Finley was once again struck by how much he resembled Albert Einstein. Schlepler had the same patches of downy white hair on both sides of his balding head, and he wore a shirt and trousers that were several sizes too large for his small frame. But it was his eyes more than anything else that reminded Finley of Einstein. They were large and brown, full of wisdom and compassion and sadness. Schlepler was a psychic who had carefully studied the human race for over seventy years and found it produced in him only deep sorrow. He had once helped police solve difficult cases. For the past eight years he had turned to horticulture, preferring the simpler pleasures and surprises of plant life to the more foreboding and dangerous insights into the human soul.

"Aurther, I need your help," Finley said after Schlepler turned his attentions back to the vines and dying flowers that clung to the red granite wall. "A patient of mine is having problems that don't seem to fit into anything I've ever encountered before."

"I'm retired, Ned. You know that," Schlepler said firmly. "My plants are my life. I have seen enough of human beings and their capacity for evil to last me several lifetimes, not to mention the one I am now finishing and plan to complete in great peace and tranquility."

"Do you believe in reincarnation?"

"Why do you ask?" Schlepler kept his back to Finley.

"My patient is taking on the personality of someone who lived in Carver County in the 1920s."

"Has your patient ever lived in Carver County?"

"No. He's never been there."

"How old is he?"

"Early thirties."

"Come over here," Schlepler said. He pointed at a piece of sheet metal. "See this? I have been experimenting with the growth patterns on these vines. Would you venture to say, Ned, that the tendrils of this vine have been completely separated by this piece of sheet metal?"

"They appear to be, yes," Finley replied awkwardly, not knowing what was expected of him.

"Wrong!" Schlepler said, pulling away the sheet metal and discarding it on the dead grass. "That appears to be the case on the surface. But, as you can see, the tendrils have managed to creep beneath the metal by following the tiny grooves where the granite blocks are joined together. Thus, they have established all kinds of intertwining connections." Schlepler moved his finger carefully along one of the tendrils to illustrate his point.

"I don't understand what you're trying to tell me," Finley said.

"Nature obviously never intended for this vine to be separated at this point, so it found other ways to circumvent the tiny obstacle I placed in its path."

"What does that have to do with my patient?"

"Probably nothing. I simply find it to be fascinating, that's all."

"Aurther, *will* you help me?"

"We must remember," Schlepler continued, ignoring Finley's question, "that what we see on the surface, in the present moment, is only an illusion. The reality is that all living things are connected to a common past. There are many lessons to be learned from nature, Ned, lessons that men like you should understand before you even attempt to probe into the human psyche. It is first of all a lesson in fate. These vines teach us that the barriers men and women place in the path of fate are ultimately meaningless. The vines will work to circumvent all obstacles until they have completely covered this wall. The things that are meant to be—will be. You must remember that."

"You're not going to help me. Is that what you're trying to say?"

"The other lesson to be learned from these plants is that there is beauty in the death of the flower, for it reveals the common root from which we all sprang, and the common future to which we all aspire through successive lifetimes. These plants are not yet done with their work," Schlepler said softly. "They will lie dormant, and in the spring they will continue to spread over this entire wall. The same is true with men and women when they have not finished with something in one lifetime. Let's go back to my room and discuss your patient."

Finley stood by the wall for a time, not certain what Schlepler had just told him or how it applied to his patient. Then he followed Schlepler over to the steps leading up to the front doors of the hospital. Inside, tranquilized patients were sitting on wooden benches and in wheelchairs along both walls of the poorly lit corridors. Some patients stared blankly at the two men as they passed. Others sat motionlessly and stared at the dirty floor. Still others babbled incoherently or waved their hands frantically in the air, trying desperately to communicate.

No matter how many times Finley visited the hospital, he couldn't get over the shock of seeing all these lonely, lost souls locked in their own peculiar, tormented worlds.

"Why do you still insist on living here?" Finley asked Schlepler. "Certainly you could find someplace where you'd be more comfortable."

"Because the truly insane people are the ones like yourself, Ned. The ones living on the outside who think they're sane. I feel much safer in here with people who suffer from no such illusions about themselves."

Schlepler turned and entered the open doorway of his room. A partially completed jigsaw puzzle of a landscape was laid out across a coffee table. Small potted plants and trays of seedlings were scattered randomly throughout the room. A library of horticulture books was jammed into one corner, its contents spilling onto the threadbare carpet that covered the floor.

"So, you think you have another Bridey Murphy on your hands?" Schlepler said somewhat impishly as he sat down in a chair by the coffee table.

"Bridey Murphy?"

"The woman who under hypnosis remembered a previous existence in Ireland."

"I don't know," Finley admitted, sitting down in another chair. "At this point, I honestly don't know what I'm working with. Most likely, there's some simple, logical explanation. But it might be something else. Something much more profound."

"What is it you want from me?" Schlepler asked, folding his hands and sitting back in his chair.

"My patient's name is Joel Hampton," Finley explained. "He's been having losses of memory, which are becoming progressively more acute. During these times, he speaks of a Katharine and a life he knew earlier in the century. I finally put him in a hypnotic trance and took him back to the 1920s. He told me he lived in Carver County at that time. He talked again of a Katharine. Then he began screaming until I was forced to take him out of the trance. I was afraid there might be permanent damage if I kept him under any longer."

"And you are absolutely certain he has never lived in Carver County?"

"Yes. He has never been near it."

"What can I do to help you?"

"I have something here," Finley said, reaching into his shirt pocket and pulling out the envelope Susan Hampton had given him. "His wife found this. I just want you to see if you can tell me anything about his past by studying these."

Finley dumped the lock of hair and the faded picture of the old Victorian farmhouse on the coffee table. He placed the envelope next to them.

Schlepler closed his eyes and gently held the lock of hair in his right palm. After several seconds he said, "This comes from a child . . . a very small child. He . . . he is happy. There is love, warmth . . ."

"You said 'he.' It's a boy?"

"Yes. He is surrounded by love but he feels different. Something inside of him is not right. It is too much sadness for a child to bear."

"What about the envelope?"

Schlepler opened his eyes and carefully studied the yellowed envelope. "There is no return address on it."

"Apparently someone tore it off."

Schlepler again closed his eyes and ran his fingers lightly over the handwriting on the front of the envelope. "Oh, there is much sadness here too, great and overwhelming sadness and pain . . ."

"Whose handwriting is it?"

"A young person . . . a woman, I think," Schlepler said. "Oh, the sadness is deep."

"Is there a connection between the envelope and the lock of hair?" Finley asked.

"Yes. Yes and no. There is a connection, but her life is sadness and pain. His is mostly love and warmth."

"Joel Hampton was adopted. Could this envelope have been addressed by his real mother?"

"Maybe. There is a connection. But wait . . ."

"What is it?" Finley asked eagerly.

Schlepler paused. "Nothing. I no longer feel it."

"What was it, Aurther?"

"Confusion. Just confusion."

"What about the picture?" Finley asked as he handed Schlepler the picture of the farmhouse.

Schlepler placed it in his right palm. He studied it for a few minutes, then again closed his eyes. His kind face grew rigid. "This is . . . oh, this is vicious . . . this is . . . horrible . . ."

"What's horrible?"

"This house!" Schlepler suddenly stood up, dropped the picture on the coffee table, and shuffled quickly over to a window where he stood with his back to Finley. "I must finish my work on the plants now," he said tersely.

"What did you see, Aurther?"

"There is so much to do before the winter frosts."

"Aurther, please, what did you see?"

"Don't go near that house!" Schlepler said firmly as he headed toward the door. "It's a place of madness. Not the harmless insanity you have seen sitting in the wheelchairs and benches just outside this room. That house is filled with a madness that destroys everything that is pure and good about life."

As he drove from Farmington to his office in Kenyon, Finley pondered the salient features of the Joel Hampton case. He was well aware that what had begun as a matter of professional curiosity was rapidly becoming something far more complicated. He had an appointment with Joel that afternoon, and he wanted to bring everything he could to it in the hope of making some kind of breakthrough.

Finley reflected on the way Joel's whole demeanor was changing, becoming more sullen and morose. Frequently, as Joel stared out the window or focused on one of the many objects in Finley's cluttered office, he would become lost in thought and oblivious to his surroundings. At other times his eyes darted nervously around the room, like a cornered animal looking for a way out of a trap.

Finley had seen that look before in patients at Farmington who were ultimately labeled "hopelessly schizophrenic" or even "incurably psychotic or psychopathic." He had also seen that look in the eyes of the prisoners of war he had worked with after their release from Japanese and Korean prison camps. One could not apply psychological labels to these men because they simply did not fit. It went much deeper than that. They had seen something so horrible that they were driven to suicide or outrageous acts of violence against others, almost as if in imitation of what they had seen and experienced. Finley saw that same look in Joel's eyes, and he knew it probably signaled the beginning of a complete nervous and emotional collapse, followed by a period of potentially violent and uncontrollable behavior.

Joel was a few minutes late for his appointment, and Finley lost no time in putting him under hypnosis. Before taking him deeper into the trance, he checked Joel's pulse rate. It registered much too high for a man his age who appeared to be in the peak of condition and in a resting position. Clearly, something was happening inside him that defied conventional psychological labels.

"Joel, can you hear me?" Finley asked, placing his patient's right arm gently on the armrest of the reclining chair.

Joel did not respond

"What year is it?" Finley asked as he checked the tape recorder. "Concentrate on the whirlpool of color and tell me what year it is."

"1933," Joel whispered, the words barely escaping from his lips.

"Good, now let's go back even further. Follow the whirlpool of color back to 1926. You live in Carver County in 1926, and you know someone by the name of Katharine. Can you tell me your name?"

Joel's lips moved slowly, but he did not respond.

Finley repeated his prompting and again asked Joel his name.

"No name," Joel mumbled.

"What are you doing in Carver County in 1926?"

"Walkin'," Joel said softly after a slight pause.

"You are walking?" Finley asked.

"Walkin'," he repeated.

"Where are you walking to?" Finley inquired gently.

"Walkin'. Walkin'. Got a locket for me darlin', for me darlin' Lady Kate." Joel suddenly started singing in the thick Irish accent.

"Who is Kate?"

"Kate, Kate. Such a lovely lady," he replied cheerfully.

"What happened to you in 1926, Joel?"

Joel moved his lips but again did not respond.

"Did something happen to you in 1926, Joel? What was it?"

"Killed . . ."

"Who was killed?" Finley asked eagerly.

His hand reached slowly, steadily, into the dried reeds and brush on the edge of the marsh. The beautiful red and brown bird was lying in the dead vegetation. He stroked its magnificent plumage. The bird gasped and shuddered and died under his gentle stroke . . .

"Who was killed?" Finley repeated.

"Killed . . . killed," Joel whispered.

"What happened to you while you were walking?"

"Rooster pheasant. Killed 'im with a rock."

Finley paused. "Where are you walking to, Joel?"

There were many sounds all around him. The crickets were chirping contentedly in a pond, and a frog leaped off a fallen log and splashed into the shallow water. Overhead, the Canadian geese honked loudly as they flew south. Dead leaves rustled in the branches of the trees as he was walking. Walking beneath a clear blue sky.

"Who is Kate, Joel?"

"Such a lady . . ."

"Were you killed while you were walking in 1926?" Finley asked boldly.

The thicket was only a few hundred feet from where he stood. Dead autumn leaves waved wildly in the wind and tumbled into the open fields. Something was in the thicket, waiting for him. He did not want to go over there, but his legs started walking in that direction. He stepped off a small embankment, entered the stubble of a wheat field, and approached the trees. "Don't go in there!" he told himself. Two arms reached out of the thicket and gestured for him to enter it. "Don't go into the thicket!" he told himself again. "Don't go!" But he went in anyway.

"Get away! Get away from me!" Joel screamed loudly as his arms flailed out, desperately fighting the air.

"Who are you fighting?" Finley asked quickly.

"Get away from me!" Joel screamed as he sat up and looked directly at Finley. "Get away or I'll kill you!"

"Joel, I'm Dr. Finley. It's 1959. You're okay. Please lie back."

"I said I'll kill you!" Joel repeated fiercely.

"I'm taking you out of the hypnotic trance. Your name is Joel Hampton and you are a lawyer. You live in Kenyon. You have a lovely wife and daughter." As he spoke, Finley looked deeply into the hate-filled eyes of his young patient. "Concentrate on the whirlpool of color as I count off the years. 1939, 1940 . . ."

Joel closed his eyes and leaned slowly back in the chair as Finley counted off the years.

"When I reach 1959, I want you to open your eyes. 1957, 1958, 1959 . . ."

When Joel opened his eyes, the look in them had changed from anger to confusion. He lay there for several seconds before speaking. "Dr. Finley, am I going insane?" he finally asked as he stared at the ceiling.

"No, but something's going on inside of you that neither of us understands."

"What's wrong with me? I seem to drift between two worlds. This one, and a nightmare world I only vaguely remember and have no power to control."

"I wish I could give you an easy answer, but I have none." Finley reached into his shirt pocket. "Have you ever seen this house before?" he asked, handing Joel the picture of the farmhouse Susan had given him.

Joel studied the photograph and handed it back to Finley. "No," he said.

"Are you certain?"

"Yes. Why do you ask?"

"Your wife found it in a box of old clothes your parents gave her. It was in an envelope with a lock of your baby hair."

Joel looked at the photograph again, then shook his head. "No. I've never seen it before."

Finley pushed himself slowly out of his chair and walked over to the rear window. Outside, a lone hawk was floating in a blue sky. Finley watched it soar in ever-widening circles until it gradually disappeared from sight. "Joel, do you believe in reincarnation?" Finley asked as he searched the sky for any sign of the hawk. He turned and looked back at Joel. "Do you believe people can live more than one life?"

"Why do you ask?"

"Because something is happening inside of you that cannot be explained by anything in the psychology textbooks. It's much more complicated. You . . . you seem to be taking on the personality of someone who lived thirty or forty years ago."

Joel stared at the ceiling. "Dr. Finley, I know that I died once before, a long time ago."

"How do you know that?"

"I . . . I can't explain it."

"Do you remember who you were or how it happened?"

"No," Joel uttered softly as he turned his head toward Finley. "But I felt myself die just before you took me out of the trance."

><><><

Susan had just placed a tray of cookies in the oven when the telephone rang.

"Susan, this is Jim Morris," a deep voice boomed across the telephone line. "Do you have a few minutes?"

"Yes, of course. What is it, Mr. Morris?"

"I've been meaning to talk to you for some time. But I've just been too busy." There was an awkward pause at the other end of the line.

"I've wanted to talk to you too, Mr. Morris," Susan said. "I wanted to thank you for giving Joel the two weeks off. We're looking forward to the vacation."

"Yes, well, my pleasure, of course," Morris stammered. "May I speak to you candidly?"

"Yes, of course," Susan replied.

"As you know, I think very highly of your husband. He's one of the best young attorneys we've ever had in this firm. And I think he has a tremendous future. But some things have happened recently."

There was another awkward pause.

"What kind of things?" Susan asked apprehensively.

"For the past month, Joel just hasn't been himself. His legal briefs are sloppily written, he forgets appointments, and there are entire days when he doesn't show up in the office. He tells the secretary he's been in the law library, but the other attorneys spend a lot of time over there and they've never seen him. I was wondering . . . well, are things all right at home? Or, if not, is there something I could do to help?"

"I don't know," Susan said. "I think Joel just needs a vacation. He moved directly from law school to the firm without a break. I think he's just exhausted."

"I hope that's all it is. It's just . . . Well, listen, if there's anything I can do, anything at all, just let me know. You know how my wife and I feel about both of you. We really want to see Joel make it here."

"Thank you, Mr. Morris. We appreciate that. Would you please tell Joel to call me before he goes home?"

There was another pause. "I haven't seen Joel for three days. That's primarily why I called."

"But I thought he was to argue the Mallory case."

"I had to send another attorney over to represent Mallory. Joel didn't show up either time he was supposed to meet Mallory at the courthouse," Morris said almost apologetically.

Susan vaguely heard him say something else. Then there was a click, followed by a buzzing noise as the connection was broken. She slowly placed the receiver back on the hook and sat down at the kitchen table to ponder what Morris had just told her.

Had her suspicions been correct? Was Joel seeing someone else? Or was it . . .

She quickly stood up and walked over to the foot of the staircase. "Aggy," she yelled up to the attic. "Get your things. I'm taking you across the street to play with Robin."

As Susan drove to the law library, she thought about how she hadn't been completely honest with Dr. Finley. She couldn't tell him about the mutilated doll or the episode with the butcher knife in the attic. She had been too embarrassed. Or possibly she didn't believe it herself. The strong, gentle man she had married seemed incapable of such things. Revealing it would seem like she was being unfaithful to Joel. But she decided the next time she met with Dr. Finley, she would tell him everything. Joel's career, their marriage, and possibly their lives were in grave danger.

Susan spotted Joel's Ford station wagon next to a city park about three miles from the law library. She parked her Chevrolet next to it. She found Joel sitting on a bench, his eyes fixed on some old Victorian homes directly across from the park. "Condemned" signs hung from two of the houses, and work crews scurried around on scaffolds, tearing off the roofs.

"Joel, what are you doing here?" she asked angrily. His gaze remained fixed on the homes. "Answer me. Why aren't you at the office?"

He had known such love and such hate in that house. There was a windmill and a huge silo and a large oak tree with a swing hanging from one of the branches . . .

"Do you know who I am?" The anger in Susan's voice had been replaced by deep concern. "Joel . . ."

As he stood by the river, he could see the house in the distance. He could hear her laughing beside him. Why, then, did he feel such fear and anger and sadness when he saw the stately old house rising out of the prairie? What had happened there?

"Joel, do you know who I am?"

He heard the voice pulling him out of the darkness, and he looked up at his wife. "Susan?" he muttered faintly.

"Are you all right?"

Joel's eyes moved slowly around the park. "What are we doing out here?" he asked weakly.

Susan sat down beside him. "What were you just thinking?"

"I don't remember."

"How long have you been here?"

"I don't know. I'm sorry, Susan. I just don't know." He leaned forward until his head was buried in his hands and his body began to shake.

Susan felt his back muscles quiver as she ran her hand gently along his spine. Then she saw the half-empty vial of sleeping pills in the grass next to his foot. "Joel, did you take these?"

Joel shook his head slowly without looking at her.

"Are you sure?" she demanded.

"I was going to take them, but I didn't have the courage," he whispered hoarsely as he looked across the park at the houses again.

Susan held him hard. "God, Joel, what is it? What is doing this to you?"

The first thing Susan heard was the metallic pinging of the raindrops against the gutters outside the bedroom window. A sudden gush of cold air blasted into the room, and the blue linen curtains billowed toward the ceiling. It was followed by the ping, ping, ping of tiny hailstones against the glass panes.

Susan rolled sleepily out of bed and half walked, half stumbled over to the window. She pulled it down with a loud thud.

Suddenly, thunder roared and lightning flashed, sending brilliant streaks of light into the room and across the empty bed. "Oh, no!" she gasped, peering into the dark hallway. "Aggy," she whispered as she rushed toward her daughter's room.

She flicked the light switch on the wall up and down, but the hallway remained in darkness.

Not again!

The small, battery-operated nightlight glowed dimly in the corner of Aggy's room, and a rag doll slumped forlornly next to a toy telephone. Susan reached blindly on the bed for Aggy as the thunder crashed overhead.

"Aggy!" she called frantically.

Susan quickly descended the staircase into the parlor. "Aggy," she called into the living room. "Aggy, are you in there?"

A small candle was burning in the middle of the coffee table. As the light flickered, it fell across the form of her daughter lying on the floor.

"Aggy!" Susan cried. She rushed over and placed her hand gently on the little girl's chest. "What are you doing down here?"

Aggy sat up slowly and rubbed her hands sleepily across her eyes. "Mommy?"

"Yes, honey, what are you doing down here?"

"I think Daddy brought me here."

"Where is Daddy?"

"I don't know," Aggy yawned.

"Let's go back upstairs, honey." Susan picked up Aggy and looked apprehensively into the darkness behind her.

As she walked toward the stairs, she heard a soft rustling noise coming from the basement. Then there were slow, steady footsteps on the basement staircase. They were followed by the soft shuffle of feet across the kitchen floor.

As the light from the candle fell across Joel, Susan saw that he was holding something in his right hand.

"Oh my God!" she gasped. She quickly turned and ran up the stairs toward the attic. She heard his footsteps behind her.

She wrenched the attic door open and slammed it shut behind her in the same motion. She quickly slid the bolt into position and leaned against the wall.

As soon as she pulled her fingers away from the lock, a fishing knife slashed through the door's new panels. It quickly withdrew, then sliced through again.

Susan stumbled over toys and dolls as she carried Aggy to the dollhouse. She pushed her through the open doorway. Outside the attic window, thunder exploded and lightning flashed across the wooden floor.

"Mommy," the little girl whimpered.

"Aggy, get as far in the back as you can! And try to be quiet!"

"Mommy . . ."

"Please, honey, do as I say. And don't say a word."

As Aggy crawled into the rear of the dollhouse, Susan heard the sharp, splintering sound of wood behind her. An arm smashed through the door, and a hand began fumbling with the bolt as lightning flashed again.

Susan shut the door of the dollhouse and quickly crawled to the other side of the room. She pressed her body into a narrow recess beneath one of the gables.

In the darkness, she could not see the attic door. She could only hear the creaking hinges and the slow shuffle of feet across the floor. She tried to control the pounding of her heart, but it raced wildly out of control.

Then she heard another sound, like a puppy crying. She listened to the footsteps as they paused briefly and moved slowly toward the dollhouse. What had first been a whimper became muffled, uncontrolled sobbing. Then the thunder exploded and lightning flooded the room, illuminating Joel as he reached for the door of the dollhouse.

"Joel, what are you doing?" Susan screamed as she stood up. "What are you trying to do to us?"

As darkness descended again, she heard the feet move in her direction. In another flash of lightning, she saw the knife in Joel's hand. She began sobbing uncontrollably, groping madly for something to protect herself. But she found only a large, locked trunk.

"What are you doing to us? God, what is it you want?"

Then something clattered across the floor. As the lightning flashed again, she saw that Joel's hand was empty.

"Ah, Katharine," a voice with a thick Irish accent called to her. "What is it ya be cryin' for, girl?"

"Joel, what are you doing?"

"Ah told ya I'd be back, now didn't I? So why so sad, girl?"

Susan felt two hands caress her cheeks. They were gentle, loving.

"Didn't ya have no faith in me?"

"Joel, please. Who are you? What do you want? For God's sake . . ."

"I got a present for ya, Kate. I brought it all the way from Carson. Do ya want to see it?" The hands continued caressing her face.

"Joel . . ."

"It's right here."

She felt one of the hands stiffen.

"I put it . . . where did it . . ."

The tone of the voice was changing, growing more angry and menacing.

"It's . . . it's . . ." Suddenly there was a loud scream, a deep, mournful lament that slowly blended with the exploding thunder.

The hands were slowly withdrawn from her cheeks, and the thunder swallowed up the sound of footsteps as Joel scurried toward the door and descended the staircase.

Susan heard the basement door being flung open violently. She slumped to the floor, sobbing quietly in the darkness.

Finley had very little to work with, only the name Katharine and a picture of an old Victorian farmhouse. He knew he needed more to start searching for someone who had possibly lived in Carver County earlier in the century, someone whose memory apparently lived on inside the subconscious mind of Joel Hampton.

He was concentrating on replaying the tapes of his sessions with Joel when Susan slipped quietly into his office. He didn't notice her at first.

"That was Joel, wasn't it?" she asked.

"Yes," Finley said, surprised by her sudden appearance.

"But it wasn't his voice."

"No. It's someone else's voice," Finley agreed.

"He talks like that in his sleep," she said. "He talks about strange people and events in that voice. Dr. Finley, what is happening to my husband?"

"I don't know, Susan. I'm going up to Carver County tomorrow to see if I can get some answers."

"I hope you find something soon," Susan said tiredly. "It's getting worse. Much worse. I'm afraid I haven't been completely honest with you. I don't know why. I guess there were just some things I didn't want to admit to myself."

"Such as?"

"You asked me, the first time we talked, if Joel had ever threatened Aggy or me."

Finley nodded. "Has he?"

"Twice now," Susan sighed. "In the middle of the night. He came after us with a knife. He was speaking in the voice on the tape recorder. He was completely out of control. We had to hide in the attic."

"Were either of you hurt?"

"No. I'm not really sure he meant to hurt us. I know that sounds insane, but he had the chance to kill me. Instead he threw the knife away and gently caressed my cheeks. He called me Katharine and talked as though he had been trying to get back to see me for a long time."

"Are you willing to have him committed?"

"I don't know. I'm afraid that would destroy him."

"You have to think of your daughter."

"She's with her grandmother. I drove her over there this morning. She's safe there. I don't know if Joel would actually hurt me. He had his chance and . . . instead he expressed his love for me, or at least for Katharine."

"I'm driving to Carver County first thing tomorrow," Finley said. "I'll leave a phone number where you can get ahold of me if anything happens. But I think you should consider having him committed."

"There's just one other thing," Susan said quietly, pulling a folded legal document out of her purse. "I found this behind Joel's baby picture, in an old photo album the Hamptons apparently put together years ago."

Finley unfolded the document and studied its bold print. "It's a copy of the adoption certificate," he said. "From some kind of private agency."

"Yes."

"No father is listed, but the mother's name is Katharine McCarthy," he said, looking up at Susan.

CHAPTER FIVE

Finley drove his 1953 Studebaker along the smooth concrete surface of Highway 75 and turned west on the bumpier asphalt surface of County Road 16. According to the map, Danvers was approximately fifty-five miles from Kenyon and forty-five miles from the Farmington State Mental Hospital.

Soon a faded sign announced "Carver County Line." A smaller sign said "Danvers, 10 miles." An old man, obviously a vagrant, sat at the base of the sign, his legs sprawled out across the gravel embankment and his hands folded on top of his baggy, navy-blue trousers. His eyes and face reflected a profound weariness. He stared straight ahead as Finley's Studebaker passed the sign and continued west.

Most of the small grain crops had been harvested, and bales of hay and straw littered the fields and ditches. A few clusters of trees also dotted the landscape, their colorful leaves swaying gently in the autumn breeze. In some areas, the jagged stubble of cornstalks protruded above the baked fields.

Finley wasn't quite sure how to proceed now that he was in Carver County. Since Danvers was the county seat, he decided he would start with the county building.

As he approached the city limits, he passed a sign that said "Danvers, pop. 212." The town was located between several foot-hills. A church steeple, a water tower, and a grain elevator rose high above the small town. Nearby, the Little Sioux River curled through the foothills and fields.

As Finley entered Danvers from the east, the other end of town was visible as it opened onto the fields in the west. Main Street itself was laid out over no more than five or six blocks.

The buildings were very old, seemingly untouched since the early part of the twentieth century. Many of the small shops and stores were abandoned, and dust had collected heavily on the display windows. A few forgotten, faded items were still visible in some of them. Other windows were boarded up, although signs advertising the wares and services of past tenants hung over Main Street.

Finley stopped next to a vacant drugstore. A thin, bearded man in a blue and white shirt and matching baseball hat was inserting a long thin pole into the frame of the faded green awning that ran the length of the store. Finley parked the Studebaker diagonally against the curb and stepped out into the bright sunlight. He paused to look down both ends of the street.

There was something almost ghostly about the abandoned stone and brick shops. A strong, pervading sense of decay clung to the brick facades, dusty windows, and signs advertising businesses that no longer existed.

A small, mangy brown and white mongrel dog suddenly leaped out of an alley, veered sharply to its right, and raced along one of the crumbling storefronts. A few feet ahead of the dog, a large rat scurried along the base of the wall. Its thin, pointed tail stuck out sharply behind its fat brown body as it disappeared into a hole where a brick had fallen out of the foundation of one of the buildings.

The dog came to a skidding halt in front of the hole. It lowered its nose and barked loudly into the darkness. Then it sniffed along the entire wall, paused once more in front of the hole, barked again and, defeated, walked slowly back down the sidewalk.

Finley watched the dog disappear into the alley. Then he approached the man who was cranking the awning out over the sidewalk. "Can you tell me where I might find the county building?" he asked.

The man extracted the pole and turned to face Finley. His Brooklyn Dodgers baseball hat, the brim tilted upwards, was shifted comically to the right side of his head. He smiled strangely and placed a stick of chewing gum in his mouth. Then, without speaking, he walked across the street and began cranking awnings up against the walls.

Finley paused for a moment, puzzled by someone who would crank the awnings out over one side of Main Street and then crank them back up on the other side. There was no threat of rain. The sky was clear blue and the only clouds looked like distant wisps of smoke hanging in the north. And, even if it did rain, the awnings were obviously too worn and tattered to offer protection.

Finley shook his head, deciding it wasn't worth pondering. He looked up and down the street, searching for the county building.

An old woman carrying a grocery bag suddenly stepped out of one of the side streets and shuffled past him. "Where might I find the county building?" he asked.

"At the end of the street," she replied cheerfully, pointing at the largest building. "Right down there."

"Thanks," Finley replied as he prepared to cross the street.

"New in town?" she asked.

"No, just on vacation. Might do a little fishing."

"Not much else to do around Danvers. Town's pretty much dead. 'Cept for us old people who find it too painful to leave."

"What happened?" Finley asked. "From the looks of these buildings, this was once a prosperous little town."

"They opened up a soybean factory and four huge grain elevators over in Tyler. Pretty much killed off everything around here. Farmers shop over there now. Barney keeps his elevator open, but he's not making much money. When the elevators go in these small towns, everything else dies right behind them."

"Tell me," Finley said, pointing at the thin man cranking up the awnings. "Why does he do that?"

"Benny? Ah, don't pay no mind to him. He struggles with anything that makes him think too hard. They used to pay him a nickel or a dime to crank out the awnings when it rained, crank them back up again when it was over. He probably don't even know most of these shops are closed. Anyhow, it keeps him busy and we all got to do something, don't we?"

The old woman switched the bag of groceries from her left arm to her right. "Good talking to you," she said. "Hope you have a nice vacation."

"One other thing," Finley said. "Have you ever heard of someone by the name of Katharine McCarthy who might have lived around here?"

"McCarthy?" She pondered the name. "Nope. Not too many by that name in Carver County. Irish settled quite a bit north of here."

"You're sure you've never heard of someone by that name?"

"Nope. Sorry," she said, walking away.

Finley immediately walked over to the county building, which was constructed out of red brick and granite blocks. Unlike the other buildings on Main Street, it had pillars next to the arched portico. Above the portico, a large American eagle clenched a bronze flagpole firmly in its beak, and its sharp talons gripped a stone ledge protruding from the wall. Someone had neglected, however, to place a flag at the end of the pole. A flag flew instead in the upper right corner of the building, next to a stone nymph reclining on the wall just below the roofline.

Finley walked up the steps and entered the building. He walked down a hallway with glistening, reddish-brown floor tiles and entered the first office he encountered.

"Yes?" a fat, middle-aged man with thick glasses asked as he looked up from a ledger on the counter. A name tag pinned to his shirt indicated he was the county recorder.

"I need some information," Finley said. "Birth certificates, death certificates, anything like that on a Katharine McCarthy who might have lived in Carver County in the 1920s or earlier. Do you have that information here?"

"Well, if she was born here or died here, I might have it. When was she born?"

"Sometime between 1890 and 1915, I think."

"You don't know the exact date?"

"No."

"Are you a relative?"

"No, I'm doing a genealogy," Finley lied, knowing the county recorder would never believe the truth.

"Well, wait here a minute," the man said. He walked toward a vault in the back of the room.

"Thanks," Finley said.

"Katharine who?" the county recorder yelled back as he paused at the entrance to the vault.

"McCarthy," Finley said. "I think she was born sometime between 1890 and 1915."

After the county recorder disappeared into the vault, Finley stood by the front desk and let his eyes wander over the area behind the counter. A large photograph of a distinguished, white-haired man in a dark-blue business suit was prominently displayed in the middle of one wall. Finley was trying to remember where he had seen the photograph before when the county recorder stepped out of the vault. He was carrying a large brown book.

"No Katharine McCarthy ever born in this county," he said, flopping the book down on the counter. "Of course, that don't mean nothing. Records weren't that good back then."

"Were there *any* McCarthys born in Carver County around that time?" Finley asked.

"Let's see," the man said, paging through the thick volume. "There was a Kevin McCarthy born in 1906. And a Jody McCarthy born in 1903. None of the mothers' names is Katharine. That's about it. Not too many Irish in Carver County. Mostly British and Scandinavians, even to this day."

"Did either of those two McCarthys die here?"

"Well, now I don't know. I'll have to check the death certificates. Just a minute," he said, disappearing again into the vault.

"While you're back there, would you check to see if a Katharine McCarthy was ever married in Carver County?" Finley yelled after him.

The county recorder reappeared shortly, carrying two large brown books. He flopped the larger one on the counter and began paging through it. "No one named Katharine McCarthy was ever married in Carver County," he said, scratching the top of his head and pushing his large eyeglasses further up his nose.

"How about the death certificates?" Finley asked.

The county recorder flipped through the pages of the other book. "Well, it says here this Jody McCarthy died three days after he was born. Diphtheria. An awful lot of that back then."

"And the other McCarthy?"

"Kevin McCarthy? Let's see. Killed in a farm accident in 1919. Fell out of a silo and broke his neck. That's a shame. Those silos can be awfully dangerous."

"That would make him thirteen," Finley said. "You have nothing on a Katharine McCarthy?"

"Nope. But like I said, it don't mean nothing." The man shut the book and set it carefully on top of the other two. "She might've lived here back then. But unless she was born here, died here, or married here, we'd have no record of her. Might not even have one then. People weren't quite so particular 'bout filing legal documents back in those days."

"Where else might I look?"

"Well, I can think of two places. You could try the high school. She might have graduated from Danvers High. In which case her picture would probably be up there someplace. Or you could try the hotel. Some of the old boys over there might've heard of her."

"Can I go up to the high school on a school day?"

"No such thing as a school day anymore. Young people here, what's left of them, are bused over to Tyler. Be movin' the county seat over there soon. Probably turn Danvers into a ghost town."

"Danvers seems awfully small to have been the county seat in the first place."

"It was."

"Then how did it happen?"

"That fella over there on the wall, John J. Sylvester," the county recorder said, pointing toward the large picture Finley had spotted earlier. "He had a lot of political pull back in the twenties. Became governor in the thirties. Good man, John Sylvester. One of the best to come out of Danvers."

Joel was driving to work when he saw a group of preschool children on their hands and knees, frantically peering into a storm sewer. Fearing that maybe one of them had somehow fallen into the sewer, Joel parked his car and walked over to them.

"What's wrong?" he asked as he approached the children.

"Samantha's puppy," the oldest boy said. He pointed into the sewer. "It fell down there."

Joel knelt down and peered through the openings in the grate. A tiny, shivering ball of fur was curled up on a ledge some five or six feet below the surface of the street. Under the ledge, a stream of dirty water flowed sluggishly across the concrete floor of the sewer.

"Stand over there," Joel said to the children. "I'll see if I can pull the grate off."

As they retreated to the safety of the sidewalk, Joel leaned over and curled his fingers around the heavy iron grate that covered the sewer opening. He pulled hard on it, but it would not move.

He paused for a moment, then curled his fingers around the grate and lifted again. This time it groaned against its iron housing and slid onto the asphalt surface of the street. The group of children edged closer to peer into the hole.

"Stay away," Joel admonished them. He lowered himself onto the iron ladder that was bolted into the wall of the sewer. "I'll be right back."

He climbed down the ladder until his feet were resting on the last rung, several inches above the stream of water. Then he reached out and gently lifted the puppy off the ledge. He stroked and comforted the puppy as he stood on the bottom rung of the ladder . . .

He had worked with animals before. A long time ago. He delivered a tiny foal as the mare lay dying on the straw-covered floor of the barn. He pulled the foal out of the mare with his bare hands. He cleaned and wrapped it in a heavy blanket and held it tight against his chest as the mare gasped and kicked and died and the blood flowed thick on the floor of the barn . . .

"Is he okay?" a girl's voice asked nervously from just outside the sewer opening.

"Ya, he be okay," Joel answered in the strong Irish accent. "He jus' be plenty scared, that's all."

He placed the puppy in his coat pocket and climbed back up the iron ladder. A fresh breeze blew gently across his cheeks as he stepped out of the sewer. He sat down on the edge of the sidewalk and dangled his feet in the hole.

"Ya see," he admonished the girl, "ya shouldn't be takin' a young pup like this away from its mother. He ain't even been weaned yet."

"Can I have him?" the girl asked as she reached toward the puppy.

"Inna minute, lass, but first ya gotta promise me ya won't take him out again. Not 'til he's older."

"I promise."

"Wait, lass. First I gotta know the names of these hooligans here. What be yur names now?"

"Samantha."

"Bobby."

"Alan."

"Frances."

The children obediently said their names as Joel pointed at each of them.

"Well, Samantha an' Bobby an' Alan an' Frances, those be some mighty pretty names. An' what be the pup's name?"

"He doesn't have one yet," the girl who had identified herself as Samantha answered shyly.

Joel handed her the puppy. "Now you leave him home 'til he has a name and gets bigger. Ain't no one should go out in the world without a name."

"Thanks, mister."

"You're mighty welcome, lad."

As the children started to leave, the oldest boy who had iden-tified himself as Alan turned and asked, "What's your name, mister?"

He should know that. That simple thing . . .

"My name?" Joel was uncomfortable with the question.

"I want to tell my mother," the boy said, "in case she asks."

"I . . . I don't know, lad. I'm sorry. Jus' take care of the pup now. Ya hear?"

Alan looked puzzled as he turned and walked after the rest of the group.

Joel pulled his legs out of the sewer opening and stood up. He leaned over and lifted the grate off the road. This time it seemed lighter, almost light enough to pick up with one hand.

He easily slid it back over the hole until it fell with a dull thud into its housing. He peered through the grate at the sluggish stream of water flowing at the bottom of the sewer.

A name? Everyone has a name. Yet he could not remember his.

><><><

The thick metal door opened with a loud groan, and Finley walked into a school hallway lined on both sides with green metal lock-ers. His footsteps echoed as the door scraped shut behind him.

The hall also contained several glass trophy cases. Black-and-white graduation pictures hung on the walls above the trophy cases and lockers. The rows of photographs covered the entire length of the hall.

Finley walked slowly, studying the faces and names of the graduating classes from earlier in the century.

"What year did you graduate?" a voice behind him suddenly asked.

"What?" Finley turned around quickly.

A thin, bald man with a half-filled bucket of water in one hand and a push broom in the other stood in the middle of the hall. "I asked when you graduated from here," he said, setting the bucket on the floor.

"I never went to school here," Finley responded.

The janitor pulled a cigar butt out of his front shirt pocket. "If you didn't graduate from Danvers, how come you're studying those pictures so carefully? Only reason people come back here anymore is to look at their graduation pictures. Or to point out their names on one of the trophies over there."

"I'm looking for someone who might have graduated from here forty or fifty years ago."

"What's the name?" the janitor asked, lighting the stub and puffing hard on it.

"Katharine McCarthy."

"Nope," he proclaimed emphatically, waving the cigar stub at the pictures on the wall. "Been dustin' those pictures for over twenty years. Never seen anyone by that name up there."

"Ever hear of anyone by that name living in Carver County?"

"Nope. Never even heard of a McCarthy livin' in this area." He leaned the push broom against the wall. "Like ya to see somethin', though."

The janitor led Finley over to one of the trophy cases that was built into the wall and framed with four pieces of oak trim stained the color of walnut. Several athletic trophies were displayed behind two sliding glass doors. The janitor carefully wiped a slight smudge off one of the doors with a rag he carried in his back pocket. He stepped back, puffed on the cigar, and admired his handiwork.

"See that?" he asked, pointing at the trophies.

"Which one?" Finley asked.

"That one there," the janitor said. He pointed the cigar at one of the larger trophies. "With the basketball player on top."

"Yes."

"Danvers won the regionals that year. Nineteen thirty-seven. Made it to the state tournament. My boy was on that team. He was the captain."

"You must have been proud of him."

"Yes, I was. He was killed in World War II."

"I'm sorry."

"We never made it to the state tournament again. Never even made it out of the district."

"Listen," Finley said gently. "I have to leave. But let me know if you remember anything about a Katharine McCarthy. I'll be staying at the hotel."

"'Course we lost the first game at state," the janitor continued, ignoring Finley. "But that didn't make no difference to us. That year everyone heard of Danvers. Made us proud to go into the big cities and tell people where we were from."

><><><

Finley walked slowly down the sloping foothill that separated Danvers High School from Main Street. As he glanced at the old gabled homes towering above the street, he had the sensation he was being watched. He had felt that way almost from the moment he first stepped out of his car on Main Street. Now, surrounded by the Victorian homes that were half concealed in the shadows of late afternoon, he felt even more uncomfortable.

Finley made his way to the Danvers Hotel and climbed a short flight of stairs that led to the outer lobby. Several old men were sitting by the window overlooking Main Street. Photographs and daguerreotypes in gold-leafed frames lined the walls next to mounted buffalo heads and deer antlers. Brass spittoons were scattered among large, padded easy chairs, and a bar with a brass foot rail was visible in an adjoining room.

Finley approached the desk clerk in the back of the lobby. "Do you have any rooms available?" he asked.

"How long ya gonna be stayin'?"

"Probably a few days."

"Well, we got rates. The longer ya stay, the cheaper the room. A dollar for one day. Six dollars for a week."

"Make it a week."

"Fill this out, then." The clerk slid a small white card across the counter. "Here's your key. Room 307. Looks right out onto Main Street. If ya leave early, be sure to return the key."

Finley filled out the registration card and gave it back to the clerk. "One more thing. I need information on someone who might have lived around here. Back in the 1920s."

"I've only been here ten years myself," the clerk said. He gestured toward the group of old men sitting by the front window. "You might talk to Oscar over there, the one lighting his pipe. He's been here most of his life."

"Thanks."

"Hey, Wally, your turn!" a voice yelled from across the lobby.

"Just a minute!" the clerk yelled back to three men sitting around a card table. "I'll be right over. Just don't look at my hand."

Finley walked over to where the old men were sitting. The one who had been identified as Oscar was packing tobacco into his mahogany pipe. He went about the task in a very ritualistic manner, attending to every detail with loving care.

"Excuse me," Finley said after Oscar had finished inspecting the bowl to make sure everything had been properly placed. "I was told you might be able to help me."

Oscar put a match to his pipe and puffed on it several times. When he was certain it was lit, he looked up at Finley. "What do you need?" he asked, leaning back in his chair, puffing contentedly.

"I need some information on someone who might have lived in Carver County in the 1920s."

"What's the name?"

"Katharine McCarthy."

Oscar considered the name carefully. "No Katharine McCarthy has ever lived in this town, leastways not that I know of."

"Are you sure?"

"I'm pretty sure." He yelled across the lobby at another old man meditating next to a cigarette machine. "Fred, you ever hear of a Katharine McCarthy living around here?"

The other man looked up and shook his head feebly.

"Nope. Sorry," Oscar said.

"Was there *anyone* by the name of McCarthy living around here back then?"

"Well, McCarthy's a common name in most places, I suspect. But not around here. Not anywhere in Carver County that I know of."

"How about a McCarthy who might have passed through here?"

Oscar puffed thoughtfully on his pipe. "Seems to me there was a construction crew that came through here in the twenties. There was a McCarthy among them."

"Was he married?"

"No, heavens, no. Those people never settle down. Finish one job and move on to the next. It's in their blood. They can't help themselves."

"Do you know where I can find out more about this McCarthy?"

"You could try Harmon over in the newspaper office. He knows something about almost everyone in Carver County. He might be able to help you. That is, if he's sober, which isn't very often anymore."

Finley looked out the window at Main Street. "Do you have any idea what happened to this McCarthy?"

"Oh, I suppose he just left with the rest of the crew once they were through here. I was in and out of the area during much of the 1920s. I probably wouldn't be the one to ask that question."

"Who might I ask?"

Outside the window a fire siren suddenly screamed, and all the old men who were nodding off to sleep raised their heads and smiled knowingly at one another.

"What's that?" Finley asked.

"Ah, it's nothing," Oscar said, banging his pipe into a metal ashtray.

"Looks like Harmon's on a toot again," another old man cackled gleefully.

"Ever have a real fire in this town, no one'll ever know about it," another laughed.

"They'll just think Harmon's hittin' the sauce again."

Within a few seconds, the notes of "Alexander's Ragtime Band" were playing on the fire siren and whistling through the streets and alleys.

"It takes some gettin' used to, I guess," Oscar chuckled. "But after you've been in Danvers long enough, ya kind of look forward to Harmon gettin' drunk and playin' music on the fire siren."

"He does this often?" Finley asked.

"Just about every day," Oscar chuckled, then once again began the ritual of packing his pipe. "You were askin' me something before Harmon started playin' his music."

"I was asking who I might talk to about McCarthy. The one you said worked for the construction crew in the1920s."

"Oh, yes. Gus," he yelled at another old man sitting by the front window, "whatever happened to that McCarthy who worked and wrestled back here in the 1920s?"

"He disappeared," Gus said.

"Just like I thought," Oscar said, turning back to Finley. "They leave right after they finish . . ."

"No, he *disappeared*," Gus interrupted. "Just didn't show up for work one day."

"What was McCarthy's first name?" Finley asked Gus.

"Judd. Judd McCarthy. A very powerful man. Probably the strongest man in Carver County. But no good."

"Why do you say that?"

"He disappeared with the company payroll."

"Are you sure?"

"Should be," Gus said, rising from his chair and shuffling toward one of the spittoons. "Cost me three months' wages."

"How well did you know this McCarthy?" Finley asked.

"Hardly at all," Gus answered, spitting into the spittoon. "We were assigned to completely different parts of the county. I just know I didn't get paid, that's all."

"When did he disappear?"

"Oh, it was in the twenties sometime," Gus answered. He made his way slowly across the lobby and sat back down in the easy chair. "I suppose it was 1925 or '26. It's been a long time. But it's somewheres in there."

"Do you have any idea where he might have gone?"

"We don't know," Gus repeated slowly as he lowered his head and closed his eyes. "He just disappeared."

Jim Morris glanced at the clock on his office wall. It was three thirty. He had been at his desk all day and he was tired and stiff. He stood up and stretched to relieve the aches in his cramped muscles and back. At the age of sixty-four, he was finding it difficult to devote an entire day to working at his desk. Retirement, just one year away, was beginning to look better all the time.

Still, there were compensations. Morris was proud of his paternalistic role in the law firm. He received far more satisfaction out of developing a young attorney than he did out of arguing a case in court. He hoped to continue guiding the younger members of the firm in his retirement years. But, thank God, he would never again have to write another legal brief.

He was looking out the window, thinking of getting in a few holes of golf before sunset, when one of the secretaries appeared at the door of his office.

"Mr. Morris, I think you'd better take a look at something downstairs," she said with a troubled look on her face.

"What is it?" Morris asked.

"I don't know how to describe it," she stammered. "It's Joel. He's . . . he's in the vault."

"Yes, I know. I sent him down there to find some files for me. What's the problem?"

"He's talking in there."

"So?"

"It's not his voice. It's not . . . Please, you'd better come downstairs."

"Okay," Morris said reluctantly.

He followed her out of his office and down the flight of stairs to the main floor of the building. Several offices had been created out of what had once been the main lobby of the Kenyon First National Bank. Secretaries and attorneys were gathered around the old bank vault where the law firm stored valuable legal documents.

"What is it?" Morris asked as he moved into the center of the group.

"Listen," someone said. "Something awfully strange is going on in there."

Morris placed his ear close to the door and listened to the garbled tones inside.

"Who's in there?" Morris asked. "Is it Joel?"

"Yes," someone replied.

"God, it sure doesn't sound like him."

Morris grasped the handle of the steel door and pulled hard on it. The door pivoted on its well-oiled hinges and slowly opened.

Toward the rear of the vault, Joel stood with his back to the door. He was indiscriminately pulling folders and legal documents out of filing cabinets and flinging them across the floor.

"Joel, what the hell is going on in here?" Morris asked as he walked into the vault.

Joel turned slowly to face him. "Ah, so it's you, is it?" he asked in a thick Irish accent. "Ah should've known ya had somethin' ta do with it." His eyes were fierce, threatening.

"What's wrong with you?" Morris asked cautiously, but firmly. The look in Joel's eyes was something he had never seen before, at least not in any sane man.

So he had been right. Even as he felt the life slipping out of his body, he knew who had set him up.

"Joel, what's wrong?" Morris repeated the question apprehensively. He stared at Joel, who was glaring defiantly back at him from the other end of the vault.

Joel started walking slowly toward Morris. "Ah shoulda known," he muttered.

"Lucy," Morris whispered without turning around. "You'd better call the police."

In the darkness he had waited for that face, any face. He had waited for days, weeks, months. Maybe even years. There was no way of knowing. But the rage had grown until there was no way to control it.

"Joel!" Morris yelled as the younger man suddenly leaped on him and wrestled him to the floor.

Morris lay on his back, staring into the angry eyes above him, as Joel clamped his hands around the older man's throat.

"Jesus Christ, he's trying to kill him!" someone yelled.

"Help him!"

"My God, he's too strong."

"Get help, quick!"

"Grab him around the throat! Pull him back!"

Morris felt the pressure on his throat increase, and a sharp pain shot through his brain and down into his chest.

"Jesus . . ."

"Hit him over the head with something!"

"I can't move his arm! He's too strong!"

Morris heard the police sirens screaming somewhere in the distance. Then he heard another sound, like the noise a large animal makes when it's cornered and about to die.

The scream blended with the sound of the sirens as a numbness surged through his body, and he was surrounded by flashes of light and color and finally darkness.

Finley was asleep in his hotel room when he heard a sound outside his door. As he turned in that direction, a shadow passed slowly over the sliver of light that slipped through the crack at the bottom of the door. The shadow was motionless. Then it slowly moved on and disappeared. Finley heard footsteps shuffle over the carpeted hall and descend the stairs.

He lay back and watched the shadows created by the lamps in the street below as they flickered across the ceiling of his room. He thought back to his discussions with the men in the lobby. He had wanted to ask Gus some more questions about the Judd McCarthy who had disappeared in the 1920s, but the old man was obviously in poor health and in need of an afternoon nap. He had fallen asleep before Finley could probe any deeper into McCarthy's disappearance. Later that evening, Finley had searched the lobby, but there was no sign of Gus or any of the other men.

As he stared at the shadows on the ceiling, Finley began to feel somewhat foolish for coming to Carver County in the first place. What was it he hoped to find in this virtual ghost town? More than likely, Joel Hampton had read about Carver County somewhere, and under the hypnotic trance, the name simply drifted out of his subconscious mind. And the thick Irish accent? Joel could have picked that up from an acquaintance or even a movie. Finley remembered reading somewhere that accents leave permanent impressions on the subconscious mind. Hypnotic suggestion could easily have removed Joel's inhibitions, and maybe he was simply mimicking an accent he had heard earlier.

Still, there was the private adoption certificate, the name Katharine, and the disappearance of Judd McCarthy. And there was something strange, almost ghostly, about the small town dying in the middle of the prairie. Finley could think of many plausible explanations for Joel's strange behavior. But as he walked the streets of Danvers, he felt in his gut that there was an almost supernatural connection between his patient and Carver County.

Suddenly, Finley remembered that he had forgotten to call Susan as he had promised. He reached for his watch on the nightstand and held it up to the light filtering in from the street below. It was twelve fifteen. Late, but he felt he should still make the call.

He put on his robe and slippers, grabbed some coins off the dresser, and padded out to the hallway. A few lights still glowed beneath the doors of several of the other rooms, but most of them were dark inside. In the lobby a single light was on above the registration desk, and the clerk was asleep on a small cot behind the counter. The light from the streetlamps outside the front window sent shadows flickering across the old photographs on the walls.

Finley stepped into the wooden phone booth next to the bar. The door creaked slowly shut behind him.

"Operator," a shrill female voice said as he placed the receiver to his ear.

"I would like to place a long distance phone call to Kenyon. The number is 589-1333," Finley said.

"Thank you." There was a slight pause. "Please deposit ten cents for the first three minutes."

Finley dropped a dime into the metal slot and listened to it jangle to the bottom of the pay phone. The line rang three times on the other end. After the third ring, a female voice whispered a sleepy "hello" into the receiver.

"Susan, this is Ned Finley. I'm calling from Danvers. I'm sorry. I forgot to leave a telephone number with you this afternoon."

"Dr. Finley, I'm so glad to hear from you. Something terrible has happened."

"What is it? What's wrong?"

"Joel went . . . he went berserk today . . ."

There was a pause, then a stifled sob.

"Susan, what happened?"

"Apparently, sometime in the middle of the day, he went crazy and destroyed a bunch of legal documents," Susan said slowly. "When they tried to stop him, he almost strangled Jim Morris. God, it was awful . . ."

"Is Morris okay?"

"He's in the hospital. At first they thought he might have suffered a stroke, but now they're saying he's going to be okay."

"Where's Joel?"

"He's at Farmington. They have him in restraints."

"Okay, I'm coming back. I'll meet you at Farmington tomorrow morning at ten."

"All right."

"Please get some sleep. I'll see you in the morning."

Finley hung up the telephone and sat in the booth thinking about what Susan had said. When he finally stepped out, the desk clerk was still asleep. A radiator hissed beneath the windows overlooking Main Street. He walked quietly up the two flights of stairs to his room, closed the door behind him, and turned on the light.

The contents of his suitcase were strewn across the threadbare carpet of the room, and his watch had been smashed on the nightstand. When he picked it up, tiny screws and gears and springs spilled out and disappeared into the carpet.

Finley lay the watch down on a vanity and looked out the window. He stared at the lampposts and signs and stone facades of the buildings on Main Street.

Then he looked back at the bed. He remembered having kicked back the covers before going downstairs. But now the bedspread was pulled back neatly over the rumpled blankets and sheets.

As he cautiously lifted the bedspread, a tiny stream of blood trickled off the mattress pad and dribbled to the floor.

He recognized the dog as the one he had seen chasing the rat earlier that morning.

CHAPTER SIX

"Where do we go from here?" Susan asked Finley as she slumped down on one of the stone benches in front of Farmington.

"They'll be doing some tests to see if it's physiological," Finley said, sitting down beside her.

"Physiological?"

"Brain tumors, things like that." Finley looked out over the hospital grounds. "But I don't think that has anything to do with it."

"On his chart, they use the term 'psychopathic tendencies' to describe Joel."

"I know. But he's not a psychopath." Finley picked up a dead leaf lying next to the bench and began crumbling it into little pieces in his palm. "A psychopathic personality develops over a long period of time. Generally the symptoms are evident in early childhood. Joel seemed to develop these symptoms almost overnight. It's something else. Right now, he's clearly dangerous, but I don't think he's psychopathic. It's probably closer to some form of schizophrenia. Maybe even something more complicated than that. I've worked with schizophrenic personalities, but never one who has retreated from reality as rapidly as your husband. He's plunging into some subconscious level of existence that I've never encountered before. Unless we get some answers and pull him out in the next few days or weeks, we may lose him altogether. We've got to find out what demons Joel is fighting before we can help him deal with them."

Susan shifted nervously, glancing at the huge granite walls behind her. "You mean, Joel may never get out of there?"

To Finley, Susan seemed so young, so helpless. Suddenly he realized he wanted to help Joel more than he'd ever wanted to help any patient before.

"There's always the very real possibility that Joel will be committed for a long time, maybe even for life. We never fully understand what forces work in the human mind, or whether they are permanent or temporary. But we'll get some answers, and I think we'll find them in Carver County."

"And you?" Susan inquired softly. "You can't just drop your practice to search for the ghosts in Joel's past. You have other responsibilities."

"I have my reasons. What I'm doing is not completely unselfish. I also have ghosts in my past." Finley paused. "Besides, I've been planning a vacation sometime this fall. Now seems like as good a time as any. My caseload is pretty light. Others will cover for me."

Neither Finley nor Susan spoke for a time.

Finley threw the remains of the leaf into the wind. "Tell me something," he said. "Was there any reason at all why your husband would have tried to kill Jim Morris?"

"No. Mr. Morris is like a father to all the young attorneys in that office. Joel idolized him."

"Maybe he thought Morris was someone else." Finley folded his hands and leaned forward on his knees. "How's your daughter?" he asked, changing the subject.

"I'm going over to my mother's this afternoon to pick her up. She's in no danger now that Joel's in there. I'm not accepting any more substitute teaching assignments until he gets better. I want to spend more time with Aggy. This has been too hard on her already."

Finley nodded. "We'll keep him sedated. In the meantime, I'll be going back to Carver County." He picked up another dead leaf and began stripping it. "You know, I'm convinced that something almost supernatural is driving Joel to do these things. Something happened a long time ago, something so horrible that many years later it's still being acted out in your husband's subconscious mind. I'm convinced of that."

"Why Joel?"

"I don't know. But now that I've been to Carver County, I feel it too. I don't know what it is. But it's there." Finley stood up, threw the leaf into the wind, and looked at the hospital. He debated whether to tell Susan about the mongrel dog, but decided against it. "Whatever it is, it's also working on me. I felt it every time I was walking the streets of Danvers. Something's very wrong in that town."

><><><

Susan watched the security guard lock the heavy iron gates after Finley walked through them. Then she stood and walked toward the stairway leading up to the front door of the hospital. She pulled hard on the huge iron handle bolted into the thick wooden door. It swung open, and she stepped into the shadows on the first floor.

The stale smell of urine and perspiration clung to the air in the poorly ventilated halls and corridors. Heavily sedated patients sat on plain wooden benches and gazed at the floor as orderlies and nurses moved among them distributing pills. Other patients, propped up in wheelchairs or strapped to large wooden chairs, sat along the outer walls.

As Susan approached the foot of the stairway leading up to the second floor, an elderly woman in a green hospital gown appeared in a doorway. The woman curled one arthritic index finger and gestured for Susan to come into the room. Susan could see that toys and dolls were scattered across the tile floor. Elderly male and female patients sat cross-legged on the floor, hugging the dolls or holding the toys up in the air for inspection.

"Come see," the old woman whispered as she stepped toward Susan. "Come see."

One side of the woman's face was paralyzed, and the flesh had folded into layers that dropped below the chin line. The eyeball was frozen open in the middle of the mass of flesh.

The old woman took another step. "Come see."

Susan stared at the unblinking eyeball as the woman moved closer, all the while gesturing with her crooked finger.

Joel doesn't belong here! They shouldn't keep him here! Susan thought hysterically.

As the old woman reached out to touch her forearm, Susan gasped and rushed up the stairs. The old woman fastened her eyeball on Susan's retreating form and kept repeating her request.

At the top of the staircase, a thick wire screen had been stretched across the entrance leading into a long hallway. The words RESTRICTED AREA were painted in black letters on a sign above the screen. Several muscular orderlies patrolled the hall, and a young nurse sat at a wooden desk in front of the enclosure.

"Who do you want to see?" the nurse asked coldly.

"My husband, Joel Hampton," Susan said.

"Do you have identification?"

"Yes." Susan reached into her purse and took out her billfold. "Here," she said, holding out her driver's license.

The nurse studied it. "Okay, but you'll have to leave that here."

"Leave what here?"

"The purse," the nurse said as she stood up. "And I'll have to check your pockets."

"Why?"

"We can't let people bring things in that the patients could use to hurt themselves or someone else. Even a simple set of keys can do a great deal of damage in the wrong hands."

Susan placed her purse on the table and lifted her arms. The nurse felt along the contours of Susan's body and thrust her hands deeply into her coat pockets.

"Okay," the nurse announced as she sat back down. "Sign here and be sure to do it again when you leave."

Susan quickly signed the register.

"Your husband is in Room 216," the nurse said, reaching for a key on the wall behind her. She stood up and inserted the key into the thick metal door in the middle of the wire screen. "Please don't go into any of the other rooms if the doors are open."

As Susan stepped into the hallway, the door clanged shut behind her. She heard the key scrape against the lock as the bolt slipped into place.

The smell of urine, perspiration, and fecal matter was even stronger than it had been on the first floor. Groans, stifled screams, and other unidentified noises drifted out from behind the metal doors on both sides of the corridor. She tried not to think of what might be happening behind those doors, or who might be making those sounds.

A large, muscular orderly met her in front of Room 216. He inserted a key into the lock and turned it slowly counterclockwise. "We keep the doors locked during the day," he said, sensing that some explanation might be necessary. "Some of the patients are occasionally allowed out into the halls. We don't want them stumbling into the wrong rooms."

"Are you going to lock it while I'm in there?"

"How long do you plan to be?"

"Not long."

The orderly noticed the nervousness in Susan's voice. "I'll leave it open. Just let me know when you leave."

Susan nodded and stepped through the doorway. Joel was stretched out across a bed on the far side of the room. A single window with thick iron bars was located near the bed. Except for the bed and two wooden chairs, the room was barren.

Susan walked over and looked down at Joel. He was dressed in a faded green hospital gown, and his arms and legs were secured to the sides of the bed by thick leather straps. His eyes were closed, and the black stubble of a beard was spreading across his face and neck.

"Joel," she whispered.

There was no response.

"It's me, Susan. Can you hear me?"

Joel continued to breathe evenly and deeply.

As Susan looked down at the still, sleeping form of her husband, she began sobbing quietly. It was incomprehensible to her that the strong, gentle man she loved could be capable of attempted murder. Early in their marriage, Joel babysat Aggy and other children in their apartment complex. He loved kids and animals and people in general. Never once did he demonstrate even the slightest violent tendencies. If anything, he was too gentle and accepting, and people frequently took advantage of his kindness. But now, he had tried to kill a man.

Susan wiped the tears from her cheek with the back of her hand. Then she stroked her husband's forearm.

"It's a terrible thing, isn't it?" a voice behind her asked.

Susan turned quickly and found herself looking into the large eyes of an elderly man standing just inside the doorway. He wore an overcoat and his hands were plunged deeply into his pockets. "Who are you?" she asked nervously.

"Don't worry, child," he replied warmly. "My name is Aurther Schlepler. I'm Ned Finley's friend. He told me about your husband."

"What are you doing here?"

"I live here."

"Are you a patient?"

"No, child, it's a matter of choice. I live here because I want to."

A loud scream erupted from the end of the hallway. It was followed by a series of garbled curses.

Schlepler walked over and looked down at Joel. "There is so much sadness and pain inside this young man. So much that he cannot understand or control."

"What do you know about my husband?"

"Only what Ned has told me. And what I feel," Schlepler answered warmly. "Come, child, let's go down to my room. I'll make you a cup of coffee and we can talk."

Susan studied Schlepler's gentle, compassionate eyes.

"Don't be afraid," he said reassuringly. "The nurse out there will tell you who I am."

Susan felt her reservations vanish as she listened to the soothing tone of Schlepler's voice, and she followed him out of the room.

The orderly stepped quickly into the doorway and pulled the door shut, sending particles of dust swirling across the rays of sunlight that entered the room through the window. The swaying branches from a tree outside sent tiny shadows flickering across Joel's beard and matted hair . . .

He remembered the streets and the brick buildings and the stone eagle. Especially the eagle with the flagpole clenched in its beak. It was the last thing they had done to the building. He had stood on a ledge and guided the eagle as it was raised by thick ropes attached to horse-drawn pulleys. And the men in the street had cheered as the eagle was attached to the side of the building. He had grinned down at them and laughed. It had felt so good to be alive. If only he could find the eagle, maybe he would remember . . .

When Finley arrived back in Danvers, he parked his car near the county building. After finding the dead mongrel dog, he had thought very seriously about leaving Danvers and working with Joel at a safer distance from the obvious threat to his own life. But after meeting with Susan and seeing Joel in restraints at Farmington, his determination to solve the bizarre psychological puzzle overcame his fears. He also realized, if someone was trying to chase him out of the small town, then he must be searching in the right place for the answers he was seeking. The desk clerk had replaced the mattress, but his response was strangely subdued.

With a glance up and down Main Street, he walked over to the hotel. Most of the old men were still sitting around the outer lobby, either playing cards, looking out the window, or dozing in easy chairs. Oscar was puffing on his pipe and watching a card game when Finley sat down next to him.

"Have you seen Gus today?" Finley asked.

"Nope. He's in Tyler," Oscar responded.

"Do you know when he'll be back?"

"Hard to say," Oscar said, reaching into his shirt pocket and pulling out a nail. "Could be a day. Could be a couple days. Could be he'll never come back."

"Why do you say that?" Finley asked.

"Ambulance took him away this morning. Gus has a bad heart. He turned all blue last night."

"Do you think if I went over to Tyler, they'd let me see him?"

"Nope," Oscar said, thrusting the nail into the bowl of his pipe. "He was in pretty bad shape when they took him out of here. Unconscious. Half dead, really. What is it ya need from him?"

"I was going to ask him some more questions about that Judd McCarthy who disappeared in the 1920s."

There was a sudden uproar from the men seated around the card table. As Finley and Oscar looked in that direction, one of the players threw his cards down in mock disgust, shoved several matchsticks across the table, and folded his hands behind his head.

"Well, I don't think Gus is gonna be much good to ya, at least for a while," Oscar said as he finished scraping the burnt tobacco out of his pipe.

"Where else might I find information on McCarthy?"

"You could try the newspaper office. Harmon might be able to help you. That is, if he's sober."

"Where's the newspaper office?"

"One block west of here."

"Thanks," Finley said.

He quickly rose from his chair and walked toward the front door. He walked one block west and crossed the street when he saw the name *Danvers Sun* on one of the display windows. The newspaper office was located in a small wooden building wedged tightly between two larger brick buildings. The windows overlooking the street were thick with dust and grime.

"Just a minute," a voice yelled from somewhere in the back as Finley entered the office. "I'll be right with you. Goddamn it, I don't know about this thing . . ." The voice trailed off into a string of profanities.

A short man with a huge potbelly soon emerged from behind one of the printing presses. He wore a visor that was much too large for his head, and his shirt and arms were covered with ink. As he walked toward the counter, he wrestled with a tray of printer's type. Finley could tell by his unsteady, wobbling gait that he had been drinking.

"Want to place an ad?" the man asked.

"No, one of the old timers in the hotel lobby sent me over. Are you Harmon?"

"Yes, I am."

"I need some information on someone who might have lived here in the 1920s. Have you ever heard the names Judd McCarthy or Katharine McCarthy?"

Harmon pushed his visor higher on his forehead and considered the names. "Nope," he said, returning his attention to the tray. "Never heard either of those names before. Listen, you sure you don't want to place an ad? We got a special this week."

"No, thank you."

"You name the price. We'll take it."

"Listen, one of the old-timers named Gus told me this McCarthy disappeared with a company payroll back in the 1920s. Think the newspaper would have reported it?"

"Possible. I didn't have the paper back then, but I suppose if it was big news, they would have reported it. Damn it, I can't seem to get this thing right," he said, still trying to manage the type case.

"Would you have copies of the papers from 1925 and 1926?"

"Might have," Harmon said, looking up from his struggle. "They'd be on microfilm in the state capital, but we could have them in the basement too."

"Any specific part of the basement?"

"Hell, I don't know. They could be almost anywhere down there. I've never had time to sort them out. Try the west wall. Ah, shit," he said as the tray fell out of his hands, spilling the type all over the floor. "The hell with it. Maybe we'll just publish the headlines this week."

Finley walked quickly down into the basement. Beneath the harsh glow of a single lightbulb in the middle of the ceiling, he could see piles of yellowish-brown issues of the *Danvers Sun* stacked on wooden shelves against all four walls. He walked over to the western wall and began sorting slowly through them.

Hours later, Finley uncovered a bundle of newspapers tied neatly together with strings and labeled "1926." He walked to the center of the room and placed the bundle on top of a table located directly beneath the overhead lightbulb. He untied the strings and began paging through the newspapers.

As his eyes moved carefully over the issue dated October 14, 1926, he found what he was looking for. Under the headline, "Payroll Stolen," the article read:

Sheriffs and police officers in four counties have been searching for three days for a certain Judd McCarthy who disappeared with the Hanley Brothers Construction Company payroll.

McCarthy, who is well known in Carver County as a barroom brawler and ruffian, was last seen leaving Danvers early Saturday morning, October 12. Company officials say he was on his way to Carson to pick up the payroll and return it to the construction site of the Little Sioux Water Reclamation Project.

Deputies who have retraced his route from Danvers to Carson have found nothing unusual. Due to his size and reputation, there is little reason to suspect he ran into foul play. The search is now extending into the Dakotas. Ben and Fred Hanley have posted a reward of $5000 for any information leading to McCarthy's arrest.

Citizens throughout the four-county area are to be reminded that McCarthy is a man of extremely violent temper.

Finley placed the newspaper on the table and looked up at the sunlight filtering through the lone basement window. At the bottom of the window well, a salamander was buried beneath a pile of dead leaves. It was straining mightily against the pane to free itself from its prison.

Finley opened his pocketknife and ran it along the outer boundaries of the newspaper article. He carefully extracted the account of McCarthy's disappearance from the page, folded it, and placed it in his shirt pocket. Then he retied the bundle, placed it on the shelf, and walked upstairs.

As he stepped through the basement door into the front office of the *Danvers Sun*, he glanced out the window. He could see that the shadows were creeping across Main Street. He guessed that it was midafternoon.

"Harmon," he called into the back of the room. He waited for a few seconds and called again.

When there was no answer, Finley stepped out into the street and walked toward the Danvers Hotel. Moments later, "Alexander's Ragtime Band" shrieked from the fire siren. The song built to a crescendo, then faded into a deep, mournful wail, and finally died out altogether.

Finley paused to look back at the newspaper office. When he turned around again, he glanced down at the tires of his Studebaker. The left rear tire was flat, the black rubber folded under the metal rim.

><><><

On the way back from her mother's house, Susan stopped by the law office to pick up some of Joel's things. She had Aggy sit in the lobby while she cleared Joel's desk and crammed everything that would fit into his briefcase.

The secretaries and attorneys who saw her smiled politely and sympathetically, but she felt uncomfortable. She hurried back to the lobby so she wouldn't have to talk to them. She made a hasty exit from the building because she wanted to get home and hide.

As soon as they were home, she sent Aggy across the street to play with her friend Robin. Alice, Robin's mother, waved and held the front door open as Aggy disappeared inside the house. Then Susan walked into the kitchen to boil water for coffee. As she was waiting, she remembered some peculiar items she had stuffed into Joel's briefcase before she rushed out of the law office. She reached for the briefcase, popped the lock, and spread the contents over the kitchen table.

She noticed a large notebook with a green cardboard cover. The single word "Why?" was printed across it. Susan recognized it as Joel's handwriting. She slowly opened the notebook.

On the first page, Joel had drawn the picture of a young woman swinging from the branch of a huge tree. Only the back of the woman was visible. At the bottom of the page, he had scrawled the name "Katharine" twice.

Susan slowly paged through the rest of the notebook. Subsequent pages revealed drawings of an old Victorian home, a thicket of trees in an empty field, two unattached arms reaching out as though to strangle someone, and other unrecognizable shapes and forms. The last page had been completely blackened with bold, violent strokes from a pencil. That page was torn in several places from the force of the pencil sweeping back and forth across the paper.

Susan studied the bold strokes for several seconds before setting the notebook down on the table. She shuffled through the other items from the briefcase and extracted a college yearbook that Joel had, for some reason, kept on his desk. Susan flipped idly through it, looking at pictures of the football team, the debating team, and the spring formal.

Joel had been an end on the football team, and his size, strength, and speed had attracted the attention of several professional scouts, even though he was playing for a small college. But a knee injury in his junior year had ended any dreams he might have entertained of playing professionally.

After the injury, Joel retreated into a shell and seriously considered dropping out of college. Then a mutual friend had set him up with Susan. She remembered how, on their first date, he had limped up to the dormitory, his knee strapped securely into a canvas brace. At first he seemed almost reluctant to be with her, but by the end of the evening, he was laughing and talking freely about himself.

Several days later she talked Joel into joining the debate team with her. Together they practiced debating in the rear of Bannister Hall, and Joel began to tell her of another of his dreams—law school. It was also in Bannister Hall that he had kissed her for the first time. His kiss was awkward, but gentle and strong.

They were embracing when Professor Holliman, the debating coach, strolled into the room. Susan remembered how Holliman had mumbled something about "failing to develop the killer instinct" in his debaters. As Holliman hung up his coat, Joel glanced awkwardly at her. Then he started to laugh. His was a laugh that came from deep in his throat, filling the room with its good-natured masculinity. She loved Joel's laugh. What wonderful times they had shared—their courtship, the early years of their marriage, and finally the joys of parenthood.

Susan was studying the picture of Joel and her in the middle of the debate team when she heard the sound of screeching brakes. It was followed by a loud scream. "Aggy," Susan whispered.

She leaped up and rushed toward the front door. "Aggy!" she screamed as she threw open the screen door.

A late model Ford coupe was stalled in the middle of the street. Two long, black streaks of burnt rubber curled out behind the car, marking its swerving course as it had come to a skidding halt. A few feet in front of the car, a teddy bear was sprawled on the road. Inside the car, an elderly woman was resting her forehead on the steering wheel.

Across the street, another woman was staring in horror at the stalled automobile. A small bag of groceries lay at her feet, the contents of which were spread out on the sidewalk.

Aggy was standing a few feet in front of the car. She turned slowly in the direction of her mother.

"Robin had to take a nap. I was coming home," she said penitently.

Finley stood beside the water tank inside the DX service station as the attendant carefully examined the flat inner tube. A white and black dog lay nearby, its head and tail curled lazily against the concrete floor.

The attendant filled the inner tube with air and submerged it in the water tank. Two tiny streams of bubbles immediately sputtered to the surface. The attendant pulled the tire out of the dirty water and carefully marked the two holes with a yellow crayon.

"Just as I thought," he said. He carried the tube over to a workbench and began patching the holes.

"What'd you find?" Finley asked.

"You didn't run over a nail," he said, scrubbing the rubber surface and applying glue. "This tire was deliberately punctured. See, the holes are on the side of the tube, not on the bottom."

"Who'd do something like that?"

"Kids probably. Aren't many left in Danvers. Ones that are here are pretty bored. Have too much time on their hands."

"Tell me," Finley said as he watched the attendant patch and then reassemble the tire, "who around here would know the most about the early history of Carver County?"

"How early?"

"First thirty years or so of this century."

"Lot of the real old boys are dead now. What is it you're trying to find out?"

"I'm trying to find information on a Katharine McCarthy and a Judd McCarthy. Ever hear of them?"

"Nope."

"Know of anyone who might have?"

"Well, if I were you," the attendant said, rolling the tire over to Finley, "I'd go out and talk to Hans Gustafson. He's an antiques dealer. Lives about eight miles east of here on County Road 6. He's been around here longer than just about anyone."

"Thanks," Finley said. "What do I owe you?"
"Fifty cents."

Outside of town, Finley passed a country church and a small schoolhouse. The windows of both were boarded up, and the vegetation surrounding them was almost level with the window ledges. Farther down the road, he passed an abandoned gas station. A tall, thin, old-fashioned gasoline pump protruded above the dead weeds.

Behind Finley's car, swirling clouds of dust rolled out into the prairie and dissipated above the fields. He glanced at his odometer and saw that he had traveled precisely eight miles out of Danvers. He checked the next two mailboxes alongside the road. The third one had a metal strip on top with the name "Hans Gustafson" painted on it.

Finley turned his Studebaker into the narrow dirt road and drove up to the farm. On the edge of the yard, a crow was perched on a weathered fence post. The bird cawed loudly and quickly flew away.

Finley parked the car next to the wooden fence and walked up to the front door. He knocked twice. When there was no answer, he turned and walked in the direction of a gentle tapping sound that filtered out of a barn on the other end of the yard. As he passed a smaller shed, he looked inside and saw an assortment of saddles, bridles, and other restored leather goods hanging from pegs. Pipe organs, trunks, violins, desks, and other unrelated pieces of furniture were neatly arranged along the floor. Finley resisted the urge to enter and explore.

Inside the much larger barn, restored carriages were lined up against the four walls. In the center of the room, an elderly, white-haired man, wearing a beret very much like Finley's, was working industriously on a carriage wheel. The western wall of the barn contained a huge sliding door that was open. Finley could see the descending sun above the distant horizon.

"Excuse me, are you Hans Gustafson?" Finley said softly, not wanting to startle the old man. When he didn't respond, Finley asked again, this time louder.

"Huh?" the old man said, looking up from the carriage wheel and cupping his hand to his ear.

Finley realized he was hard of hearing. "Are you Hans Gustafson?" he asked loudly.

"Ya, I'm Hans Gustafson," the old man said in a strong Norwegian accent.

"The service station attendant in town told me you might be able to help me find someone."

"Vait a minute," Gustafson said, turning up the volume on his hearing aid. "Der. I turn dis off ven I'm vorking. Now, vat is it you vant?"

"I need some information on two people who might have lived in Carver County in the 1920s. Can you help me?"

"Da twenties. The vife and I ver back in da old country den. Who are ya lookin' for?" Gustafson placed a large chisel on top of the carriage wheel as he spoke.

"Have you ever heard the name Katharine McCarthy?" Finley asked.

"Nope," Gustafson said firmly. "Never heard dat name."

"What about Judd McCarthy?"

"Now I tink I've heard dat name. But I don't know vere."

"He disappeared in the 1920s with the Hanley Brothers Construction Company payroll," Finley said, reaching into his pocket and handing Gustafson the article he had cut out of the *Danvers Sun*.

Gustafson took a pair of bifocals out of his pocket, fitted them to his nose, and read the article. Then he handed it back to Finley. "Vell, yes, I've heard about dis before. But dis newspaper article tells you more'n I know 'bout Judd McCarthy."

"Did any other McCarthys live around here back then?"

"Nope," Gustafson said, turning the carriage wheel over on the workbench. "But dis is a Scandinavian county. Der vas a lotta prejudice 'gainst da Irish in da old days. They settled farther northa here."

Finley pulled the photograph of the old Victorian farmhouse out of his pocket. "Have you ever seen this in Carver County?"

Gustafson studied the photograph carefully. "It looks like von a da farms by da old Sioux line railroad. Rich farmers at von time. Made a lotta money. Den vent broke like da rest of us in da thirties."

"But you don't know who might have owned it?"

"No. Could've been a couple dozen farms over der dat looked like dis in da old days. Don't look dat good no more, dough. Most of dem are gone or 'bandoned. Corporations keep buyin' up da land." Gustafson turned the photograph over and studied the back. "Dis picture vas taken 'round here. Dat much I can tell you."

"Why do you say that?" Finley asked.

"See dis?" Gustafson pointed to a faded impression of a gramophone with the initials "PH."

"Yes."

"Means 'Hornsby Studios'," Gustafson said, handing the photograph back to Finley and leaning over the carriage wheel. "Phillip Hornsby. He had a picture studio in Danvers back in da twenties and thirties. He died in da late thirties. Drank himself to death." Gustafson carefully moved his index finger along the wooden grain of one of the axles. Then he bent over to examine it more closely.

"Well, thank you very much," Finley said, placing the photograph back in his pocket and preparing to leave.

"You know, I vas tinking," Gustafson said, looking up again. "Dat name McCarthy. Der vas a Maureen McCarthy who lived 'round here. No one could ever forget her. But dat vas back in da 1890s."

"What can you tell me about her?"

"Vell, she came over from da old country. Round 1895, I tink. Quite a high-spirited young woman. Used ta drink with da men in Danvers. Long 'for dat vas considered proper."

"What happened to her?"

"Vell, let me see now," Gustafson said, pondering the question. "She vurked for a time on da Graham farm. Den der vas a lotta talk 'bout her. You know how women are 'bout someone who's prettier'n da rest a dem."

"Was she married?" Finley asked.

"No. Seems to me der vas some big scandal. She vent to prison, I tink. No, vait, I 'member now. She vas committed to an insane asylum."

"Why?"

"Now dat I don't know. But she vas certainly different. Loved a good time. Laughed a lot. But I couldn't tell you vy she vas sent to an asylum."

As Gustafson resumed working on the carriage wheel, Finley glanced through the open doorway at the descending sun.

"You have a beautiful view of the sunset," Finley said.

"Ya," Gustafson said, looking up from his work. "It makes da prairie look so serene an' peaceful. But der are a tousand shattered dreams out der. Lyin' just a few inches under da topsoil. I've buried most of dem in my lifetime."

As the sun descended behind the horizon, shadows crawled over the brown stubble of the fields. With one last burst of energy, the sun turned the clouds into brilliant shades of purples and oranges and fiery reds. Then, in the distance, three clusters of trees slowly darkened as the last rays of sunlight splashed across the prairie and over the carriages that lined the walls of Gustafson's barn.

The moonlight filtered through the window of Joel's room at the Farmington State Mental Hospital. The pale light fell across the thick iron bars and sent elongated, distorted shadows across the bedspread.

Joel lay with his arms and legs securely attached to the sides of the bed. The growth of beard was spreading rapidly across his face, concealing his once-handsome features and giving him a fierce, menacing appearance. The moonlight reflected off the few gray hairs in his dark beard.

A steady moaning sound drifted into the room from the other end of the corridor, and an occasional muffled scream filtered through the metal door. Outside, the crickets chirped noisily in the dead grass.

An orderly entered the room and gazed down at Joel. He checked the leather restraints and quickly exited.

Joel slept peacefully as the moon slipped slowly across the black sky, and the elongated shadows created by the iron bars crawled steadily across the bedspread.

If only he could find the small town with the eagle on Main Street . . .

Late that evening, Ned Finley sat alone in the lobby of the Danvers Hotel. Behind the counter, the clerk was asleep on his cot. Two radiators hissed next to the windows overlooking Main Street.

The lobby was dark except for a light that glowed behind the counter and the ones that filtered through the windows. Finley sat in one of the easy chairs and watched the lights flicker over the old photographs on the walls.

The lights from the street fell across a picture of men proudly surrounding a horse-drawn fire wagon. Another photograph depicted the Danvers Hotel much earlier in the century. As a steam-powered automobile chugged down the dirt road, hotel guests eyed it suspiciously from the upstairs windows. The large photograph of former governor John J. Sylvester, occupying its place of honor in the middle of the eastern wall, was in the shadows. Sylvester's eyes glowed from behind his mustache.

After returning from the Gustafson farm, Finley had placed a call to Farmington. He left a message for Aurther Schlepler. If a Maureen McCarthy had been committed to an "insane asylum" in the 1890s, it would undoubtedly have been Farmington. There was no other mental institution within a hundred miles of Danvers.

Finley was hoping his earlier conversations with Schlepler had stirred the elderly psychic's compassion. He hoped Schlepler would agree to comb through Farmington's catacombs for any record of a Maureen McCarthy. Finley knew that going through proper channels to get this information would take time, and he sensed that he didn't have much time. Joel was rapidly slipping into some kind of unreachable psychotic or schizophrenic state from which he might never return.

As Finley sat in the lobby, he felt the ominous, ghostly presence of the many faces that stared at him from the photographs on all four walls. He also considered the full impact of what he was trying to prove now that he was back in Carver County. He was in search of a man who had lived in the 1920s and who maybe, just maybe, lived on inside the subconscious mind of a young attorney some thirty-three years later. Reincarnation? The supernatural? Once again, the whole thing struck him as being too far-fetched, too improbable to be taken seriously by anyone, much less by a psychologist who had been trained to look for plausible explanations for his patients' behavior.

For a moment, Finley wished he hadn't grown so fond of Joel and Susan. Maybe he should have driven up north for two weeks. Done some fishing. Maybe by that time Joel would have regained his senses. Sometimes these conditions were temporary, and they just had to work themselves out, with or without the help of a trained psychologist.

Still, at the very least, there was something very strange about this small town. The dead dog, the punctured tire, his feelings of being watched and followed—*something* was amiss in Danvers. But did it necessarily involve Joel?

The desk clerk began to snore loudly as Finley rose from his chair and walked up the two flights of stairs to his room. Most of the other rooms along the hallway were dark. He glanced at the new watch he had purchased that day and noticed that it was twelve thirty.

As he reached into his pocket for the key, he looked down at the sliver of light that crept under the door of his room. He stepped back, remembering that he had turned the light off when he went down to the lobby earlier that evening. He crept back to the door, knelt down, and placed his ear within a few inches of the keyhole. He could hear the distinct sound of footsteps and the clatter of vanity drawers opening and closing on the other side. He quickly stood up, unlocked the door, and threw it open.

A thin man with one arm flopping uselessly by his side stood next to the bed. He whirled around as Finley stepped into the room. The man's eyes darted nervously from side to side as he looked for an avenue of escape.

Finley recognized the man as one of the card players he had seen in the lobby. He had dealt cards with his right arm, while his left arm hung limply in his coat pocket.

"What's going on here?" Finley demanded as his eyes moved slowly over the clothes and personal belongings that were strewn across the floor.

The intruder's eyes continued to dart around the room.

"Who are you?" Finley said.

The man still did not speak.

"Who the hell are you?" Finley repeated angrily.

"Burt," the man whispered nervously as he tucked his left hand into his coat pocket.

"What are you doing in my room?" Finley demanded.

Burt stayed silent.

"Listen," Finley said emphatically, "unless you give me some answers, I'm going to haul you over to the sheriff's office. Maybe he can get you to explain why you've been destroying my things."

"I was told to do this," the man replied.

"Who told you to do this?"

"I don't know."

"What do you mean you don't know?"

"There was a note in my mailbox. Couple days ago. It had a hundred dollars in it," he sputtered.

"And?"

"It said I would get another hundred dollars if I could get you out of town. There was no signature."

"You expect me to believe that?" Finley asked.

"Please, I'm no criminal," Burt pleaded. "I needed the money. I can't work. Not with this." He pulled his left hand out and held it up to Finley. The fingers were curled into a small ball at the end of a thin wrist.

"Did you recognize the handwriting?"

"No! Please, don't tell Wally! I can't afford to get thrown out of here. There's nowhere else to go!"

Finley glared at the man. "You didn't have to kill a dog to get me out of town," he said finally. "There was no need for that."

Burt looked stunned. "I don't know what you're talking about," he said.

"The dog you killed and threw across my bed, damn it! You know you did it. Don't play any more games with me!"

Fear and confusion played alternately across Burt's eyes. "I didn't kill no dog, mister," he said quietly. "I threw your clothes on the floor and smashed your watch and put an ice pick in your tire, but I don't know nothin' about no dog."

"Don't lie to me!"

"Look." The man held up his limp arm again. "How could I kill a dog with this?"

Finley paused. His eyes moved between the paralyzed arm and the man's face. "You didn't kill a dog and spread him across my bed?"

"No!"

"You're not lying to me?"

"No, please, I've never killed anything in my entire life. I'm just trying to survive, that's all."

Finley sensed the sincerity in the man's plaintive denial. He studied his eyes for a few more seconds and stepped back from the doorway.

Burt darted swiftly past Finley and disappeared into the darkness at the end of the hallway. Finley quickly walked back into his room. He locked the door, turned off the light, and walked over to the window that overlooked Main Street.

His encounter with the intruder had temporarily eliminated the doubts Finley had pondered earlier while he sat in the lobby. Clearly, he was on to something important enough for someone to try to drive him out of town. But he still didn't know if it involved Joel Hampton or something else entirely. And who was it that wanted him out of Carver County? How far would that person go to see to it that he never found what he was looking for?

Finley leaned against the windowsill and watched the street-lights play across the abandoned stores below. For a moment, he thought he saw someone standing in the shadows on the other side of the street. But he realized it was only the moonlight catching the silhouette of the stone eagle and projecting it onto the wall of the store adjacent to the county building.

CHAPTER SEVEN

"The record of Maureen McCarthy's confinement at Farmington," Schlepler said. He placed a cardboard box on his coffee table, sat down, and began toying with the pieces of a picture puzzle.

Finley sat down in another chair and read through the papers in one of the files. "It says here that she escaped from Farmington."

"Yes," Schlepler said as he inserted a piece of the puzzle into the autumn landscape scene.

Finley ran his index finger slowly across the yellowed page. "She was 'committed to Farmington for lewd and immoral conduct.' What did she do?"

"Someone had her committed," Schlepler said without looking up. "The signatures are at the bottom of the page."

Finley moved his eyes to the bottom of the document. "'Witnesses . . . Frank Graham, Helga Graham, Oscar Sumners, Agnes Sumners . . . April 14, 1895.' Four signatures were enough to have her committed?"

"If they were very influential people."

"What do you make of this?" Finley asked. "What kind of 'lewd and immoral conduct' are they talking about? And why would it give these people grounds to commit her to a mental institution?"

Schlepler reached for the document and laid it flat on the coffee table. "There are several things about this document that raise one's suspicions about the motives of everyone involved. You will note, for example, that she was confined to the western wing. In the nineteenth century, Farmington's western wing was reserved for unwed mothers who were considered morally unfit to live in the community."

"So that's what they accused her of," Finley said.

"Yes. She was most likely pregnant when she escaped."

"Was it common practice in the 1890s to put unwed mothers in mental hospitals?"

"No, but a young woman with powerful enemies might end up in one, especially if she had no one to defend her. In this case, as you said, she was a young, rather attractive Irish woman in a Scandinavian county. Undoubtedly, her manner of living tempted some of the husbands of Danvers's finest, and she made many enemies in the process. The world back then was not quite so willing to accept a high-spirited, independent woman."

"Why do you suppose these *specific* individuals signed this?" Finley asked.

"That is very difficult to say. It's possible they were merely appointed to carry out the wishes of their community. Or perhaps they had their own personal reasons for wanting her declared insane."

"Why do you say that?"

"Intuition maybe. I also found this." Schlepler handed Finley a small piece of stationery with a note scratched on one side.

"'Dear Maureen,'" Finley read. "'I can't believe they are doing this to you. I'm sorry. Love, Maynard.'" Finley paused to contemplate the meaning of the note. "Who do you suppose Maynard is?"

"Now that is another of the great mysteries in this whole affair," Schlepler said. "Like the vines growing on the walls outside that window, the lives you are dealing with here are becoming progressively more intertwined. One can only hope that the death of the flower will reveal the common root from which they all sprang." Schlepler inserted two more pieces into the autumn scene. "Ned, why are you so involved in this case? Certainly you have worked with other schizophrenic or psychotic personalities. Why is this one so special? Is it because of Tony?"

Finley nodded weakly. "I suppose. At least that's part of it."

"You aren't even sure he was your son. Why punish yourself?"

"Those who were close to his mother told me he was my son, and he was looking for me when he died. Or committed suicide . . . ."

"You didn't even know of his existence until it was all over. Shouldn't his mother have told you, if she wanted you to know?"

"I lost all contact with her. Deliberately, I suppose. But I have no idea what she told him about me. Perhaps he assumed the worst. Perhaps he had a right to do so. But he was obviously trying to find out the truth before he died . . . Every son has a right to know his father, Aurther."

Schlepler sighed. "And you think something like that might be happening to Joel Hampton?"

"I don't know. I'll be the first to admit I'm losing some of my objectivity in this case. I'm sure you noticed the resemblance between Joel and the picture I have of Tony. But, like I said, that's only part of the reason."

Finley stood and walked over to the window. Outside, the moonlight played gently over the fields, and light cloud formations drifted lazily beneath a star-filled sky.

"I've been in this profession for almost thirty years," Finley said as he leaned against the windowsill. "And I'm more aware than anyone of the inadequacies of contemporary psychological theory. Oh, we find convenient labels to attach to various forms of deviant behavior. But we know—every psychiatrist or psychologist who ever lived—that terms like 'schizophrenia' or 'paranoia' or 'psychopathic tendencies' are only partial explanations for human behavior. It goes much deeper than that."

Schlepler looked up from the puzzle. "And?" he inquired.

"I've always felt in my gut," Finley continued, "that there are other explanations for some of the behavior we see around here." He turned away from the window and gestured toward the hallway. "I've always wondered if maybe we live on the edge of a thin, but impenetrable veil between this life and other lives we've lived. For some reason, in Joel's mind, that veil appears to have been pierced and he's slipping over to the other side."

"Do you feel this is a universal phenomenon?" Schlepler asked as he lit a pipe that had been lying on the table next to the puzzle.

"I don't know what you mean, but it's possible that many so-called psychological traits are really the results of earlier patterns of behavior and experiences from previous lives. And it's equally possible that unresolved traumas from past lives work their way up through our subconscious minds, frequently manifesting themselves in forms of antisocial behavior. Of course, I have no proof for this."

"Your colleagues will never accept such a theory, Ned. Even if there might be some truth to it, they will think you have somehow taken leave of your senses," Schlepler said, puffing on the pipe. "They might even go so far as to excommunicate you from the profession."

"Psychology is still an infant," Finley said. He looked back out the window at the clouds. "It has much to learn about itself. What I'm suggesting is no more far-fetched than what Freud was arguing half a century ago. Perhaps in another half century the theory of past lives and their influence on contemporary behavior will be equally acceptable. Or at least plausible."

"If Joel Hampton is struggling to resolve some issues that were unresolved in a previous existence," Schlepler replied, "and you can prove it, perhaps you might have a breakthrough here."

"Maybe," Finley agreed. He rubbed the back of his neck and continued to look out the window. "At the very least, I've never before worked with a patient who so clearly reflects memories of a past life. If that doesn't qualify as a breakthrough, certainly it must at least give us reason to pause and reflect upon what we are doing here at Farmington. Freud taught us to go back to earliest childhood to find the source of all aberrant behavior. Perhaps he didn't teach us to go back far enough. Maybe we have to go back even beyond the moment of conception."

After his conversation with Schlepler, Finley walked down Farmington's dark corridors. He climbed the stairs to the second floor and entered the room where Joel was strapped to his bed. Susan was sitting in a chair next to her husband. Behind them, the moonlight filtered through the window and fell across the blanket that covered Joel's body. A small light cast a faint blue glow in one corner of the ceiling.

"Has there been any change?" Finley asked.

Susan shook her head.

"I've asked the nurses to keep him tranquilized, at least for now," Finley said. "They'll be moving him down to the first floor, so it'll be more pleasant for you to visit him. When we get some more answers, we'll cut back on the medications and see what he remembers."

Susan reached into her coat pocket and pulled out the green notebook. "I found this yesterday," she said. "It's Joel's. It was on top of his desk. He must have been doodling in it before Jim Morris sent him down to the vault."

Finley sat down in the other chair and began paging slowly through the notebook. He ran his fingertips lightly over the last page, which was completely darkened by bold, sweeping pencil strokes. He felt the perforations where the strokes had left grooves and small tears in the paper.

"What do you make of it?" Susan asked.

"It looks like some kind of a record of the thoughts that have been tormenting your husband. There is tremendous violence and passion in these drawings. Also great confusion." Finley flipped back through the notebook. He paused at the drawing of the old Victorian home. "Unless I miss my guess," he speculated, "this is the same farmhouse as the one in the photograph you found."

"Has Joel ever seen that photograph?" Susan asked.

"Yes, but not long enough to remember all this detail. Unless, of course, he has a photographic memory."

"No," Susan shook her head. "Joel's very intelligent, but he doesn't have a photographic memory."

Finley glanced at the bed. "Then he's probably been in Carver County before. Maybe even in the 1920s."

"Why do you say that?" Susan asked.

"An antique dealer told me this was most likely one of the old farmhouses out by the Little Sioux River northwest of Danvers. He also knew of a Maureen McCarthy who lived in Carver County in the 1890s. She was eventually committed to Farmington. I don't know if she is connected to all of this, but my instincts tell me she might be."

Finley pulled out the note that Schlepler had found in the Farmington basement and handed it to Susan. "Aurther Schlepler found this. He's a friend of mine."

"I know. He stopped by," Susan said.

"Aurther is a psychic," Finley explained. "Before he retired, he often worked with police on murder and missing persons cases. I thought he might be able to help us. I hope it was okay for me to bring him into this."

"Anything you need to do to help Joel is fine with me," Susan said as she read the note. "Who's Maynard?"

"I don't know. But he obviously has some connection to Maureen McCarthy. And maybe to your husband."

Both Finley and Susan looked at the pale full moon floating outside the window. Then Finley looked back at Susan. He had noticed a kind of listlessness and weariness creeping into her manner and demeanor, and it worried him. He was altogether too aware that the spouses of the mentally ill were frequently subjected to so much stress that they also became psychologically traumatized. He had worked on cases where the patient was eventually cured, but the patient's spouse slipped into a suicidal state of depression.

"How are you doing?" he asked. "You've been dealing with an awful lot of stress."

Susan nodded weakly. "I'm tired," she said. "But I'll be all right."

"Are you sure?"

"Yes, don't worry about me, Dr. Finley. Worry about Joel." Susan paused and looked back at her husband. "Dr. Finley, do you suppose it's possible that Joel is incurably insane?" she asked.

"I'd like to think that isn't the case," Finley answered, putting his arm around her shoulder. "Come on. Let's go downstairs and get a cup of coffee."

As they walked out of the room, Joel's right hand clenched and slowly unclenched. There was a slight, almost imperceptible movement on his dry lips.

Maynard? He had heard that name before. He was a young boy. Just big enough to walk. He was sitting in the shadows at the bottom of a stairway. Bright light from the next room poured out onto the floor. It was only a few feet away from where he was sitting. He hadn't been able to sleep and he had walked down the long flight of stairs. But he saw the light and heard the man's voice and thought maybe he shouldn't go in there. So he sat down and he listened as a man and a woman talked in hushed tones. That's when he heard the name "Maynard." It was followed by the woman's voice. She was crying. The man said something, but the crying didn't stop. He stood and walked back into the darkness at the top of the stairs. Long into the night he heard the crying. And he remembered the name Maynard.

The next day Finley returned to the county recorder's office to ask some general questions about the early history of Carver County. The county recorder provided some information, but he suggested that Finley pay a visit to Marsha Williams in the Danvers library. He said she had converted the library into a historical archive.

The library was a small granite structure located along a foothill north of Main Street. Two polished stone pillars were set solidly in blocks on both sides of the front entrance. Above the entrance, large stone letters spelled out the name, "Andrew Carnegie Library." As Finley opened a large glass-paneled door and stepped into the entryway, he was greeted by the faint smell of glue. The door creaked shut behind him and made a long, mournful groan as its wooden edge slipped tightly past the metal jam.

Finley climbed a short flight of stairs to another wooden door with glass panels. He opened the inner door and walked into the main floor. A short, trim, elderly woman was working behind a large, pulpit-shaped desk in the middle of the room. She was repairing several old manuscripts and leather-bound books that were organized neatly across her desk. Four glass display cases were spaced symmetrically around the room. Other historical artifacts and collections were displayed on built-in oak shelves.

"Yes?" the woman inquired cheerfully, looking up from a leather binding she was gluing to the back of an old Bible.

"Are you Marsha Williams?" Finley asked.

"Yes, I am," she replied.

"The county recorder said you might be able to help me."

"What is it you need, young man?"

"I'm looking for a 1920s map of Carver County. I'm trying to find out what would be the shortest route between Danvers and Carson in 1926."

Marsha finished running her finger carefully along the newly glued edge of the binding. Then she set the Bible on a table behind the front desk.

"What do you know about the history of Carson?" she asked as though eager to begin a lecture on the subject.

"Not very much," Finley replied. "The county recorder told me it was kind of a boomtown. Sprang up quickly and died just as fast."

"Well, Carson was part of the last major period of railroad expansion in this area. The town just kind of grew up alongside the intersection of the Little Sioux Railroad and the Great Northern Railway. The Great Northern pulled out of this area almost as soon as the last track was laid. Rerouted its lines through Tyler. The Little Sioux line folded a couple of decades later, in the twenties. Carson sprang up and died so fast that no county roads were ever built to connect it to Danvers."

"How did people get from here to Carson?" Finley asked.

"By railroad, when the trains were running. Schedules were kind of irregular in those days. Otherwise they traveled on foot or horseback. They just followed the railroad tracks—the Little Sioux line. Used to be an old Indian trail in the 1800s. People walked it all the time."

"Where can I find this railroad?"

"Well, they don't use it anymore. Haven't for years. Railroad buffs walk it every once in a while, but there's no traffic on it.

Weeds and marshes have pretty much covered the old ties and tracks. Come over here. I'll show you where it is." Marsha stepped out from behind her desk and led Finley over to the western wall of the library. A discolored map was prominently displayed in the middle of the wall above the bookshelves. It was labeled "Carver County 1933."

Marsha unhooked a wooden pointer hanging next to the book-shelves. She raised its metal tip and ran it along the surface of the map. "This is Danvers here and this is Carson," she explained. "The Little Sioux line ran right alongside the Little Sioux River, just west of here about two miles. Farther north, it veered away from the river and angled off in a northeasterly direction toward Carson."

"How far is it between Carson and Danvers?"

"Oh, there are roads that go that way now. Dirt roads. Kind of bumpy, but they'll get you there. Probably about thirteen miles."

"No, I mean how far is it from Carson to Danvers along the railroad?"

"It's exactly nine miles. Are you planning to walk it?"

"Yes, I think so," Finley said, studying the map. "Incidentally, have you ever heard of a Katharine McCarthy who might have lived around here in the 1920s?"

"No. No one by that name," Marsha responded, carefully considering the name. "I'd probably remember that name if she'd lived here."

"What about a Judd McCarthy?" Finley asked. "Have you ever heard of him?"

"Oh my, yes, he was a ruffian and a scoundrel. He disappeared with some payroll money. My brother was with the group that went looking for him."

"Did they ever find him?"

"No."

"Did they ever find a body?"

"No. They figure he headed for the Dakotas."

"Didn't he disappear somewhere along the Little Sioux line?" Finley asked, gesturing at the map.

"Well, he was in Carson when they last saw him. He could have headed out in any direction from there. Most likely he went west with the money, not south along the railroad."

Finley continued perusing the map. "It seems kind of strange to me," he speculated, "that they would send a man on foot to

THE SEARCH FOR JUDD McCARTHY

pick up the payroll. It would seem much safer to have the payroll shipped by railroad car right to the construction site. Didn't the Little Sioux line run right through the Hanley Brothers Construction site?"

"Yes, it did. My, you do know a lot about the history of Carver County," Marsha said admiringly.

"Only what I read in a newspaper article," Finley replied. "It said something about the construction site for the Little Sioux Water Reclamation Project. I assumed that meant next to the Little Sioux River."

"Yes, it certainly did. And of course you're right. Normally they did ship the payroll by armored car, right to the construction site."

"Why didn't they this time?"

"Well, if I remember correctly, the normal procedure was for the payroll to come via the Great Northern. Actually, it was another smaller railroad that leased the line from the Great Northern after they rerouted their tracks to Tyler. The payroll would then be transferred to the Little Sioux line in Carson and accompanied by armed guard to the construction site just outside of Danvers."

"It seems strange that they would normally take so many precautions, and yet this time they sent one man to pick up the payroll."

"I think there was some question about that," Marsha mused as she looked up at the map. "Fred Hanley said he didn't want the payroll sitting in Carson until the next train came through on the Little Sioux line. And I guess the men hadn't been paid for a while and there were some grumblings. So he sent McCarthy."

"Alone?" Finley asked.

"Yes."

"It seems to me they would at least send several armed men."

"McCarthy had a reputation. Apparently Hanley didn't think anyone would try to mess with him."

"Were they certain that someone *didn't* try to mess with him?" Finley asked.

"Oh my, yes," Marsha said as she walked back to the front desk. "No body was ever found. And there was no sign of a struggle. My brother told me they were convinced McCarthy had fled into the Dakotas with the money. They put out a reward for him, you know."

"Yes, I know. Did anyone ever collect it?"

"Nope."

"Well, thanks for your time," Finley said. He glanced once more at the map and then walked toward the inner door.

"Are you going out to walk the Little Sioux line?" Marsha called after him.

"Yes, I am."

"Be careful."

"Why?"

"It's overrun with wildlife. Snakes and skunks all over the place. They probably won't cause you no harm unless you step on them. But you should be careful."

"Thanks," Finley said as he opened the inner door and walked down the short flight of stairs to the outer door.

Marsha watched the glass-paneled doors swing shut behind Finley. Then she looked down at her desk and uttered, "Oh, drats. He didn't sign the register."

She turned it slowly around on top of the desk. There were only two signatures entered between the neatly lined spaces. She pulled the pen out of its wood holder next to the book and scratched something in one of the empty spaces.

"There," she said, admiring her handiwork. "That should do it. 'Tall man with brown beret.' He can sign beneath that if he ever comes in again."

Finley parked his Studebaker on the gravel shoulder of a country road some two miles west of Danvers. Small rocks crunched beneath the weight of the automobile as it came to a halt next to the stubble of a cornfield. Dust billowed out from beneath the car, swirled across the ditch, and dissipated above the jagged cornstalks.

Finley stepped out and looked across the field. In the distance a long, winding embankment protruded from the prairie, arching out of sight in a northerly direction. The abandoned railroad line curled across the Midwestern landscape like a huge snake slumbering beneath a layer of weeds.

Finley had no idea what he hoped to accomplish by walking the Little Sioux line. Clearly, there were many suspicious events surrounding the disappearance of Judd McCarthy. But did his disappearance have anything to do with Joel Hampton? At the very least, Finley rationalized, even if his journey to Carson accomplished nothing else, he would familiarize himself with some of the sights McCarthy had seen prior to his disappearance. Maybe something along the way would help provide a clue to the mystery. Or maybe he'd find something he could use to prod Joel's subconscious mind to determine once and for all if there was a connection between his young patient and Judd McCarthy?

As Finley picked his way through the furrows and cornstalks, he could hear the distant popping sound of a tractor's cylinders. In the extreme northern end of the field, a thin stream of smoke poured steadily out of a small John Deere. As Finley approached the embankment, he had to walk across several black, newly plowed furrows. On the other side of the furrows, he climbed the embankment and walked to the top of the railroad tracks.

Dry, matted vegetation covered most of the wooden cross ties and rusty iron tracks. Dead crab grass, dandelions, and other weeds filled the areas between the rotting ties. Tall sunflowers grew alongside the embankment, their brown and yellow heads tilted upwards at the bright sun that moved lazily across the sky. Thick brush on both sides of the embankment concealed old barns, sheds, and abandoned farmhouses. Farther north, the embankment disappeared into a marsh.

As Finley's feet crunched through the vegetation, he studied the surrounding countryside. The Little Sioux River ran almost parallel to the embankment for the first mile of the journey to Carson. Finley could hear the gurgling waters as they drifted slowly south.

From what he had seen on the map in the library, Finley judged he was about two miles into his trip when he saw some deep trenches that had been dug almost to the very banks of the river. At the bottom of one of the trenches, a concrete culvert had been partially exposed by the constant erosion of rain and floodwaters. Piles of discarded lumber and steel molds lay scattered around the bottom of the trench, and an abandoned railroad car rested on two rusty rails several feet above the culvert. Finley studied the general layout of the trenches, the culvert, and the railroad car. He realized he had stumbled upon the remnants of the Little Sioux Water Reclamation Project.

Finley walked down the embankment and sat on a weathered packing crate located next to a pile of lumber at the bottom of the trench. He took a large handkerchief out of his back pocket and slowly wiped the beads of perspiration from his brow. From somewhere in the distance, a windmill groaned plaintively to the blue sky. The only other sound was that of the breeze blowing through the weeds and grass in the trench.

As he folded his handkerchief and put it back in his pocket, Finley noticed a slight movement underneath one of the piles of lumber. He leaned over to get a closer look, then lifted a rotting wooden pallet and found himself staring into the sleepy eyes of a huge snake. He froze as the snake glared at him. Then he dropped the pallet and scurried back up the embankment. The sound of the groaning windmill accompanied him for several hundred yards as he moved in the direction of the marsh.

It was midafternoon when Finley entered the city limits of Carson. The town was much smaller than Danvers. There was no sign of human activity as Finley walked down Main Street and entered a building that had a sign over the doorway that read "Carson Chronicle." A sign inside directed him to the second floor of the small wooden structure.

At the top of a steep flight of stairs, Finley entered a stuffy room with two heavy wooden tables located in the middle of the floor. No one else was in the room, but rows of yellowed newspapers were stacked on shelves in bookcases that lined all four walls. Above each of the shelves, a hand-lettered sign conveniently indicated the year in which the newspapers had been published. Finley paged through a pile shelved under the year 1926. When he found what he was looking for, he carried the newspaper back to one of the tables and slowly paged through it. The paper was dated October 14, 1926.

On the second page he found a brief article under the headline, "Local Wrestler Defeated."

> Local residents were treated this past Saturday afternoon to an old-fashioned dogfight between Judd McCarthy, a wrestler of some repute from the Danvers area, and Farmer John Tobin, said to be the biggest and strongest man in Carson. When the smoke had cleared, McCarthy was the victor and also the winner, rumor has it, of a considerable amount in wagers. A picture of the exhausted combatants appears elsewhere in this week's edition of the *Chronicle*.

Finley paged eagerly through the paper until he found the caption, "Exhausted Participants in Wrestling Match Shake Hands." There was a hole just above the caption, where someone had carefully run a pocketknife or razor blade along the edges of the photograph, neatly extracting it from the page.

Finley stared at the hole, puzzled that someone would cut out such an obscure, seemingly insignificant newspaper photograph. Then he placed the paper back on the shelf, descended the stairway, and walked out to Carson's Main Street. Overhead, the sun was beginning to dip toward the western horizon. He knew he would have to start back to Danvers or risk walking the last miles of the railroad line in total darkness.

On the outskirts of town, Finley again climbed the embankment and began the journey back to Danvers. As he walked, pheasants ran through the thick brush, and an occasional gopher scurried across the railroad ties before disappearing into its hole.

Finley continued to ponder the meaning of the missing newspaper photograph. Everything he knew about Judd McCarthy now made him suspicious. McCarthy's life had many layers of meaning, or so it seemed. Nothing about it was normal. Even if it turned out that there was no connection between McCarthy and Joel, Finley was becoming increasingly obsessed with the Irish laborer who had disappeared while transporting a company payroll from one small town to another.

In an abandoned farmyard some fifty yards from the embankment, the gray gable of a barn protruded above a cluster of elm trees. It was surrounded by shattered cornstalks that had been destroyed by a hailstorm. The stalks were bent toward the ground, and the tassels and ears of corn hung limply above the black, leaf-strewn furrows. A weather vane in the shape of a rooster adorned the top peak of the ancient structure. The front door of the barn hung precariously from one hinge.

Intrigued, Finley stepped off the embankment and walked over to the barn. Inside, sunlight streamed through the many holes in the roof and walls, illuminating the dust that hung suspended in the air and casting long shadows across the straw-covered floor. A green tractor was rusting against one wall, and plowshares were lined up in neat rows along another wall. In the middle of the floor, a stone grinding wheel was leaning heavily against a wheelbarrow. Several burlap sacks containing seed corn were stacked behind the grinding wheel.

As Finley walked toward the center of the barn, there was a loud rustling sound overhead. It was followed by the frantic noise of flapping wings as three sparrows flew out of the rafters and darted across the rays of sunlight, causing particles of dust to swirl wildly in the air. Two of the sparrows flew out through large holes in the roof. The third sparrow smashed into one of the dust-covered window panes. It beat its wings frantically against the glass, then flew through a hole in the roof and disappeared.

A wooden cabinet that was secured by a huge, rusty padlock aroused Finley's curiosity. He pried at the lock halfheartedly, then lost interest and wandered back in the direction of the wheelbarrow. It was filled with an assortment of junk. Tattered fragments of leather harnesses and bridles, twine, old stoneware jars, rusty nails, and several horseshoes were intertwined at the bottom. Finley placed some of the smaller items in his pockets, then turned and walked toward the door.

As he was about to step out into the sunlight, he heard the distant popping sound of a rifle. Seconds later, a window shattered, and pieces of glass exploded across the floor. Other bullets splintered the barn's rotting panels.

Finley dropped to the floor as the popping noises built in intensity, and broken glass and splinters of wood sprayed the straw all around him. The popping noises continued for several more seconds, then grew more distant and finally faded away.

"Get those patients out of there," one of the orderlies yelled from the top of the staircase leading down to Farmington's main floor. "We're bringing Hampton down."

Joel stood at the top of the stairs. He was dressed in a faded green hospital uniform, and his arms were strapped to a large leather belt that circled his waist. The thick, black beard now covered his face and neck. He stared straight ahead, unblinking, almost catatonic.

Two brawny orderlies each grabbed an arm and led him down. Another orderly and a young nurse scattered the patients at the bottom of the staircase.

"Where are you taking him?" the nurse asked.

"Room 111," the orderly replied as he came off the last step.

"Who authorized the transfer?"

"Finley."

"Is he safe?"

"He hasn't caused us any problems. Just sleeps or lies in bed staring at the ceiling. He'll be under sedation as long as he's down here."

The nurse shook her head in disgust. "I don't how what they expect us to do. We've already got more patients than we can possibly handle. Now they give us one who has psychopathic tendencies."

"Only following orders," the orderly shrugged.

The nurse shook her head again. "Bring him this way."

The old woman with the paralyzed face suddenly stepped out of an adjacent room. She curled her index finger and whispered, "Come see, please, come see . . ."

"Sophie, get back in that room!" the nurse admonished the woman.

"Please, come see."

"Sophie!" the nurse scolded. "Get back in there, right now!"

Joel's head turned slowly in the direction of the old woman. He stared into the paralyzed layers of flesh . . .

Something had happened to him shortly after he stepped off the hill. No, it was not a hill. It was . . . a railroad embankment. A long, narrow railroad embankment winding across the prairie. He had stepped out of the marsh and . . .

"Christ, I can't budge him!" one of the orderlies muttered angrily as he tugged at Joel's arm.

He was beginning to remember why he was walking on the railroad embankment. But what had happened to him in the thicket? Why had he forgotten everything from the moment he had entered the thicket until he found himself in this strange room, surrounded by these even stranger people?

"Do you need some help?" the nurse asked as the two orderlies tugged on Joel's arms.

"He's stiff as a board," one of the orderlies muttered. "I can't even bend his elbow."

"Wait!" the other orderly said.

"What is it?"

"He's starting to relax. Give him a couple seconds."

The muscles in Joel's arms and shoulders began to relax noticeably. He stared straight ahead as the two orderlies led him toward the darkened hallway to the right of the staircase.

He was beginning to remember it all . . .

It was almost dusk when Finley entered the marsh just outside of Danvers. Dead leaves, carried by autumn breezes, drifted across the countryside. Overhead, a flock of Canadian geese flew south in V-formation, the lead goose bellowing a challenge to the departing sun as his flock disappeared from sight. Reeds on the edge of the marsh swayed gently. In the sloughs, the chirping of the crickets became louder and more intense. Frogs, startled by the crunching sound of human footsteps, leaped off fallen logs and splashed into the water.

Finley didn't know what to make of the incident in the barn. It could have been kids shooting at an old building, not knowing he was inside, or it could have been something more sinister. He decided to put it out of his mind and concentrate on the terrain, looking for anything he might use later to probe more deeply into Joel's memories.

The marsh covered less than two acres, and Finley soon stepped out of the tall reeds and stood on the edge of an empty wheat field. In the west, the sun was touching the horizon and casting long shadows across the wheat stubble. Ahead of him, the river flowed parallel to the embankment, disappearing into the foothills just outside of town. In the distance, the church steeple, grain elevator, and water tower protruded above the prairie. In the silence of early evening, the mournful lament of a windmill drifted across the countryside, mingling with the sound of the crickets.

Suddenly Finley saw something in the shadows of a thicket of trees to the east of the embankment. In the departing sunlight, it looked like a human figure standing among the colorful leaves and tall weeds.

Finley crossed the field and paused at the edge of the cluster of trees to peer into the shadows. What he had taken to be a human figure was instead a large birdhouse suspended at the top of four long wooden poles. A rusty bicycle with one wheel missing was propped up against the birdhouse's supports. Nearby, a swing set tilted awkwardly toward the ground, and an old plow and disc harrow rusted among the weeds.

In the middle of the thicket, the concrete foundation and basement of a farmhouse yawned out of the black soil. Weeds and grass grew out of the cracks in the walls, and the floor of the basement was littered with broken glass jars and puddles of water. A small shed, seemingly untouched by the devastation that had vented its rage on the farmyard, stood nearby.

"Tornado," Finley whispered to himself as he wandered around the yard.

On the northern side of the basement's foundation, Finley reached down into the weeds and extracted the shattered face of a child's doll. At that moment, he felt the ground beneath him shift ever so gently. The slight movement was followed by a loud groan as boards cracked and splintered all around him.

Finley tried to step back, but the boards gave way beneath his feet and he plunged down into the darkness.

CHAPTER EIGHT

As the sun climbed the eastern horizon, it cast a pale gray light over the fields outside of Danvers. The dead leaves hung motionlessly in the elm and oak trees.

Overnight, dew had settled on the trees, and as the sunlight entered the groves, the beads of moisture glistened and sparkled, accentuating the colors and veins of the leaves. As the sun rose higher, the tiny beads evaporated, and the leaves began to flicker ever so slightly in the early morning breezes. Within an hour, they were rustling against one another and dancing in the trees.

In the tornado-ravaged farmyard, the sunlight fell across the splintered boards and pierced the deep hole Finley had fallen into. Under his weight, the rotting boards that covered the opening of an old cistern had collapsed, and he had fallen through. Some of the boards had fallen in behind him, splashing into the water that covered the bottom of the chamber. One of the pieces of lumber hit him on the head as he fell, momentarily stunning him.

When he came to, he was sprawled across a pile of rocks and lumber, with only his head and shoulders above water. He decided to wait until daybreak before making an attempt to get out. He constructed a small platform out of the rocks and lumber. Leaning against the wall and dangling his feet in the dirty black water, he had sat on the boards throughout the night. He dozed off occasionally, but mostly he stayed awake, listening to the crickets in the darkness above him.

As the sunlight gradually filtered into the cistern, Finley studied his predicament. He was at the bottom of a concrete chamber, the mouth of which was perhaps ten feet above where he sat. Even by standing and stretching, he could only reach to within five or six feet of the rim. He decided that perhaps by standing on a pile of rocks and other debris, he'd be able to reach the top and climb out.

Two frogs and a large garter snake lay in the shallows of the water on the other side of the cistern. In the darkness, he had sensed a slight, undulating movement across the surface of the water. As the moonlight filtered into the deep hole, he decided it was nothing more than the black, striped body of a harmless garter snake. In the morning, he was relieved to find that his original guess was correct. He had nothing to fear from his fellow prisoner.

Finley reached into the water and began stacking rocks, lumber, and other debris against one of the walls. He discarded the unusable objects, but most he patiently loaded onto the pile. As he plunged his hands into the water, the frogs and snake scurried away. Once he grabbed a broken bottle and cut his index finger. He wrapped his handkerchief around the wound and continued.

When he had extracted everything usable from the bottom of the cistern, he stepped gingerly onto the pile, balancing himself carefully against the walls with his arms. At the top of the stack, he stretched mightily toward the rim and the sunlight. Still, he was three or four feet short, and there was no way he could leap off the pile of debris to gain the extra distance he needed to climb out.

He reached for one of the thicker pieces of lumber that dangled above his head. He pulled on it and found that it was firmly attached to something outside the mouth of the cistern. He reached high on the slab, grasped it firmly with both hands, and stepped off the pile.

Finley pulled himself up slowly and reached out with one hand for the rim. As he almost grasped the edge of the rim, there was a loud groaning sound overhead, then a sharp crack like a tree limb breaking off, and he tumbled back into the water, still clutching the rotting piece of lumber with one hand.

He fell hard and, for a few seconds, was completely submerged. When he surfaced, the frogs and snake were swimming frantically around him. One of the frogs croaked a loud, belligerent note of defiance as Finley retrieved his brown beret and crawled back to the top of the pile of rocks and debris.

He rested for a time while he studied the walls of the cistern, looking for any holes in the concrete surface that might provide footholds. But there were none. He looked up at the sky and the clouds that were drifting past the opening. The clouds seemed almost close enough to touch. In the distance, he heard the distinct popping sound of a tractor motor. As he rested, the sound came closer and closer to where he was sitting. When the tractor seemed only a few hundred feet away, it suddenly backfired, then coughed and sputtered and was silent.

"Help! I'm in here!" Finley yelled. He felt both foolish and relieved at the same time. "Help! I'm trapped in here!"

He could hear his own voice echo across the cistern, and he was afraid the sound might be muffled between the concrete walls. Then he heard what sounded like a metal door slamming shut.

"Help!" he hollered, this time even louder.

The sound of his voice was interrupted by the put-put-put of the tractor. The motor grew louder, then faded and disappeared in the distance.

For the next few hours, Finley examined the walls of the cistern. He ran his fingers carefully over the surface to make certain he hadn't overlooked any metal rungs that he knew were cemented into some cisterns. He even went so far as to pound against the walls with a large rock, hoping that perhaps he could chip out two or three small footholds to help him climb out. When nothing worked, he sat back down on the pile of rocks.

The irony of his situation did not escape him. He had gone to Carson in search of a man who had somehow disappeared mysteriously. Now, unless he could figure something out, he too would vanish and would probably never be heard from again.

It was too ironic, too coincidental, almost amusing in an insane way. He pondered whether Aurther Schlepler's fates were trying to tell him something. Perhaps they didn't want him to find out what had really happened to Judd McCarthy, and why his spirit seemingly lived on inside Joel Hampton's tortured psyche.

The thought made Finley very angry, and he stood up to consider new ways of escaping from his prison. He reached into his pocket and extracted three of the large nails he had pulled out of the rusty wheelbarrow back in the abandoned barn a few miles outside of Carson. He put two nails in his mouth. He reached high on the wall with the third and began pounding on it with a large rock. The rusty nail snapped almost immediately.

He was able to drive the second nail about an inch into a small crack in the wall before it too snapped. The third nail sunk about two inches into the crack and held firm. Finley grasped the head of the nail with his right hand. As the metal dug deeply and painfully into his palm, he raised himself slowly off the rock pile, using his feet to provide leverage against the wall. As he reached out for the rim a few inches above his hand, the nail suddenly broke loose, and again he went tumbling down the pile of rocks and into the black water.

This time, as he surfaced out of the dirty water, he found himself looking up at a puzzled face at the top of the cistern. The man's battered straw hat and gray overalls were clearly outlined against the sky.

As the frogs and the snake swirled around him, and the water ran out of his hair and down his cheeks, Finley stared in disbelief at the farmer.

"What the hell you doing down there?" the farmer asked.

"I'm taking a bath," Finley replied, not quite knowing why he said it.

"Do you need any help getting outta there?"

"Yes, for Christ's sake, I've been stuck here all night."

"I'll be right back," the farmer said as his face disappeared from the opening.

Within minutes, he returned and slid a ladder into the cistern. It scraped against the rim as it slid deeply into the water. Once more Finley retrieved his beret. Then he quickly scrambled up the ladder.

"How'd ya get down there?" the farmer asked as Finley crawled past the broken pieces of lumber and sat down just outside the opening.

"I was looking around the farmyard when those boards collapsed under my weight."

"You're mighty lucky."

"Why do you say that?"

"Tractor broke down out there," the farmer replied, pointing at a John Deere tractor that stood at the end of some long black furrows. "I came over to the shed to get some tools to fix it. Heard ya poundin' on the walls of the cistern."

"Is this your land?" Finley asked.

"Well, it's on my land," the farmer replied. "But I didn't even know that cistern was there. Weeds covered it so much over the years. I'll bring over the grader and fill it with rocks so no one else'll fall in."

"Before you do," Finley said, "I want to get something out of the bottom."

"What's down there?"

"Do you have a burlap bag?" Finley asked. He started to climb back down the ladder.

"Why?" the farmer yelled after him.

"There's something down here I want to take back to town with me," Finley's muffled voice filtered out of the cistern.

"What is it?"

"This," Finley said. He crawled back up the ladder and rolled a human skull over the rim onto the grass.

"What the hell!" the farmer said. His eyes grew wide as he stared at the skull that rolled past his feet. He ran toward the shed as Finley again descended into the cistern.

Joel sat in a wheelchair next to a window on the first floor at Farmington. Behind him, some patients wandered around the hallway jabbering incoherently to one another. Other patients, completely lost in their thoughts, shuffled across the tile floor as soft, gentle music from an overhead intercom system filtered through the halls and corridors.

Joel's arms and legs were strapped to the metal frame of the wheelchair as he stared out the window at the strange, bizarre world just beyond the walls of the hospital.

He knew where he was. He had passed it during his wanderings in the early 1920s. He remembered the red granite walls rising out of the prairie and the strange stories and legends about the people imprisoned inside. But why was he now a patient? What had he done that he should be committed to a mental hospital? And what was that strange world unfolding just beyond the window where he sat? He had seen cars before. But not like the ones that cruised past the huge open gate on the edge of the hospital grounds. And he had seen airplanes. But not ones that streaked through the sky, leaving long white tails streaming behind them. He watched the white vapor disintegrate in the sky, and he knew he had entered a world more mystifying than anything he had ever dreamed possible. More terrifying in its own way than any nightmare. Still, he knew he must escape and enter that world if he was to change what had been left undone. He had to get back to Kate. He needed her now, more than ever before. Now that he was alone in this strange world, how his soul cried out for Kate . . .

"Come on, Hampton, let's get you back to your room," an orderly said as he reached down to unlock the wheelchair.

He would escape and somehow get back to Carver County . . . and to Kate. And he would find those who had done this to him . . . He would learn why he, Judd McCarthy, now found himself staring out the window at this strange world . . . Now that he remembered his name, it was time to go back . . .

"Where'd you find these?" the county coroner asked Finley while he studied the skull and other human bones spread out across an examining table in the basement of the county building.

"In an old cistern, about three or four miles west of here," Finley answered. He peered closely at the skeleton that was slowly taking shape beneath the bright lights that illuminated the table.

"You don't know which farm?" the coroner asked.

"Nope, but I can take you out there. Looks like a tornado destroyed it many years ago."

"About three miles west of here?"

"Yes."

"Must be the old Johnson place," the coroner said. He poked a small light into the mouth cavity of the skull and scrutinized the brown teeth. "What were you doing out there?"

"Looking for worms," Finley lied. "I was going fishing."

"Fish don't bite that well so late in the year." The coroner switched off the light and stepped back from the table.

"Tell me," Finley said. "How long has that skeleton been there?"

"Hard to say," the coroner said as he wiped off his hands. "Probably at least thirty, forty years judging from the decomposition of the bones and teeth. But it could be much longer. Hard to say, really."

"It looks like the skull was fractured in three places. Arm was broken too," Finley said, pointing at the bones just above the right wrist.

"Yup, sure was."

"Think the fall would have done that?"

"Not very likely," the coroner answered, pointing to the three cracks in the skull. "Fall probably would have caused one of these. No way it would've done this much damage to his head. No, he was hit repeatedly over the head with something. Probably a large rock."

"Murder?"

"Most likely. A fall wouldn't have done that," the coroner repeated emphatically.

"How tall do you suppose he was?" Finley asked.

The coroner picked up a notepad he had been writing in earlier. "Well, these are only my preliminary observations, based solely on what we have in front of us. But he's probably a male Caucasian, cause of death—a blow to the head. Age, probably fifty or sixty . . . and he's, oh, couldn't be no more than five feet seven inches."

"Are you sure?" Finley asked.

"Give or take an inch or two."

"Are you positive he wasn't a younger man? Probably well over six feet?"

"How much younger?"

"Probably thirties. Forties at the most."

"Nope. Frame and bone structure don't match that at all. He's closer to sixty and much less than six foot tall. Why do you ask?"

"I was reading about someone who disappeared around here in 1926. He was probably in his thirties, well over six feet."

"Well, this isn't him," the coroner said. He picked up the burlap bag and dropped it into a wastepaper basket, then began packing the bones in a metal storage crate. "Most likely just some old hobo who was killed and his body dumped in a convenient spot."

Finley was feeling tired and disappointed as he walked up the flight of stairs into the hotel lobby. Behind him, dark clouds spread across the sky, sending ominous shadows across Main Street.

When he found the bones, he was certain he had solved the mysterious disappearance of Judd McCarthy. When the bones turned out to be the skeleton of an older, much shorter man, Finley once again questioned his motives for getting so involved in this case. He knew he couldn't devote his whole life to solving McCarthy's disappearance. First he had to prove that there *was* definitely a connection between Joel and the Irish laborer.

Inside the lobby, the lights were turned on and two card games were in progress. Gus was sitting quietly in one of the easy chairs, staring out the window at the shadows that were moving across the storefronts on the other side of the street. Finley sat down beside him, and the two men looked out as the wind whipped against the huge window panes, causing them to creak and groan in their casings.

"Feeling better, Gus?" Finley asked.

"Yup," Gus answered as he chewed on a wad of tobacco.

"Do you remember who I am?"

"Yup. You're the fella who was askin' me 'bout Judd McCarthy the other day. Day before they took me over to the hospital."

"Can I ask you some more questions about him?"

"What is it you want to know?"

"You said you worked with him."

"No, I said I worked for the Hanley Brothers Construction Company. But I didn't work with McCarthy. We were assigned to different parts of the county."

"But you do remember when he disappeared?"

"Oh, yes, that I remember," Gus laughed softly to himself. "He took the payroll and left town. Cost me three months' wages."

"Were you certain there was no other explanation for his disappearance?"

"Nope. He picked up the payroll in Carson and took off into the Dakotas."

Outside, the rains began to beat heavily against the large windows.

"Do you think it's possible that McCarthy ran into foul play on the way back from Carson?" Finley asked.

"Nah, he was too big. Too tough," Gus said as he spit a dark stream of tobacco juice into a spittoon next to Finley's feet. "Nobody'd mess with him."

"You don't think there was any other explanation?"

"Nope. He left with the money," Gus said emphatically. "Judd McCarthy wasn't vicious or mean. He just didn't have any sense, that's all. Probably just took the payroll over to the Dakotas and spent it."

Large, pea-sized hailstones began to beat against the windows and bounce on the street.

"What did McCarthy look like?" Finley asked as they watched the hailstones grow bigger.

"Oh, he was big. Very big."

"Over six foot?"

"Oh my, yes. Closer to six-and-a-half feet."

"How old was he?"

"Must have been in his early thirties . . . You know, if you want to see what he looks like, there's a picture of him over there on the wall."

"Where?" Finley asked eagerly.

"Here, I'll show you," Gus said, struggling to get up from his chair. He shuffled across the room and paused to peer closely at the gold-leaf-framed photographs. He pointed at one of them.

"That's McCarthy right there. Big fellow in the middle. The one leaning on a shovel."

Finley stepped closer to the photograph and studied the eyes and face of a huge, grinning, dark-haired laborer. Judd McCarthy was staring back at him from a group of workers who were lined up in front of a newly constructed building on Main Street. Mc-Carthy's large dark eyes glowed with intensity and good humor. His huge right forearm leaned rakishly on the handle of the spade he had thrust several inches into the dirt.

"Like I told ya," Gus said as he turned to leave. "He's well over six foot tall."

Finley studied the photograph for several more minutes. Then he walked back and sat down in the easy chair. Outside, the hail had stopped failing, but the rains continued to pour heavily. The cloud cover had blocked out the sun completely, making it seem more like late evening than midafternoon.

"Does it always rain this hard around here?" Finley asked.

"Get the heaviest rains in the state," Gus said. He reached into his tin of chewing tobacco and extracted a pinch with his index finger and thumb. He packed the small wad firmly in the area between his lower lip and front teeth. "Good thing most of the crops are in. Hail'd do 'em in for sure."

"Any problem with flooding around here?"

"Only around the Little Sioux River. Farms out there get flood-ed most every spring."

"I noticed an unfinished culvert out that way, a few miles out-side of town. Looked like someone started to build it a long time ago and then just gave up. I assumed it was the Little Sioux Water Reclamation Project I read about in the newspapers."

"You assumed right," Gus said.

"How come they didn't complete the project?"

"Ran out of money. John Sylvester started it with the Commu-nity Development League in the twenties. Hanley Brothers was called in later to help out. Always ran on a pretty tight budget. When McCarthy disappeared with the last payroll, that wiped it out for good."

In the dark skies, lightning flashed across the cloud layer and thunder clapped, causing the lights in the ceiling to dim.

"Seems kind of strange that they would lay so much of the culvert and then stop a few hundred yards short of the river," Finley speculated as he watched the lights glow brightly again.

"Just ran out of funds, I guess. Later there was the Great Depression and people had other things to worry about."

Suddenly the lights went out in the lobby.

"Dammit," Gus sputtered in the darkness. "Just when I had a good mouthful." He spit anyhow, in the general direction of the spittoon near Finley's feet.

"Gus?" Finley said.

"Huh?"

"You just hit my leg."

✕◇✕◇✕

A large rainbow arched across the prairie as Finley parked his Studebaker outside Farmington's gates. Susan was waiting for him in Joel's room. Joel was sleeping peacefully on the bed, his arms and legs again restrained.

Finley sensed immediately that Susan was probably in the early stages of depression. The sullen, listless demeanor, the sense of resignation, the slow, weary movements and glazed eyes—Finley had seen those symptoms before, both in his patients and in himself. The product of two alcoholic parents, he had slipped into periodic depression until he left home at the age of sixteen. Those early experiences created in him deep misgivings about marriage. They also made him sensitive to the early signs of depression in other people.

Finley sat down next to Susan and placed a hand on her shoulder. "How are you doing?" he asked.

"I'm fine," Susan said without looking in his direction.

"Maybe you shouldn't spend so much time up here. Maybe you should relax more . . . at home?"

"I'll be fine," Susan repeated. The tone in her voice was weak and unconvincing.

Finley gestured at Joel. "How's he doing?"

"They've taken him off the sedatives."

"Has he talked to you at all?"

"No."

Finley and Susan sat silently for a time while they looked at Joel.

"Aurther Schlepler came by earlier," Susan said. "He asked how you were doing. He seemed very concerned about both you and Joel."

"Did he come by for any specific reason?"

"No, he was just worried. He said he couldn't sleep two nights ago. He sensed that you were in trouble. Before he left, I called the hotel and the clerk said he had seen you just this morning. I told Aurther and he seemed reassured, but he's terrified of a picture you showed him earlier."

"The picture of the farmhouse you found in Joel's baby clothes. Aurther said it was 'a place of madness.' He warned me not to go there."

"Have you found the house yet?"

"No."

Outside Joel's room, an old man in a white hospital gown shuffled past. He paused to raise his finger in the air as he babbled something incoherently at the ceiling. A nurse grasped him gently by the elbow and led him down the hallway.

"Susan," Finley said. "I would like to try something with Joel, if it's all right with you."

"What do you have in mind?"

"I want to find out once and for all if there is a connection between him and Judd McCarthy."

"Are you planning to hypnotize him again?" Susan asked nervously.

"There's no need. Joel is in his own hypnotic state. I just want to ask him some questions."

"Do you think it's wise? He seems to be improving."

"He's not getting any better. He may look calmer, but he's slipping deeper into a catatonic state. If he regresses any deeper, we may never be able to bring him back."

"What if he becomes violent again?"

"We can handle the violence. In one respect the violence is a good sign. It means he's fighting whatever it is that's pulling him deeper and deeper into the past."

Susan stared at her husband's sleeping form. "What do you have in mind?"

"I'm going to ask him what he knows about Judd McCarthy. I'm going to take him back from Carson to Danvers along the Little Sioux Railroad. I'm convinced if I can figure out how Mc-Carthy disappeared, I'll know why his memory still lives inside your husband, if that is in fact the case."

"Haven't you done that before?" Susan asked.

"I have more of the details now. Maybe one of those details will trigger something in Joel's subconscious mind and give us a clue as to what's happening with him."

Susan glanced at the open doorway, where the old man was again wandering down the hallway, babbling at the ceiling. Then she looked back at Finley. "What do you want from me?"

"Nothing. Just your permission."

"If you think it'll help Joel, yes, of course."

Finley walked over to the side of the bed. He looked closely into Joel's face.

"Judd McCarthy," Finley began boldly. "You are in a whirlpool of color that has stopped at October 12, 1926. What's happening to you on October 12, 1926?"

Joel continued to sleep peacefully.

"Judd McCarthy, it's Saturday, October 12, 1926. You are in Carson to pick up the Hanley Brothers Construction Company payroll. Do you remember what's happening to you on the way back from Carson?"

A short, deep sigh escaped from Joel's lips and his chin quivered slightly.

"Judd," Finley said, leaning over the hospital bed. "You wrestled someone in Carson. Do you remember who it was?"

"Tobin," Joel whispered.

Tobin reached for him with both huge arms, but he knew enough to keep moving. Tobin was too big, too overweight. He knew if he kept moving Tobin would tire out. Tobin lunged at him and fell and rolled through the dirt. The dirt mixed with Tobin's sweat and clung to his body. When he got back up he looked like a brown bear. A huge, dirty brown bear reaching out as though to maul someone. He heard the ticking of a clock in the background as Tobin lunged, fell, and again rolled through the dirt.

"Do you remember a Farmer Tobin?" Finley asked.

"It's a mighty good day for a war, lad," Joel whispered in an Irish accent. "'Tween Norway and Ireland."

"Did Tobin have anything to do with your disappearance, Judd?"

"Tobin, your mama must've been a grizzly bear," Joel laughed softly.

Tobin lay face down on the street, unable to move. Then he rolled slowly over onto his back, his huge chest heaving and gasping for air. His long arms were sprawled out on each side of his body. His face and chest were smeared with dirt. Tobin was beaten and he, Judd McCarthy, was the wrestling champion of Carver County. Then he heard the laughter. It grew louder and louder, thundering off the ground and echoing against the railroad depot. It was his own laughter. He had pinned Tobin almost without having touched him. Tobin had worn himself out by rolling in the dirt. The laughter grew even louder as he reached down to help Tobin stand up. Tobin glared at him from the ground, his nostrils flaring.

"I whipped him, Kate," Joel whispered. "Make 'im kiss the Blarney Stone too if I could throw 'im that far."

"Who is Kate, Judd?"

Kate was waiting for him down by the river. Kate with her white bonnet and the cotton dress that lifted gently in the breeze. And he was walking . . . walking beneath a clear blue sky . . .

"Who is Kate?" Finley repeated.

"There's the farm. Kate's down by the river," Joel whispered cheerfully.

"What's happening to you just outside of Danvers?"

The colorful leaves whipped off the trees in the thicket and flew out into the prairie. He knew he shouldn't go in there. Someone was waiting for him. Someone he knew. He didn't trust that face. No, it was the eyes he didn't trust. He remembered those eyes. But it didn't end in the grove. Not yet . . .

"Judd McCarthy," Finley asked boldly. "Who killed you that Saturday when you were on your way back from Carson to meet Kate?"

It's . . . oh, Jesus, God, it's dark. There's just no way . . . Oh, Jesus, let me out . . . Kate . . . Kate . . .

"Kate! Kate! Kate!" Joel screamed as he struggled against the leather restraints and tried to sit up in bed. The veins in his forearms bulged mightily, and his fists clenched and unclenched with fierce strength as he fought against the leather straps.

"Judd, you're all right! You're all right!" Finley yelled. He pushed hard on Joel's chest, trying to force him back down.

"Jesus, God, it's dark!" Joel screamed as his right arm suddenly tore free.

"Susan, get the nurse! Quick!" Finley tried to control Joel's thrashing right arm, but Joel lifted him bodily off the floor.

As Finley was struggling to hold onto Joel's arm, a nurse rushed into the room. She tore back the sheet and plunged a syringe into Joel's exposed thigh. Joel fought for several more seconds against the other restraints, then his eyes slowly closed and he fell back onto the mattress.

Finley quickly strapped his arm back into the restraint, and Joel's forearms and clenched fists soon relaxed. He began to sleep peacefully under the influence of the strong sedative.

"Are you all right, Dr. Finley?" the nurse asked.

"Yes, I'm fine," Finley responded as he caught his breath.

"Do you need anything else?"

"No, just keep him on sedatives. You know how to get in touch with me if anything happens."

"Yes, Doctor," the nurse said before walking out of the room.

Finley turned toward Susan, who was standing at the foot of the bed. Her eyes reflected a strange, confused mixture of love and fear as she stared at her husband. "I'm sorry, Susan," Finley said softly.

"What did it prove?" she stammered.

"It proves that Judd McCarthy's memories definitely live on inside your husband. There's no question about it now."

"Why do you say that?"

"McCarthy wrestled someone by the name of Tobin the day he disappeared. Apparently he won a lot of money on the match. Your husband just mentioned Tobin's name. Joel would never have known that unless he shares McCarthy's memories."

Susan slumped down in the chair beside the bed. "What kind of a man was this McCarthy?"

"I don't know," Finley said, sitting down next to her. "I only know him from what I've read and from what some of the old-timers in Danvers told me."

"What did they tell you?"

Finley considered evading the question, but thought better of it. "They say he was a violent man with a strong temper. Some accuse him of disappearing into the Dakotas with a company payroll. Others speak more kindly of him."

"What do they say?"

"An old man I talked to in the hotel said McCarthy wasn't vicious or mean. He said he just didn't have any sense."

Susan shuddered. "The man inside my husband acts more like a madman."

"Susan, it's hard to really know a man when you only meet him through old photographs, stories, and newspaper articles. But I like McCarthy. I don't know why. I think something horrible happened to him, something so horrible that he refused to die in his own lifetime. Instead, he continues to live on inside your husband."

"Why?"

"That I don't know. Maybe Joel is his son. I've seen a picture of McCarthy in the Danvers Hotel lobby. There is a resemblance."

Susan stood and walked over to the bed. She gazed into Joel's face, then looked back at Finley. "What does all of this mean for him?" she asked, trying to control her emotions. "You said once that this could be permanent unless we get some answers soon. Does this mean it's too late?"

Finley stood slowly and leaned against the rail at the end of the bed. "Susan, your husband is caught between two worlds— his own and Judd McCarthy's. Right now, I don't think he knows who he is, or whether he's living in the 1920s or the 1950s."

"But he's definitely drifting more and more into that other world, isn't he?"

"Yes, he is," Finley admitted.

"So is it too late?" Susan asked again.

"No, I think we still have some time. But I don't know how much."

Susan looked at her husband. "Where do we go from here?" she asked.

"Back to Carver County," Finley said firmly as he strode toward the doorway. "Maybe you can join me later? I'll call to set up a time and place to meet."

Susan glanced at Finley as he left the room. Then she looked down at her husband. "Joel?" she asked as she rubbed his forearm. "Do you know who I am?"

Joel's eyes blinked sleepily open.

"It's me, Susan. Do you remember me?"

Joel turned slightly and stared into his wife's eyes. "Kate?" he asked.

"No, I'm Susan Hampton," she replied, the tears welling up. "Joel, I'm your wife."

"Wife?" Joel whispered. The word seemed to confuse him. His eyes closed and then opened again. "Wife?" He repeated the word three more times.

"Yes, I'm your wife," Susan reassured him as she stroked his hand.

"Kate, Kate," Joel sighed dreamily.

From deep in his chest, Susan heard a sound like an enraged bull bellowing in defiance. The sound grew louder and louder, until it filled the room and echoed into the hallway. She stepped back in horror as the nurse again rushed into the room and thrust a syringe into Joel's thigh.

CHAPTER NINE

As he drove back to Danvers, Finley thought about the scene in Joel's room. Clearly, the name Tobin was somehow locked in Joel's subconscious mind. Unless he had stumbled across some obscure newspaper account of the wrestling match between Tobin and McCarthy, which seemed extremely unlikely, the name Tobin could only have come from his memories of a previous life in Carver County.

The possibility that traumas from a previous life might have caused Joel's psychological and emotional collapse was no longer that far-fetched. Indeed, the clear connection between Joel and McCarthy created a renewed excitement in Finley. Now he was convinced that he was on to something that defied traditional psychological explanations.

His excitement was tempered only by his knowledge that the final revelations might come too late, long after Joel had slipped into a permanent catatonic state. Finley's feelings for Joel and Susan made that possibility more agonizing and personal than he wanted it to be. He had always tried to maintain an objective, professional relationship with his patients. Such walls were necessary when one confronted severe, often incurable mental illnesses and other lesser psychological problems on a daily basis. But those walls had fallen in this case, and he found himself caring deeply for both Susan and Joel. Such feelings might impair his professional judgment, but he knew they would also give him the motivation and determination he needed to pursue this matter to the end. He decided to do just that, no matter what the consequences might be to himself and his professional career.

The next morning, Finley made a quick call to Susan. He was evasive about why he wanted her to join him in Carver County. His primary reason was just to get her away from Farmington. He described an area near the Little Sioux River and asked her to meet him there later that day.

Finley immediately walked out to his car and drove over to the library. Marsha Williams was standing on a small stepladder when he entered the main floor. She was adjusting several large photographs that hung crookedly on the wall. Stern-faced married couples from the late 1800s and early 1900s stared out of most of the photographs, their faces reflecting a humorless, almost puritanical resolve. Beneath each photograph, a small white label identified the couple. The largest label was reserved for the portrait of John J. Sylvester, which hung in the middle of the wall, as it had in both the county recorder's office and the Danvers Hotel lobby.

Marsha was so preoccupied with her task that she was oblivious to the stepladder that was swaying and lurching beneath her feet. Finley walked over and steadied it.

"Oh, thank you," she said as she looked down at Finley's brown beret. She continued to adjust the picture frames until she was satisfied with the way they were hanging. Then she stood erect on the top rung, put her index finger to her lips, and admired her handiwork. "There, they look so much better, don't they?" she said, scrambling down.

"Yes, they certainly do," Finley agreed as he folded the stepladder.

"Bring it right over here," Marsha said. She led Finley to a small closet behind the desk. "Just put it in there."

Finley placed the stepladder inside and shut the door.

"My," Marsha sighed, "it would be so much easier if I had a man to help me around here." She pondered the idea for a few seconds, then reconsidered. "No, he would just be getting in my way, I'm afraid." She turned briskly and walked behind the desk.

"Miss Williams . . ."

"Now you come over here, whoever you are," she admonished Finley. "Before you do anything at all, sign the registration book. We're applying for a state grant and they want to know exactly how many people visit us each year."

"Where do I sign?" Finley said, walking over to the desk.

"Right here. And sign again in the space below it." Marsha pointed at the space where she had earlier written "tall man in brown beret."

Finley scribbled his name in the two adjacent spaces in the book. Before he was able to put the pen back in its holder, Marsha spun the book around and studied the signature. "Ned Finley?" she asked.

"Yes."

"Well, Mr. Finley," she said cheerfully, extending her tiny hand and smiling at him, "I'm Marsha Williams and I'm pleased to meet you. What can we do for you today?"

"I was wondering if you could tell me more about that map over there," Finley said, pointing at the large county map on the wall. "I would like to know more about the people who lived along the Little Sioux Railroad in the 1920s. I don't think I showed you this the first time I was here," he added, handing the photograph of the old farmhouse to Marsha. "Do you know if this farm was located anywhere in Carver County back then?"

Marsha considered the photograph for a moment. "I don't know," she said thoughtfully. "Picture looks like it was taken from across a field. Farm is almost too far away to tell." She turned it over and looked at the picture of the gramophone and the initials "PH" on the back. "The picture was developed in Danvers. That much you can be sure of. That's the mark of Hornsby Studios. Phillip Hornsby."

"Yes, I know," Finley said. "But do you have any idea who might have owned this farm?"

"Well, it was most likely a farm along the Little Sioux line. They all looked pretty much the same. Big Victorian homes. It could have been any one of them."

"Could you show me where some of those farms are located?" Finley asked, gesturing at the map.

"Yes, of course." Marsha took the long pointer down from the wall and raised the metal tip toward the map. "All of these darker areas are the farms and homesteads from the twenties and early thirties."

"Looks like there were at least forty farms between Danvers and Carson," Finley said.

"At least."

"How many of the owners can you identify?"

"Probably ten or twelve. Some of those farms were rentals. Others were bought and sold many times over the years."

"Tell me about the ones closest to Danvers."

"Well, this is the old Johnson farm . . ."

"The one destroyed by a tornado?" Finley asked.

"Yes, how did you know that?"

"I was out there the other day."

"Oh, I see," Marsha said. She seemed a little disappointed that Finley already knew something about the farm she was describing to him. She quickly turned her attention again to the map. "This is the Bentley farm and . . . I don't know who owned this one right here, but this one is the Graham farm. And right across the river here is the Mosley farm."

"What was this Graham's first name?" Finley asked.

"Fred, I think. No, no, that's not it. It was, let me see." She paused, trying to remember the name. "It was Frank. That's it. Frank and Helga Graham."

"Did they live out there in the 1920s?"

"Oh my, yes, they certainly did," Marsha said. She continued to run the marker along the map. "And this is the Helgeson farm. Now this one I don't remember. No, I do. This is the Sumners farm and this . . ."

"Wait," Finley said. "That farm there. You said it was the Sumners farm."

"Yes, I believe that's their place."

"What were their first names?"

"I don't remember much about them."

"Miss Williams, do you know anything at all about a Maureen McCarthy who lived around here in the 1890s?" Finley blurted out.

"I think I've heard that name before. Why do you ask?"

"She was committed to the Farmington State Mental Hospital in the 1890s. The Sumnerses and the Grahams were the ones who signed to have her committed."

"I would have to do some research on that. Much of what we have is uncatalogued. Would you want me to call you if I find anything?"

"Yes, please do. I'm staying in the hotel . . ."

Suddenly, the fire siren began wailing outside the library, and the notes of "Amazing Grace" filtered in through the thick windows.

"Oh my, that's too bad," Marsha said, glancing toward the street.

"What's too bad?" Finley asked.

"There must have been a funeral. Harmon gets drunk and kind of sentimental whenever someone dies in Danvers. He'll be playing 'Amazing Grace' for a couple of days now. I wonder who died." She scratched the back of her neck and a sad, distant look crept into her blue eyes. She looked quickly up at the map and began pointing at the remaining farms. "That's the Jenstad farm there and . . . there's one more that I remember. Oh, yes, one of the earliest homesteads in Carver County. Jerry Tobin lived right there for many years."

"Farmer Tobin?" Finley asked excitedly.

"No, a brother, Jerry Tobin. Kind of a strange man. Kept to himself the last fifteen or twenty years of his life. I don't know much about him except by reputation. Seems to me people said he was kind of crazy."

><><><

Gus was sitting alone at a large oak table when Finley entered the saloon adjacent to the lobby of the Danvers Hotel. Gus was sipping on a beer as he studied a mural painted across one entire wall of the barroom. In the mural, Buffalo Bill sat on a huge golden stallion that stood on its hind legs and pawed at the air as its magnificent white mane flowed in the wind. On the other end of the mural, an Indian chief was mounted on a smaller black and white pony. The Indian chief was sadly watching a long train that raced through the middle of the mural, scattering a herd of buffalo across the prairie. Dead and dying buffalo littered the areas on both sides of the railroad tracks.

"Gus, I need your help again," Finley said as he sat down.

"Do you see that?" Gus said, pointing at the mural.

"See what?"

"Buffalo Bill."

"Yes."

"He had blue eyes."

"So?"

"Whoever painted that mural painted his eyes brown," Gus said as he sipped his beer.

"Gus, what do you know about a Farmer Tobin?" Finley asked.

"The wrestler?"

"Yes. What kind of man was he?"

"Oh, he was big, tough, but gentle as a newborn calf."

"Do you think he had it in for Judd McCarthy?"

"In what way?"

"Do you think Tobin might possibly have been involved in McCarthy's disappearance?"

"You mean, was he in cahoots with McCarthy?"

"No. Do you think he might have killed McCarthy when he was coming back from Carson with the payroll?"

Gus coughed and spit into a red handkerchief. "Judd McCarthy and Farmer Tobin were like brothers outside the ring," he said, clearing his throat. "They boasted about killin' one another, but there was nothin' to it. They were a lot alike. Kind of big and dumb. Neither one of them really fit into town life. Preferred the country."

"I've heard that Farmer Tobin had a brother who was a little crazy."

"Yup. Jerry Tobin. Lived a few miles outside of town. But you shouldn't jump to any conclusions."

"Why's that?"

"Jerry Tobin fell from a barn in the early twenties. Lay flat on his back for the next twelve years of his life before he died. Couldn't even get outta bed. Just lay there with a broken neck askin' anyone who came through the room to kill him. That's how he was crazy. He wasn't capable of killing anyone himself."

"Are you . . ."

"You'd better go over to the counter," Gus said, pointing at the doorway leading into the lobby. "Wally's wavin' for you to come over there."

Finley turned and looked in the direction of the lobby. The desk clerk was holding up a black telephone and pointing at him. "For you," he yelled.

Finley walked quickly to the counter and took the telephone from the clerk's extended hand. "Hello, this is Ned Finley."

"Mr. Finley," a cheerful female voice said. "Land sakes, it's a good thing you signed the register this time. Otherwise I'd never have known your name."

"Miss Williams?"

"Yes, this is Marsha Williams, up in the library. I found something just after you left this morning."

"You found information on Maureen McCarthy?"

"No, I couldn't find anything on her. But you asked if I knew the first names of the people who owned the Sumners farm. Remember?"

"Yes."

"Well, their names are Oscar and Agnes Sumners. I really should have known that," Marsha said, admonishing herself. "My memory just isn't what it used to be."

"They're the ones who had her committed to Farmington," Finley said. "What kind of people were they?"

"I didn't know them. But others who lived out that way and wrote down their memories for our archive said they were rich farmers. Then they went broke. Agnes Sumners hung herself in the thirties."

"But you don't know what their relationship might have been to Maureen McCarthy?'

"No, but I did find something else you might be interested in."

"What's that?"

"Well, remember the first day you came into the library?"

"Yes."

"You asked about a Katharine McCarthy."

"What did you find out about her?" Finley asked.

"I couldn't find anything about her. But when I was looking up this information on the Sumnerses, I found that they had a daughter. Her name was Katharine too. Katharine Sumners."

"What do you know about her?"

"Nothing, really. I'll see what I can find for you."

"Thanks very much, Miss Williams," Finley said, handing the receiver to the clerk. He walked back into the saloon and joined Gus next to the mural.

"Important?" Gus asked.

"I don't know," Finley said. "Gus, did you ever hear of a Katharine Sumners who lived in Danvers?"

"Yup. Lived on a farm just northwest of here."

"Whatever happened to her?"

"Went east, I think."

"Who lives out there now?"

"Someone by the name of Walker. I don't know her first name."

"How do I get out there?"

"Just drive northwest of here about three miles. It's not too far from the Little Sioux line. It's a shame, isn't it?" Gus said softly.

"What's that?"

"Buffalo Bill," Gus said, sipping his beer. "They shoulda painted his eyes blue."

><><><

Finley parked his Studebaker on the gravel shoulder of a country road. In the distance, on a slightly elevated foothill, a ghostly gray, Victorian farmhouse was visible in a cluster of trees. A damaged windmill and a silo with the dome missing were located on opposite sides of the farmhouse. Finley recognized the windmill as the one he had heard groaning across the empty fields on the day he had walked the Little Sioux line to Carson.

He stepped out of the car and pulled the photograph of the farmhouse out of his pocket. He held it up to the horizon.

"It's the same house!" he said emphatically. "The picture must have been taken from this road!"

He climbed back into the car and drove toward the entrance to the farmyard. He had to turn sharply to enter the dirt road that led up to the house. The Studebaker's tires fit tightly into two ancient ruts that were covered with weeds. Finley parked next to a weathered lath fence that surrounded the yard. He waited for the dust to settle and then stepped out of the car.

There was a sense of lost grandeur and dignity in everything about the old house. Shingles were missing from the roof, paint was peeling off in large scabs on the exposed walls, and the windows were caked with dirt. From somewhere, perhaps from the interior of the house or maybe carried on the wind, Finley thought he heard the distant sound of music, a lilting romantic melody played on an ancient gramophone. He glanced at the gables of the house, and what appeared to be a human face moved quickly past one of the windows and disappeared.

Several large trees surrounded the house. A steady autumn breeze stripped away the leaves and sent them drifting out into the prairie. A swing, hanging by one rope from the huge branch of an oak, swayed ever so gently. A gray, sunbaked wagon, shorn of one wheel, was lying in waist-high vegetation next to the oak.

To the west of the house, the windmill creaked high overhead. Two of its metal blades had broken off and fallen to the ground, where they lay next to a rusty water pump. On the other side of the house, clinging vines grew almost to the top of the silo. It reminded Finley of a huge tombstone withering above the ruins of the farm. Close by, a partially exposed concrete wall and wooden door protruded out of a hillside.

Finley listened to the sounds of the wind rustling through the leaves. Then he looked up at the gables to determine if he had indeed seen a human face, but the windows were empty. Above the gables, several wood shingles flapped steadily against the roof.

He walked up the jagged stone pathway to the front porch. A courting swing hung from two corroded chains bolted into the ceiling of the porch. The swing squeaked on its hinges as it swayed slowly in the breeze.

Finley knocked on the door and waited. Moments later a thin, older woman opened the door a few inches and squinted out into the sunlight. There was a distant, almost senile look in her eyes as she peered at Finley.

"Yes?" she asked in a meek voice.

"Are you Miss Walker?" Finley asked.

"Yes, I'm Gina Walker."

"Miss Walker, I'm trying to gather some information on a family that once lived in this house. Can you tell me anything at all about the Sumners family?"

"I'm sorry. That was long before my time."

"Anything you can tell me about them would be greatly appreciated," Finley said. "Anything at all."

"I'm sorry. I know nothing about them," the woman said as she started to shut the door.

"Please . . ."

"You'll have to excuse me now. I'm busy."

The door scraped past the jamb and a bolt clicked shut on the other side. For several seconds, Finley stood on the porch and stared at the door. Then he turned and walked down the pathway.

Before climbing into the Studebaker, he looked back at the farmyard. A sudden gust of wind caught the swing that hung from the oak tree by one rope, causing it to glide forward a few feet. As the windmill groaned, and the breezes played across the shingles and whistled through the weathered siding, Finley thought he again heard a romantic melody from somewhere inside the farmhouse.

"Christ, he looks mean with that beard," one of the hospital orderlies said as he looked down at Joel Hampton.

Joel's eyes were open and he was lying on his back, staring at the ceiling.

"Maybe you should shave him?" the young nurse said as she adjusted the straps around Joel's forearms.

"Not on your life. I read his chart. I don't want him biting off my fingers."

"Then you shouldn't complain about the way he looks," the nurse admonished him. "You never know what the patients can hear."

"Well, I only know that I don't intend to shave him. Not with those eyes staring out of that beard. It looks like the devil himself staring back at you."

As the nurse and orderly walked out of the room, Joel continued to stare at the ceiling. He unclenched his fist and slowly twisted his right forearm in the leather straps.

He had learned that by clenching his fists as the orderlies tightened the straps, he could move his arms more freely once they left the room. It was only a matter of time now before he would slip out of the restraints and escape. He would sneak down the empty corridor, scale the fence outside the hospital, and disappear into the night. They would look for him, but he would keep to the riverbank. And he would work his way up the Little Sioux River to Carver County. He would look for the thicket and the old farmhouse. He would find those who had done this to him. He would make them pay. And then he would keep the promise he had made to Kate . . .

When he returned to Danvers, Finley drove back to the library. Marsha Williams was reading a yellowed newspaper behind her desk. She looked up as Finley approached.

"Mr. Finley, did you get my message?" she inquired cheerfully.

"What message?"

"The one I left for you at the hotel."

"No," Finley said. "I haven't been back there yet. I just got back from the Sumners farm."

"Well, I remembered something unusual about that family," she said as she held up the newspaper. "I hope you won't be disappointed, but Katharine Sumners died in 1927. In a boarding house fire back east. This article describes the funeral."

Finley quickly read through the article. "Where is this Peace Lutheran Cemetery?" he asked.

"Three miles south of here, on the Mill Dam Road."

"Thank you," Finley said, setting the newspaper back on the desk.

"I have something else to show you," Marsha said. She stood and led Finley over to the photographs that hung on the eastern wall. "That's them, right there," she said, pointing at the stern visages of a married couple who stared out of a black and white photograph.

"Who are they?" Finley asked.

"Oscar and Agnes Sumners. It says on the back that this photograph was taken in 1914, on their thirtieth wedding anniversary. I found it in our uncatalogued collections in the basement when I was looking for the information you requested. One of the volunteers who used to help out here must have taken it in without telling me."

Finley studied the grim, humorless faces. "They don't look any too happy with one another, do they?"

"Those were conventional poses in the early part of the century. It wasn't considered proper to smile."

"You don't have a photograph of Katharine Sumners here, do you?" Finley asked.

"No, in fact I can't find anything at all on her, except for the newspaper article you just read."

Finley drove his Studebaker along a dirt road that curved gradually to the top of a small foothill. On each side of the road, harvested fields of hay lay in neat rows awaiting the balers. The Peace Lutheran Cemetery was located in a cluster of trees at the very top of the foothill.

Finley parked his car and walked through the metal gateway into the cemetery. A bronze statue of a Union soldier stood on a large granite block in the middle of the rows of gravestones. The soldier held his rifle and bayonet in a horizontal position as he ran into battle. Some twigs from a bird's nest protruded over the top of his cap.

Finley began walking among the gravestones, looking carefully at the names and dates inscribed on the granite surfaces. Many of them were extremely old, dating back to the middle of the nineteenth century. In a distant corner, he located the Sumnerses' family plot.

There were three gravestones, all level with the ground and partially concealed by weeds and dead leaves. Finley knelt down to clear away the debris from the graves of Oscar, Agnes, and Katharine Sumners. As a lone bird chirped in a nearby tree,

Finley's eyes moved slowly back and forth over the inscriptions, which read: Oscar Sumners (October 2, 1860–December 12, 1920), Agnes Sumners (May 2, 1862–July 14, 1933), and Katharine Sumners (January 16, 1899–April 30, 1927).

Finley stood beside the graves, staring at the weathered inscriptions and pondering the significance of the dates. When he looked up, he could see the Danvers water tower, grain elevator, and church steeple rising out of the prairie. A peacefulness and quietude lingered over the cemetery, reminding him of an old proverb he had heard in his youth. He couldn't remember the exact words, but he knew it was something to the effect of "No matter what good or evil men have done, the silence of the grave claims them each and every one."

Finley looked down again. Already the wind had deposited some new dead leaves and pine needles over the inscriptions. Then he noticed something unusual on Katharine Sumners's grave. A round object protruded above the leaves. He reached in and extracted the wire meshing from a small wreath. Some dead flowers still clung to the thin strands of wire.

Finley carefully examined the wreath before placing it back on the grave. He immediately walked toward the cemetery gate and climbed into his car. He drove back to Danvers, turned left on a gravel road northwest of town, and parked next to an empty field.

Susan was waiting for him by the banks of the Little Sioux River as they had planned. She was sitting among the dead leaves. At the river's edge, Aggy was playfully throwing small stones and pebbles into the water. She laughed gleefully as the cold water lapped against her bare feet, and her toes sunk deeply into the sandy bottom.

Susan looked up as Finley approached. "Why did you ask me to meet you here?" she said.

"Aurther told me you were helping him go through some more of the old files in Farmington's basement. I wanted to see if you had been able to find anything new on Maureen McCarthy," Finley replied evasively. "I thought this would be as good a place as any to meet."

"You must have had other reasons for having me join you here," Susan insisted.

"I wanted to get you away from Farmington," Finley admitted. "I was concerned about your own mental health. But I also wanted to see if you found anything on her. I still think she's one of the keys to solving this whole affair."

"We found nothing. She just seems to have disappeared."

"On purpose, no doubt. She was probably afraid they would take her back to Farmington."

"How about you? Have you learned anything more about Judd McCarthy?"

"No, but I did learn where the photograph of the old farmhouse came from."

"Where?" Susan asked eagerly.

"It's located not too far from here, near the Little Sioux Railroad. The farm was owned by Oscar and Agnes Sumners."

"Weren't they the ones who signed to have Maureen McCarthy committed?"

"Yes, they were one of the couples. They also had a daughter, Katharine Sumners. I just came from the Peace Lutheran Cemetery, where they're all buried."

"Is this the 'Katharine' Joel was talking about?"

"I don't know. Judd McCarthy was definitely planning to meet someone named Katharine when he got back from Carson," Finley said. He glanced down at the river flowing a few feet below where they were sitting. "I believe he was going to meet her right about here."

"And you think it was Katharine Sumners?"

"I don't know. Susan, what was the birth date on the back of Joel's adoption certificate?"

"May 4, 1927."

"Are you sure?"

"Yes, why?"

"Katharine Sumners died on April 30, 1927."

"Then she couldn't possibly be the Katharine McCarthy who signed the adoption papers," Susan said.

"Doesn't seem that way, unless there was a mix-up in the dates. I suppose there could be one other explanation."

"What's that?"

"Maybe this is just another dead end."

"Then why would the picture of the Sumners farm be hidden in a box of Joel's baby clothes?"

"I don't know," Finley admitted.

For a time, they sat and quietly watched the river flow steadily south.

"Dr. Finley," Susan said abruptly, "you once said that you had your own reasons for taking an interest in Joel. I know it's none of my business, but do you mind telling me what those reasons are?"

Finley shifted nervously. He glanced at Aggy who was still playing by the river's edge.

"I'm sorry. It's none of my business," Susan said, sensing Finley's reluctance to talk about his own past.

"No, it's okay," Finley said. He picked up a twig and began breaking it into tiny pieces. "I don't talk about it often. But I guess we're friends now . . ."

"You really don't have to . . ."

"No, it's okay. I don't mind . . . I've never been married. I guess you know that. Part of it has to do with my childhood, I'm sure, which was an unhappy one. I've always preferred the bachelor life. No ties, nothing to stop me from wandering when I want to. But I have known women. One of them bore me a son, or so it was rumored. He was a young man when he died. I was told he was looking for me. I didn't even know of his existence until years later. Apparently he was having emotional problems. I always wished I'd known . . . maybe I could have helped."

"Do you see something of your son in Joel?"

Finley nodded. "I never knew my son, but after I found out about him, I always wondered what he must have thought of me. Somehow I feel that Judd McCarthy was also a better man than the people in Carver County say he was. And if Joel is his son, well . . ."

"You seem to be convinced that McCarthy was Joel's father."

"No, but the possibility exists. And if I can be of any help in clearing McCarthy's name . . . I guess maybe it helps me deal with my own past."

"I'm sorry about your son," Susan said.

"It's kind of hard to think of him as my son. He's more . . . like a patient I couldn't help. I send flowers up north sometimes, for the grave . . ." Finley paused and contemplated something. "Which reminds me, there's something else that's very strange about this business with Katharine Sumners."

"What's that?" Susan asked.

"A wreath was on her grave. Although she died in 1927, someone is still putting flowers on her grave."

"Who?"

"I don't have the slightest idea," Finley admitted. "But there must be someone around here who still cares about her."

><><><><

It was late afternoon when Finley drove back to the hotel. Inside the lobby, he paused beside the photograph of the construction crew. He studied the rugged, smiling face of Judd McCarthy. Then he walked over to Gus, who was dozing in one of the large chairs.

"Gus?" Finley said as he sat down.

"Huh?" Gus opened his eyes sleepily.

"Would there be a photograph of Katharine Sumners somewhere in the lobby?"

"Very doubtful," Gus said, struggling to keep his eyes open.

"Why?"

"She was very shy, mostly kept to herself."

"Tell me, is there any chance she might have been seeing or dating Judd McCarthy?"

"Never," Gus said emphatically. "McCarthy was a low-level drifter. Had no goals in life. The Sumners? They were rich. There were other reasons, too."

"Such as?" Finley asked.

"McCarthy was interested in a different kind of woman," Gus laughed softly to himself. "If you know what I mean."

As Gus fell back to sleep, Finley looked out at the dark shadows that were beginning to fall across Main Street. Then he stood and walked out of the lobby.

He walked up the small foothill to the high school, opened the huge glass door, and stepped inside. The poorly ventilated school smelled of dust and mildew. His heels echoed on the tile floor as he walked past the metal lockers and turned left into an adjacent hallway.

Finley walked to the very end, where some graduation pictures hung above the glass trophy cases. In a black and white photograph, labeled "Graduating Class of 1918," he found Katharine Sumners in a group of twenty or thirty graduating seniors.

She was not a beautiful girl, but there was something about her that was gentle, subtly attractive, and mysterious. In the middle of the more somber faces, she smiled shyly out at Finley. Something in that smile told him he would have liked her. It was the same feeling he got when he looked at the picture of Judd McCarthy. In fact, there was something about the two smiles that was very similar.

The night orderly walked into Joel's room and used his index finger to probe the area between the leather restraints and Joel's arms and legs. Satisfied that the restraints were neither too tight nor too loose, he pulled the bedspread over Joel's stomach and chest.

The orderly then glanced out the barred window at the clouds that were drifting across the sky. One dark cloud slowly blocked out the moonlight. In the distance, a single light glowed weakly above a cluster of trees that surrounded a farmyard.

The orderly turned and walked out of the room. The hallway was dark except for some green lights that glowed weakly along both walls. The orderly glanced down the hall at the night station. A nurse sat behind the large circular desk. Her back was turned as the orderly walked in the opposite direction and entered another room.

In the second room, a frail old man was asleep on the floor next to the bed. He was curled up in the fetal position.

The orderly shook his head in mock disgust. "Jason," he said, "when are you going to learn to sleep in your bed?"

The orderly lifted the old man and laid him gently on the bed. He watched as Jason curled up into a tight ball, clutched a blanket to his cheek, and began snoring softly.

"I wish they were all as docile as you," the orderly chuckled. He suddenly realized he didn't have the hospital chart with him. "Damn," he muttered, "I must have left it in Hampton's room."

He walked quickly back to the hallway. The night nurse was still sitting with her back turned to the corridor.

In Joel's room, the moonlight had broken through the heavy cloud formations and was shining brightly through the window. The bedspread was lying on the floor next to the bed.

The orderly stared at the wrinkled sheets and leather straps that curled across the empty bed. "Jesus Christ!" he muttered. He rushed out of the room. "Hampton's not in his room!" he yelled to the nurse.

CHAPTER TEN

Early the next morning, Finley drove out to the abandoned water reclamation project. He had developed some hunches about the project, and he wanted to determine whether or not his suspicions were correct. He walked a few feet into the yawning black hole of the main culvert and chipped several pieces of concrete off the inside wall. He drove back to Danvers and deposited the fragments in the county engineer's office. Afterward, he walked over to the library to collect everything he could find on John J. Sylvester, the Hanley brothers, and the Little Sioux Water Reclamation Project. He made himself comfortable at a large table in the basement archives and spent the better part of the morning reading through the materials he had collected.

Boxes of uncatalogued donations were stacked throughout the basement. Some artifacts had apparently been gathering dust on makeshift shelves for years, while other shelves contained neatly organized rows of historical records and documents. On two folding tables, stacks of carefully labeled folders attested to Marsha Williams's on-going efforts to bring some semblance of order to the collections.

It was almost noon when Finley walked up the stairs to the main floor. Marsha was sitting behind her desk when he entered the room.

"I was just reading through this book on Carver County history," Finley said, placing a small, hardbound volume on the desk. "Do you know anything about the author?"

Marsha picked up the book and glanced at the title. "Oh my, yes. This was written by my neighbor, Myra Stevenson."

"Well, there's something curious about this book—"

"Poor Myra," Marsha said, interrupting Finley.

"Why do you say that?"

"Myra wanted to be a poet," she said sadly. "Sent her poems in for years, but never had one accepted. Then shortly after she died, *Harper's* sent her a letter saying one of her poems had finally been accepted for publication."

"That's too bad."

"Oh, not really," Marsha exclaimed cheerfully. "They were ghastly poems. Now, what is the problem with this book?"

"Well, the section on John J. Sylvester says nothing about the ten years of his life before he became governor."

"I suppose Myra just decided to concentrate more on the years when he was a state celebrity. Mr. Sylvester had a short, but illustrious career in politics," Marsha said proudly. "He was the only person to ever get out of Danvers and really make something of himself. He even thought of running for president, you know."

"No, I wasn't aware of that," Finley admitted.

"It's a shame. Such an honorable man. He would have made a fine president," she said dreamily. "And what it would have meant for this town."

"Well, what I really need is some background information on the public works projects in Carver County in the 1920s," Finley said.

"Myra didn't mention that in her book?" Marsha asked, somewhat perplexed.

"No."

She quickly flipped through the pages of the small volume. "That is strange," she said, looking up at Finley. "The Community Development League under Mr. Sylvester almost built this town."

"Wasn't that organization involved with the water reclamation project?"

"It certainly was."

"What was that project supposed to accomplish?"

"Oh, that was one of Mr. Sylvester's many dreams for Danvers. Come over here and I'll show you what he had in mind." Marsha led Finley over to the large Carver County map. "Now, you must remember that Mr. Sylvester was a visionary. He had hoped to make Danvers the most prosperous town in the county. Since the big railroads were already abandoning us, he came up with another plan, a very expensive one. But he hoped it would mean economic prosperity for the people of Danvers for years to come."

"What was the plan?" Finley asked as she unhooked the long wooden pointer from the wall.

"The plan was to divert the floodwaters of the Little Sioux River, both to alleviate the flooding problem and also to get the overflow to other parts of the township where it was desperately needed." Marsha began running the pointer over the map. "Now, you must remember that the farmers along the river were flooded out almost every spring. It cost them and the people of this area a fortune in lost crops and damaged farmland. Mr. Sylvester's plan was to build a huge culvert under the prairie to collect the floodwaters and divert them to two different areas."

"Is that what those lines represent?" Finley asked, pointing at two broken black lines that branched off from the point where the main culvert joined the river.

"Yes, this one here was to take the waters farther east where they would be stored in a reservoir to be drained off by the farmers during the dry years. Curiously, although we get all kinds of rain along the river, there have been years when the farmers east of here haven't had enough water to grow a thing."

"What about the other culvert?"

"Well, now here is where you see that Mr. Sylvester was a dreamer and not at all a practical man. This culvert was to use the floodwaters to power an electrical plant southeast of Danvers. The plant was never built. It was much too impractical."

"Why?"

"A power plant could only have been used in the spring when the overflow came off the river. The rest of the year there wouldn't have been enough water to power its turbines. And the problem with the other culvert was that even if you got the floodwaters over to the farmers east of here, there was still the problem of digging irrigation ditches so they could get the water to their crops. It was all highly impractical and much too expensive."

"If there were so many problems with the project," Finley asked, "how come the people in Danvers went along with it?"

"Mr. Sylvester was a dreamer. People got caught up in his visions and went along with them, even when they were impractical. They knew he had their best interests at heart. And his dreams were better than most of the realities they were accustomed to."

Finley studied the thin black lines that wandered in two directions away from the river. "You wouldn't have anything on the financial dealings of that organization, would you?" he finally asked.

"Which one?"

"The Community Development League and the Little Sioux Water Reclamation Project."

"Yes, I think I do have something on that. Just a minute." Marsha walked over to the basement door and disappeared down the stairs. She returned shortly with a large, leather-bound volume. "This is volume two of *The Public Works Projects in Carver County (1920–1930)*. It's the original copy. Now, what exactly is it that you need?"

"The cost breakdown of the water reclamation project. Also, anything on its financial dealings with the Community Development League."

Marsha flopped the book open on a table and carefully paged through the handwritten volume. "There should be a section here on the financial records of that project. Yes, here it is. Oh my!"

"What's wrong?" Finley asked.

"Those pages have been torn out!"

After leaving the Carnegie library, Finley walked over to the county building. He walked down a short flight of stairs into the basement and approached the front desk of the county engineer's office.

"Do you have the test results on the concrete samples I brought in?" Finley asked the engineer who was sitting at a desk in the back of the room.

"Yes, I have them right here," he said. He slowly stood up, walked over to the front desk, and laid a small piece of paper on the counter. It had a series of handwritten formulas and notations scribbled down the middle of the page. "What would you like to know?"

"Would that concrete stand up under stress?" Finley asked.

"Depends on what you were planning to use it for," the engineer said as he adjusted his glasses.

"The sample was taken from a culvert, a flood-control project."

"No. It's well below minimal engineering requirements. Water pressure would blow it out in a few years."

"Does that mean the entire culvert was built with inferior concrete?"

"Not necessarily. It means that this section is inferior. You would have to take samples from several sections to determine if the entire system is defective."

"Thanks," Finley said.

He walked back out to Main Street and got into his car. He drove west toward the water reclamation project. He parked on the shoulder of a country road, took a large flashlight and burlap sack out of the trunk, and walked across the fields to the Little Sioux line.

Finley walked along the tracks until he came to the abandoned railroad car. The reddish gray siding was warping and buckling beneath the bright sunlight, and the iron wheels were set firmly on two tracks that disappeared into the weeds and foliage. The name "Little Sioux Railroad" was painted in faded white letters that were turning gray and blending into the color of the wood siding.

Finley walked down the embankment toward the scattered piles of old lumber and iron molds that littered the bottom of the trench. He was careful to leave considerable room between himself and the rotting wooden pallet where he had seen the huge snake.

A gust of wind whistled through the warped siding on the railroad car as he paused next to the yawning mouth of the culvert. There was an ominous silence from the dark interior as it stretched for miles beneath the prairie topsoil. Weeds and grass clung to wide cracks in the sides and floor of the culvert. Scattered puddles of water held dead leaves that had drifted into the tunnel opening.

Finley switched on the flashlight and stepped into the culvert. As he walked deeper into the interior of the flood control system, he chipped tiny pieces of concrete out of the walls and deposited them into the burlap sack. The fragments came out easily, looking more like sand and gravel pouring out of the huge cracks in the walls.

In some sections of the culvert, boulder-sized segments of the walls had broken free and fallen to the tunnel floor. Occasionally, a frog or lizard darted across the puddles as he moved deeper into the tunnel, following the flashlight beam into the darkness.

The culvert suddenly angled off sharply in two directions. Finley realized that this was where the two tunnels separated, one heading east toward the reservoir, and the other bending in a southeasterly direction toward the power plant.

He directed the beam of light as far as he could into the two openings. In the second tunnel, his flashlight illuminated the white, gleaming teeth of several rats as they scurried across the floor and glared back at him defiantly. Their high-pitched squeals echoed against the walls as they disappeared into the tunnel's depths. Finley focused his flashlight on their retreating tails. Then he took one last sample of concrete from the wall and walked back in the direction of the entrance.

As he approached the mouth of the culvert, he heard another sound mingling with the distant squeal of the rats. Ahead of him, there was the distinct rumbling of heavy machinery moving around just outside the entrance. The rumble grew progressively louder, then became strangely muffled as he rounded the last curve in the tunnel wall.

Where bright sunlight should have greeted him at the opening, there was instead a huge wall of black dirt filling the culvert from floor to ceiling. Beyond it, the sound of heavy machinery faded as Finley ran the beam of his flashlight across the glistening, black topsoil.

Behind him, the rats' screeching pierced the silence of the abandoned flood control system.

Joel climbed the red granite wall surrounding Farmington and fled into the countryside. Thick clouds covered the moon as he ran through the harvested fields. Occasionally, he stepped on corn and wheat stubble, and the pain shot up into his ankles and calves. Still he ran, following an instinct that kept his legs moving long after he was exhausted.

When the moonlight broke through the clouds, he sought refuge in the sparse brush and clusters of trees that dotted the wide expanse of the prairie. When the clouds once again moved across the moon, he stumbled to his feet and ran, moving always, or so he thought, in the direction of the Little Sioux River.

He was disoriented from lying so long in the hospital bed and from the strangeness of the world around him. The prairie he remembered had large unplowed areas of open land and tall prairie grass. They were all gone, as was so much of what he had once known.

Finally he collapsed on the edge of a thicket. His hands and knees sank into the damp grass and weeds as he gasped for breath. Slowly, he rolled to a sitting position and fell back against a tree. He stared up at the clouds and stars . . .

How far had he come? Unless he had completely lost his sense of direction, surely he could not be too far from the river. He would have to be there before morning. They would be looking for him, and the brush and trees along the riverbank would be the best place to hide. After he rested, he would find those who had taken everything away from him. Everything, including his life. Then he would find Kate. He remembered her golden hair, and he could almost feel her breathing gently against his chest as he held her close. He needed her now, more than ever before.

Suddenly, he heard the barking of a dog and the sound of crunching weeds. Seconds later, a young Labrador retriever shot out of the underbrush and came to a halt a few feet away from where he was sitting. The dog barked again, then snarled menacingly.

"Ah, so ya be a tough guy, huh?" Joel laughed softly. He reached a hand out to the dog. "Come on over here. Ah ain't gonna hurt ya."

The Labrador backed away and crouched down in one of the furrows of the plowed field. A soft, almost imperceptible noise rumbled deeply in the dog's throat as it stared at Joel.

"Come over here, old buddy," he whispered gently, still holding his hand out. "Ain't nothin' here gonna hurt ya. Ah just wanta say hello, that's all."

As the saliva dripped off its tongue and glistened in the moonlight, the dog slowly raised itself to a sitting position. It glanced into the open fields, then crept over to where Joel was sitting.

"Ya sure make a lotta noise for a little fella," Joel said as he scratched the top of the dog's head. "Sounded like a grizzly bear pounding through those trees. 'Most scared me half to death."

The dog laid its head on Joel's lap, and the saliva quickly soaked through the thin fabric of the hospital uniform. It felt good to have company out in the darkness of the prairie.

"Strange sky up there tonight," Joel said softly. He paused as he heard another noise in the thicket behind him. He turned quickly to see a light flash on in a farmhouse buried deep in the trees. A woman, her nightgown silhouetted against the bright light behind her, stepped up to the screen door.

"Charlie, you comin' in here tonight?" she yelled. "Or do I have to come out and get you?"

Fearful of being discovered, Joel picked up the dog. He held it under one arm while he grasped its snout so it couldn't bark. The dog's legs and body thrashed frantically beneath Joel's strong grip. A frightened whine filtered out of its throat.

"Charlie, what you got out there?" the woman yelled from the porch.

A male voice from inside the house suddenly yelled, "Ah, he's probably just chasin' some damn rabbit. Let 'im be."

"But it looks like rain."

The dog struggled even more wildly in Joel's arms, and he increased the pressure on its chest and snout.

"He's been out in the rain before," the man's voice yelled disgustedly. "Ain't gonna hurt him one damn bit."

"But . . ."

"Get back in here!" the man bellowed.

Joel heard the screen door creak slowly shut, and the light went out. He heard the steady drone of voices, and then there was silence again.

He bent over to place the dog on the ground. "Now, old buddy, don't ya make no noise as I be leavin'. Ah don't want ya gettin me in trouble."

The Labrador collapsed in a heap as he set it down. "What be the matter with ya?" Joel inquired, turning the dog over gently. He felt its chest. There was no movement beneath his hand. "Ya be all right?" he asked with deep concern. He lifted the dog and tried to look into its glazed eyes. Its body was limp and its head flopped to one side.

"Ah, no, ah only meant ta keep ya quiet," Joel lamented. He placed his ear to the dog's chest, but there was no heartbeat. "Ah didn't mean ta kill ya."

He placed the dog on the ground and covered it with dirt and weeds. He shook his head and patted the mound. "I didn't mean ta do it, lad. I'm mighty sorry."

A light flashed on in the farmhouse and the screen door suddenly burst open. A huge man in pajamas stomped out onto the back step.

"Goddamnit, Charlie, get in here!" the man yelled into the darkness. "She ain't gonna let me get no sleep until you quit chasin' that rabbit an' get in here!"

Joel stood and crept along the edge of the thicket, moving toward the other side of the house. Behind him, he heard footsteps crunching through the underbrush. He looked all around and ran once more into the open fields.

Was he that strong? So strong he had killed something without meaning to. Maybe that's why he was at Farmington. Maybe there had been others.

✕✕✕✕

Susan heard the telephone ringing almost as soon as she stepped out of her car. Aggy was still sitting in the backseat, clutching two large Halloween pumpkins.

"Honey," Susan said as she fumbled with her purse and rushed toward the front door, "you wait in the car. I'll answer the phone and then I'll take you over to Robin's."

"Can we carve the pumpkins tonight, Mommy?"

"I don't know. It's kind of early. We'll have to see." Susan inserted the key into the lock and turned it. The phone was still ringing loudly in the kitchen as she stepped through the front door.

She rushed across the living room and yanked the receiver off the kitchen wall. "Hello," she said.

"Mrs. Hampton?" a male voice inquired.

"Yes."

"Mrs. Hampton, this is the security division at the Farmington State Mental Hospital. I'm calling to tell you your husband escaped last night—"

"What?" she gasped, fear rising in her throat.

"He went missing around midnight, right after the last bed check. We're searching the hospital now. It's quite possible he's still inside. But we thought we should let you know. For your own safety."

For a moment, Susan was unable to speak. "Have you contacted Dr. Finley?" she asked finally.

"We've called the Danvers Hotel several times, but they haven't seen him since early morning. We left a message for him to call us as soon as he returns."

"What do you want me to do?" Susan asked weakly.

"Just stay home. Keep your doors locked. The police are looking for your husband. If he is coming in your direction, we'll get him. But keep your doors locked, just in case."

"What . . . why . . .?"

"Your husband is considered to be a dangerous man, Mrs. Hampton. We don't know if he would try to hurt anyone. But we don't want to give him the chance."

Susan composed herself and spoke more calmly into the phone. "Do me a favor, please?"

"Yes, Mrs. Hampton."

"If you get in touch with Dr. Finley, have him call me."

"Yes, ma'am."

"Thank you."

Susan placed the phone back on the wall and sat by the kitchen table, staring blankly out the window. Then she remembered she had left Aggy in the car. She quickly walked outside. As she approached the car, she saw that Aggy was no longer in the backseat.

She looked frantically down both ends of the street. "Aggy!" she yelled. "Aggy, where are you?" She continued to yell Aggy's name as she paced up and down the sidewalk.

"What is it? What's wrong, Susan?" Alice asked as she stepped out of her house and rushed out to the street.

"I can't find Aggy. Is she over there with Robin?

"No. I haven't seen her all day."

"I left her in the car while I answered the phone! I told her to wait and I would take her over to play with Robin. When I came out, she was gone!"

Susan felt the panic build. *Joel loved Aggy. He would never do anything to hurt her, would he?* She took a deep breath and tried to control her fear.

"You look over there," Alice said, pointing down one end of the street. "I'll check the other end."

Susan felt almost paralyzed with fear as she started down the street. Suddenly she heard a weak voice behind her.

"Mommy, were you calling me?"

Susan whirled around.

Aggy stepped through the screen door onto the porch of their house. "I was upstairs getting some toys to bring over to Robin's," she said meekly.

Susan suddenly felt the full weight of the terrible pressure she had been laboring under for the past few weeks, and her shoulders and arms began to shake uncontrollably.

Why? Why us? My God, what have we done?

The tears seemed trapped inside of her, unable to burst through the walls she had built to protect herself. There was only the shuddering sensation she could not control, and the horrible feeling of being completely alone.

"Susan, my God, what's wrong with you?" Alice asked, placing a consoling hand on Susan's quivering shoulder.

Susan tried to say something, but her head was aching and the words would not come. She reached for her throbbing forehead, but her hand was shaking so badly she quickly thrust it into her coat pocket.

"Susan, are you all right? What is it? Should I call someone?" A strong note of panic crept into Alice's voice. "Should I call a doctor?"

Susan shook her head vigorously.

"Are you sure?"

"Yes . . . please . . ." Susan breathed deeply, and the shaking in her shoulders and arms began to subside.

"Look, come over to our place for a few hours. Until you pull yourself together," Alice insisted.

"No!" Susan said firmly. She took another deep breath. "I'll be all right."

"What is it? Is it Joel?"

Susan nodded weakly.

"What's wrong with him?"

"He tried to . . . and now . . ." Susan could not find the right words.

"Are you two having problems?"

"Joel had a breakdown of some kind. He's hospitalized at Farmington. He's . . ." Susan paused again, unable to explain to Alice what was happening to Joel and her.

"I knew something was wrong," Alice said gently. "Frank and I heard strange noises over there in the middle of the night. What is it? Are you two fighting?"

"No, he's . . . I mean, yes. Joel's been under tremendous pressure. He thinks he's . . ." Susan wanted to explain to Alice that Joel was undergoing some strange transformation in which he was taking on the personality of someone who had lived in the 1920s. But she knew Alice would not understand. "He just needs a rest."

"Are you sure?"

"Yes."

"I can't talk you into coming over for coffee?"

"No." Susan glanced down at Aggy, who had crept over to the sidewalk. Aggy placed one hand on her mother's coat. "I have to make supper," Susan said.

"You can eat over at our place," Alice offered.

"No, thank you. We have a lot to get done tonight."

"Susan," Alice said reassuringly. "These things happen. Frank and I almost split up three times. People get over these things. It just takes time."

Susan nodded. She knew there was no way to make Alice understand.

"Let me know if you need anything, okay?"

"Thanks," Susan replied as Alice walked away.

"Are you sure it's nothing else?" Alice turned and asked again.

"Yes."

Susan watched Alice disappear behind a tall bush. Then she looked down at Aggy.

"Mommy, what's wrong with Daddy?" Aggy's eyes were filled with fear and confusion.

Susan thought about diverting her daughter's attention to some other subject. But she realized there were some things even a four-year-old girl should know to protect herself.

"Honey," Susan began slowly. "There's something wrong with Daddy. He's . . ."

"Is Daddy dead?" Aggy asked sadly.

Susan dropped to one knee and held her daughter close. "No, honey, your daddy is not dead. He's . . . very sick. And you and I are going to be alone for a while. Until he gets better."

"Did Daddy hurt you?"

"No, why do you ask?"

"Because you're crying." Aggy pushed herself gently away from her mother. "The last time you cried was when Daddy chased us into the attic."

"That was an accident. Daddy didn't mean to scare us." Susan looked into her daughter's eyes. "Honey, you have to do one thing for me."

"What?"

"If you see Daddy at any time," Susan said slowly, "you mustn't talk to him or go near him. Come to me or go over to Robin's."

"Why?"

"Because your daddy is sick . . ." Again Susan searched for the right words to explain Joel's actions.

"Will he hurt us?"

"He might," Susan admitted. "He doesn't want to. But he could hurt us."

"Will he hurt my dolls again?"

"No, but you must remember what I told you. Don't talk to Daddy or go near him if you see him. Then he won't hurt you."

"Okay, Mommy."

Susan picked up Aggy and carried her to the front porch. "When Daddy's well, honey, then you can talk to him again." She set Aggy down and they walked through the front door holding hands. "Now, you go upstairs and play while I make something for us to eat."

"Okay, Mommy," Aggy said somewhat sadly. She trudged up the steps and disappeared at the top of the stairs.

Susan locked the door behind them. The telephone receiver was hanging limply from the wall when she walked back into the kitchen. She placed it back on the hook and walked over to the cupboards. She indifferently selected a can of tuna fish and placed it on the counter. Then she idly rummaged through a drawer, looking for a can opener.

Suddenly she heard a noise behind her, and she whirled in that direction. She held her hand to her pounding heart as the basement door swung open a few inches, then groaned to a slow halt. Susan gulped and sighed deeply as she realized the lock had apparently not caught, and the door had creaked open by itself.

She walked over and reached for the metal knob. As her hand touched it, she remembered that Joel had come out of the basement after he had carried Aggy downstairs. He had disappeared again down there after threatening them in the attic.

Just what was down there that so intrigued him?

Susan peered into the darkness as she walked down the flight of wooden stairs. At the bottom, she groped for the overhead light switch. After moving her hand in a circular motion several times, she managed to grasp the thin cord. She pulled hard on it and the harsh glare of a lone lightbulb flooded the room.

The concrete floor was littered with the wreckage of glass jars, boxes, and pieces of furniture they had been keeping in storage. Even the water heater had been bludgeoned and slashed repeatedly with some sharp object. In the middle of the wreckage, Susan noticed the shattered remains of several of her steak knives.

As she bent over to examine one of the knife handles, she again heard the basement door creak open. She turned quickly and found herself looking up at Aggy, who was silhouetted against the light from the kitchen windows.

"What are you doing down there, Mommy?" she asked innocently. "Is Daddy down there?"

><><><><

Finley ran the flashlight beam over the huge pile of topsoil that covered the entrance to the culvert. Then he turned and walked back into the depths of the tunnel.

At the point where the tunnel branched off in two directions, he paused and focused the light into the darkness. He decided the tunnel to his left was probably the main culvert system, the one that had most likely been completed before the water reclamation project was abandoned. The rats' squeals drifted out of the other culvert, so reason would suggest that he take the main culvert and not the one the rats had turned into their private sanctuary.

But if the rats were this deep into the system, he reasoned, they must have come in from the opposite end from where he had entered it. If so, there must be another opening somewhere southeast of Danvers.

Finley threw the burlap sack over his shoulder and walked into the second tunnel opening as the rats scurried into the darkness ahead of him. As he walked deeper into the culvert, he played the flashlight beam over the circular walls. He walked rapidly, holding firmly onto the sack, his sole weapon should the rats lose their fear of him.

A veteran of many World War II combat experiences, Finley was not a man to panic easily, but the thought of being trapped underground with thousands of rats chilled him to the very bone. As he walked, he fought to control the fear as the flashlight reflected off the gleaming white teeth of the rats staring down at him from the holes and cracks in the walls of the culvert.

Long, drooping cobwebs hung from the walls in some sections, and the flashlight beam occasionally illuminated small black bats, their sharp claws embedded in the pitted ceiling. The disturbed bats would chortle in unison as Finley approached. He decided the bats were more evidence that there was probably an opening somewhere up ahead.

He walked for what seemed like several miles. Finally, ahead of him, he saw a large mound of dirt that had tumbled into the culvert, closing it off completely. He ran the flashlight beam over the pile of debris. Then he turned the flashlight off and peered into the mound, looking for any light that might reveal an avenue of escape.

Behind him, he heard the soft padding of tiny feet on the floor. He switched on the flashlight and quickly pivoted. As he aimed the beam down, several large rats hissed at him before retreating into the darkness. He ran the flashlight back and forth in the direction where they had fled. Just beyond the beam of light, the rats continued to hiss.

Finley was annoyed with himself for having chosen this tunnel. Obviously, there was no avenue of escape through the large pile of debris. And the real question was whether or not he could go back to try the other branch of the culvert. The batteries in the flashlight were weakening, and it was obvious that it was his only real defense against the rats. Once the batteries died, they would lose all fear.

Suddenly he heard a soft rustling sound, and he directed the flashlight at the floor. The beam fell on two rats scurrying up the mound of dirt. At the top, they burrowed into the black soil and disappeared.

Finley climbed up the pile of debris to the ceiling. He tore aside several small chunks of concrete and thrust his arm into the soil. A portion of the ceiling had remained intact on the other side of the mound. He tore at the remaining rocks and chunks of concrete until he had created a small opening just below the ceiling. He grabbed his sack and slowly squeezed through the opening. Once again he aimed the flashlight into the darkness. The culvert curved gradually out of sight, just beyond the beam.

Finley scrambled down the other side and surveyed the area in front of him. Large puddles of water had accumulated on the floor, and rusty steel reinforcement rods were stacked against one wall. He walked past the pile of metal and moved deeper into the culvert.

He had gone another mile or two when he saw a glimmer of light ahead of him. As he moved closer, the light began to glow brightly on the tunnel floor. Almost immediately, he stepped through a weed-strewn opening and into the sunlight.

He found himself standing on the side of an embankment. In the distance, the Danvers church steeple, grain elevator, and water tower rose out of the foothills. In front of him, the black furrows of a newly plowed field stretched across the prairie.

As Finley looked back into the culvert, a lone rat scurried out and disappeared into the brush.

><><><><

Finley caught a ride with a farmer who was driving to Danvers on a Ford tractor. The farmer dropped him off on the northwestern edge of town, about a mile from where his Studebaker was parked. Finley crossed the fields and followed the railroad tracks back to the water reclamation project. At the mouth of the culvert, huge tire tracks crisscrossed over the top of the freshly turned soil, then angled south across the field that separated the embankment from the river.

Finley followed the tire tracks to where they intersected with a gravel road farther south. Large clumps of black dirt had fallen off the rubber wheels and were scattered over the road. There were no tracks in the field on the other side of the road. Finley looked down both ends of the road as far as he could see. There was no sign of the heavy equipment that had bulldozed and closed the culvert entrance. He decided it must have been loaded on trucks and hauled away.

Finley immediately drove back to Danvers. He pulled the sack out of the trunk of the car where he had stowed it and carried it into the basement of the county building. The county engineer was sitting at a desk in the back of the room.

"I've got the samples for you," Finley said, setting the sack on the counter.

"Be with you in a minute," the engineer said as he scribbled some notations on a large chart in front of him. Then he joined Finley at the counter. "What do you have here?"

"More concrete samples from the flood control project I told you about earlier," Finley said, dumping the contents of the bag on the counter. "You said I would have to collect samples from several sections to determine if the entire system was defective. Here they are."

The engineer picked up the small fragments and crumbled them between his thumb and index finger. "You don't have to run these through analysis," he said as the pieces fell onto the counter. "It's obvious that whoever mixed this didn't know what he was doing. See, it falls apart in your hand."

"So a flood control project constructed from this concrete would definitely be defective?" Finley asked.

"No question about it. Much of it would wash away and collapse in a few years. Certainly within a decade or two."

"Thanks," Finley said. He started to put the samples back into the sack. "Incidentally, who was responsible for burying that culvert three miles west of here?"

"What culvert?"

"The water reclamation project."

"They buried it?" the engineer asked, surprised.

"Just this morning," Finley answered.

"I don't know nothin' about that. State's been meanin' to do it for some time now, but I sure didn't know they were planning to do it today."

"How come they let it sit for over thirty years? Then all of a sudden they decide to bury it?"

"It's a health problem." The engineer glanced over at a woman who had stepped up to the other end of the counter. "Be right with you, ma'am."

"No hurry," the woman said. She set her purse on the counter and walked across the hall to a water fountain.

"What kind of a health problem?" Finley asked.

"Rats. All over that system. Get out into the fields and into the towns. 'Bout time they do something to get rid of them."

"Who had the authority to bury it?"

"State health authorities, most likely. They been after the county to do it for years. Probably just decided to do it themselves, since we've been kind of slow about it. Haven't had the money."

As the engineer walked over to assist the woman, Finley swept the rest of the concrete samples into his sack. He walked quickly back up the stairs.

It was late afternoon when he stepped out onto Main Street. A slight chill was in the air and the blue skies of Indian summer were yielding gradually to the grayer tints of late autumn.

Finley threw the sack into the trunk of his car and slid into the driver's seat. As he inserted the key into the ignition, he heard a sinister rattling sound behind him. Without moving his body, he turned the rearview mirror ever so slowly downward. A huge rattlesnake, coiled on the backseat, appeared in the mirror.

Finley threw his body down across the front seat. The snake lashed out at the movement and missed. Finley quickly opened the passenger door and crawled out. He slammed the door shut behind him.

Outside the car, he looked through the rear window at the rattlesnake as it slithered and recoiled.

$$\times\!\!\times\!\!\times\!\!\times$$

"Someone sure meant to scare the hell out of you," the policeman said to Finley as they stood in a small office in the basement of the county building. The dead rattlesnake was stretched out across a long wooden bench next to them. "But they sure weren't out to hurt you."

"Why do you say that?" Finley asked.

The policeman took a pen out of his shirt pocket and pried the snake's mouth open. "Snake has no fangs. Someone pulled them out with pliers."

"What the hell?" Finley said as he looked at the two bloody holes at the top of the snake's mouth.

"Some people'll go a long ways for a joke," the policeman said as he took the pen out of the rattlesnake's mouth.

The snake's jaws slowly closed as Finley glanced suspiciously in the direction of the county engineer's office. "I didn't know there were any rattlesnakes in this area," he said.

"There aren't. Someone must have brought this one over from the Dakotas."

"Tell me something," Finley said, looking back at the policeman who was writing up his report in a black book. "Whatever happened to John J. Sylvester?"

"The governor?"

"Yes. A book I was reading didn't give the date of his death. In fact it didn't say anything about his later years."

"Probably a good reason for that," the policeman said, closing his book.

"What do you mean?" Finley asked.

"He ain't dead yet. Owns the bank right across the street. Has for years."

"How old is he?" Finley asked, surprised.

"Probably late sixties. Maybe early seventies. He was the youngest governor the state ever had. That's probably why he's still around."

"What about those pictures of him hanging all over town? When were they taken?"

"Probably ten, fifteen years ago. Hasn't changed that much. Maybe a little heavier."

"That explains a lot of things," Finley said.

"Explains what?" the policeman asked.

"Nothing," Finley replied. "Listen, the next time you talk to the county engineer, tell him they buried the water reclamation project much too early."

"Why?" the policeman asked, perplexed.

"Because all the rats aren't in there yet."

He had made it safely to the banks of the Little Sioux River long before daybreak. From there, he had followed it upstream for perhaps eight or ten miles. As the sun came over the horizon, he took refuge beneath the exposed roots of a large tree that grew along the riverbank. Then he had fallen asleep.

He woke to the gentle sound of the sluggish water as it lapped against a log at the river's edge. For the rest of the day, he sat there.

He remembered how very much he had liked to sit on the banks of the Little Sioux River, watching the gentle waters flow toward the Mississippi and the Great Sea beyond. That thought had always brought out the wanderlust in him. That is, until he met Kate. She was the first woman he'd ever loved. There had been others, but not the kind a man would ask to marry. He had to find her again. But first he would find those who had done this to him.

It was late afternoon when he heard the loud honking overhead. He peered through the exposed roots at a flock of Canadian geese weaving gracefully across the sky. They seemed to be following the course of the Little Sioux River as they disappeared from sight. For a moment, his spirit responded to the majestic freedom of the geese flying gracefully south, and he wished he could join them.

The hospital uniform was covered with dirt, and his feet were bloody from the sharp wheat and corn stubble he had run through the previous evening. He laid his head back on the riverbank and fell asleep again.

He dreamt of the geese and the river, the river that opened onto the largest body of water he had ever seen, a body of water that stretched beyond the horizon and seemingly into the sky itself. He felt himself being pulled away into that river.

But then he saw the girl in the swing. Always before, she was sitting with her back turned toward him. Now she was looking in his direction. It had been so long, but he still remembered those soft eyes and the shy, gentle smile.

And he knew, although the river beckoned, that it was not yet time for him to go . . .

CHAPTER ELEVEN

Finley left the county building and walked across the street to the Danvers State Bank. It was the oldest structure on Main Street. High above the brick portico, the date "1880" had been inscribed.

Fake stone columns climbed the granite walls on both sides of the door, and tiny stone nymphs skipped across the top of the wall, just below the roofline. A green lightbulb glowed weakly above the entrance.

A middle-aged woman in a black and white business suit was pulling the shade down over the front window as Finley climbed the stairs and opened the door.

"I'm sorry, we're closed," the woman said politely.

"I have an appointment with Mr. Sylvester," Finley said as he walked into the lobby.

"You must be mistaken," the woman replied. She tried to stop Finley from walking any further into the bank.

"Mr. Sylvester is expecting me," Finley said firmly as the door closed behind him.

"But you can't!" the woman blurted out.

"Let Mr. Finley in, Miss Phillips!" a deep baritone voice suddenly boomed across the lobby.

As Finley looked in that direction, a tall, heavyset man stepped into an open doorway in the rear of the lobby. He stood with one hand in his coat pocket, while the other hand held a long cigar. As the swirling smoke dissipated, John J. Sylvester posed in the doorway like a Shakespearean actor about to step out onto the stage.

Sylvester's white hair and mustache were accentuated by piercing blue eyes that stared at Finley. He wore a dark blue business suit, and his large frame was illuminated by the light from a window behind him. An aura of power and nobility clung naturally to John J. Sylvester.

"Please let Mr. Finley come in to see me, Miss Phillips," his voice boomed out again as he raised the cigar slowly and dramatically to his mouth. "He is right. We have an appointment."

As Sylvester disappeared behind the cloud of smoke, Miss Phillips stepped aside. A look of disdain crept into her eyes as Finley shuffled past in his dirty tan pants and sweater. His dirt-caked shoes left muddy tracks across the floor.

Sylvester was sitting behind a large walnut desk when Finley stepped into his private office. His left arm was cocked confidently at his side as he sat motionlessly in a black swivel chair. "Sit down, Mr. Finley," he instructed politely, but firmly.

As Finley sat down in a chair in front of the desk, his eyes swept across the photographs that lined the walls. Sylvester stared out from most of them.

"I understand you have a keen interest in local history," Sylvester said, his blue eyes fixed on Finley. "What is it you want from me?"

"I think you know what I've been looking for," Finley said, trying to avoid Sylvester's intimidating gaze.

"Why don't you tell me, so we may both be enlightened?" Sylvester said. He placed the cigar in a large metal ashtray and leaned back in his chair.

"I think you know that I've been investigating the disappearance of Judd McCarthy. I know you had something to do with his disappearance and death. But I'm not exactly sure how you were involved."

"If my memory serves me correctly," Sylvester said, seemingly unperturbed, "McCarthy disappeared into the Dakotas with a company payroll."

"That was a smokescreen, as you very well know. Some powerful people had him put away. You were one of them."

"Why don't you tell me what you think you know? Then I'll see if I can help you."

"I know you inherited this bank in the 1920s," Finley began. "You were a young man, full of ambition, but the bank was only marginally successful as a business. Then you became President of the Community Development League, which controlled city funds for growth and expansion. You were also involved with the Hanley Brothers Construction Company and the Little Sioux Water Reclamation Project. It was a perfect opportunity for you to filter city funds and construction funds into your bank, and you did so with the help of Fred and Ben Hanley."

"And how did we succeed in this venture?" Sylvester asked somewhat sarcastically. He picked up his cigar from the ashtray and relit it with a silver lighter.

"By inflating labor costs and contract costs, at the same time using inferior materials for the water project. It gave the Hanley brothers a wider profit margin, and it gave you the necessary capital to expand your bank's investment capabilities. The people in this town believed in you, and you took them for a ride."

"Can you prove this?" Sylvester asked coldly.

"There's no need to prove it," Finley said. "You would never be prosecuted for a crime that took place thirty-three years ago."

"Then what is it you want from me?"

"Undoubtedly the metropolitan papers would love to get their hands on a business scandal involving a former governor. Especially one who was so popular and who was held in such high esteem by his constituency."

"Money? Is that what you want?" Sylvester asked, leaning forward. "Is this blackmail, Mr. Finley?"

"I only want the truth. What happened to Judd McCarthy on October 12, 1926? If you tell me that, I'll leave you alone."

"I don't know what happened to him," Sylvester said, sitting back in his chair.

"Then I'll just have to go to the newspapers," Finley said, standing to leave.

"No, wait. Much of what you have said is true, but I don't know what happened to McCarthy. I'm busy now," Sylvester said, gesturing toward the outer lobby. "I must help Miss Phillips. If you will come back this evening, I will tell you everything I know. Then you can decide for yourself whether or not it will be worth pursuing this affair."

Finley studied Sylvester's sharp blue eyes. "What time?"

"Make it eight o'clock," Sylvester said. He smiled strangely and squashed his cigar in the metal ashtray. "I promise to have some answers for you."

That evening Finley paced nervously outside the bank building. Main Street was dark except for the oblong streetlights that glowed dimly on the corners and in the middle of the blocks. The smell of hay and straw drifted in from the surrounding countryside.

After he had paced for almost half an hour, Finley walked up the flight of stairs to the front door of the bank building. The green light was glowing dimly above the portico. Through the window, he could see a thin sliver of light above the partially open doorway of Sylvester's office. He tested the front door, found it open, and walked into the dark lobby.

Sylvester was seated at his desk when Finley entered his office. He had just finished sealing a letter and was running his palm across the back of the envelope.

"You're late, Mr. Finley," Sylvester said, looking up. "This is for you." Sylvester handed Finley the letter, then leaned back in his chair and lit a cigar.

Finley examined both sides of the envelope. "What is it?"

"Just some things you might want to know. I have another letter here, too." Sylvester patted a smaller envelope on his desk. "You'll know what to do with it after our conversation."

Finley sat down in front of the desk and looked suspiciously around the room.

"You have nothing to fear, except of course your own imagination. I am the last survivor of those who were involved in the events you described this afternoon. There is no one else."

"Are you ready to tell me what I need to know?" Finley asked.

"Yes, but first I want to apologize for what happened to you this afternoon. I understand you found a rattlesnake in the backseat of your car. I did not order that. It happened without my approval."

"And I suppose you didn't order the flood control system to be buried with me inside?" Finley asked sarcastically.

"You were inside the culvert?" Sylvester asked, seemingly surprised.

"You know I was," Finley said firmly.

"No, I did not," Sylvester said. He stood and began pacing between his desk and a small window that looked out onto an adjacent alley. "I'm glad you managed to get out. I know you don't believe that, but I didn't know you were inside the culvert."

Finley watched Sylvester suspiciously, not knowing whether he was witnessing a sincere confession or a carefully rehearsed role played by a skilled actor and master politician. "Did you have anything to do with the dead dog that was spread across my bed?" Finley asked.

"The panther has four paws. Burt was one of them, but there were others. It should not concern you. I tried many ways to get you out of town so we wouldn't need to have this conversation. I could have had you killed many times, but I chose not to. You are a most stubborn detective. I commend you for that."

"What happened to Judd McCarthy?" Finley asked. "That's all I want to know."

"Yes, Mr. McCarthy," Sylvester mused as he puffed on his cigar and looked toward the lobby. "You know, you can only see a tiny part of Main Street from this office. Not enough, really. But I have sat in that lobby many times, late at night, looking at the abandoned stores and shops out there. You have no idea of the dreams I had for this small town . . ."

"Those dreams didn't seem to stop you from embezzling money through the Community Development League," Finley said.

"No, you are wrong," Sylvester said, returning to his desk. "The league was a sincere effort on my part to help this town. It all went sour when the Hanley brothers came into it."

"What happened?"

"The water reclamation project could have turned this entire town around. It could have meant economic prosperity for the rest of this century. But Ben and Fred Hanley turned it into their own private boondoggle. Their greed is what destroyed it."

"And you went along with them?"

"Only much later, when there was no turning back. I was inadvertently sucked into their schemes. By the time I learned what was really going on, full disclosure of what they were up to would have meant the end of my career, the end of my dreams for this town. I only went into politics for one reason, you must understand that."

"What was that reason?"

"To funnel money back into Carver County through the state government. It was my way of paying these people back for what they had lost on the water project. I know you think of me as an evil and vicious man, but I can assure you it was Ben and Fred Hanley who pulled the strings. They made it possible for me to get into politics. And then they made it necessary for me to get out."

"How?" Finley asked.

Once again Sylvester started pacing. "Without my knowledge, and with me as an ignorant participant in their sordid schemes, they bilked everything out of the league. By October of 1926, there was nothing left to embezzle except for the final payroll, which involved a great deal of money. They came to me with a plan. When I refused to go along with them, they threatened to plant incriminating evidence against me, then leave town. I had no choice. I went along with them."

"Was McCarthy sent for a phony payroll?" Finley asked.

"Yes. How did you know that?"

"I was only speculating."

"The payroll McCarthy carried with him from Carson was worthless paper cut to the size of currency. They set him up."

"And then they had him killed?"

"No, there was someone else involved . . ."

"Who?" Finley demanded.

"Let me finish what I was telling you about my political aspirations, Mr. Finley. Then we will return to your interests in Judd McCarthy." Sylvester paused to light another cigar. "We split the payroll—Ben, Fred, and myself. I used the money to finance my first campaign for the state senate. With his share, Fred moved to the East Coast and retired. Ben moved to Florida. I wasn't to see either of them for years. Then, in the thirties, Ben approached me when I was thinking of making a bid for the presidency. He wanted a political favor. It would have involved another scheme in which thousands of innocent people would have lost their money and their dreams. I refused. Ben then said he would go to the press with the story of my involvement in the community league and water reclamation project. That's when I decided against running for the presidency. I told him I was through with politics and there was nothing I could do to help him, even if I wanted to. He gave up and went back to Florida. I had carried the heavy burden of those sins for too long. I had no desire to add to them. You must remember that these people believe in John J. Sylvester," he said loudly and dramatically, gesturing toward Main Street. "Mr. Finley, if you take those dreams away from these people, they will have nothing left!"

"I have no desire to take anything away from the people in this town," Finley said firmly. "I only want the truth."

"Did you see that green light outside the front door?" Sylvester asked.

"Yes," Finley said.

"I keep it burning day and night for the people in this town. It is the last bit of hope I have to give them. You have seen them wandering the streets, jobless, half crazy, drinking themselves to death, trying to live with shattered dreams. That small light above John J. Sylvester's bank is the last bit of hope they have. You must not take it away from them!"

"I told you, I only want to know what happened to McCarthy," Finley said. "Then I will leave here and I will never say a word to anyone."

"Can we really count on that?" Sylvester asked as he sat down behind his desk. "Human nature is a devious thing. You may leave this office with the best of intentions, and yet someday find it expedient or financially attractive to tell the true story of John J. Sylvester. I'm not sure we can afford to let that happen."

"You have my word. Just tell me what happened to McCarthy."

"No, I cannot trust you, Mr. Finley," Sylvester said as he pulled a small revolver out of the top drawer of his desk. "I have been too trusting of men in the past, and I've paid dearly for it. I do not intend to make that mistake again."

"What do you plan to do?" Finley asked, startled.

"As you can see," Sylvester said, holding the pistol up dramatically, "I have just taken a pistol out of my desk drawer."

"Do you plan to save your reputation by killing me?" Finley asked calmly as Sylvester pointed the pistol at him. "If so, everything you have just told me is a lie."

"It was very foolish of you to come into a bank after closing hours," Sylvester said, ignoring Finley's question. "It will be easy for me to explain to the authorities that I was working late and you surprised me. Thinking you were a bank robber, I shot you. It's a perfect alibi."

"Before you fire that gun, would you at least tell me who killed McCarthy?"

"Someone else despised him for reasons even I don't know or understand."

"Does it have something to do with Katharine Sumners?" Finley asked boldly.

"That's enough, Mr. Finley. Our conversation has come to an end. It is time for you to take leave of us now."

"But . . ."

"No more talk. Please stand and turn toward the doorway."

Finley slowly did as he was told.

"Now, walk toward the door," Sylvester commanded sternly from behind the desk. "I have a heavy conscience, and you are about to help me relieve it."

"Do you really think this will relieve the burden on your conscience?" Finley asked as he walked across the office.

"Yes, I'm sure it will do it a great deal of good," Sylvester said. "Stop right there. That's far enough. You must remember that I tried in every way to discourage you. I did not mean to hurt you in any way. And I certainly never meant to kill you."

"Then why are you doing this?" Finley asked as he stared at the streetlights glowing outside the bank building.

"Because there is always a chance that you will leak something to the newspapers," Sylvester said from behind him. "I am an honorable man. I have made only one major mistake in my life, and you have discovered it. My honor is important to me. It is even more important to those people out there. I would not want for them, or for me, to live without it."

"So you're going to kill me to protect your honor?"

"No, you are wrong again. Just look at that street out there so you will know why I am doing this."

As Finley stared at the dim lights outside the abandoned shops and stores on Main Street, a gunshot boomed across the office. He shuddered, stiffened, and then slowly turned around.

Sylvester was slumped across his desk, the revolver clasped in his right hand and a bullet hole in his temple.

"You're free to go, Mr. Finley," the policeman said as they stood in Sylvester's office. The policeman had just finished reading the letter Sylvester placed on his desk shortly before he shot himself. His body had been removed earlier by ambulance, but a dark pool of blood still glistened on top of the desk.

"What does the letter say?" Finley asked, trying not to appear too curious.

The policeman folded the letter carefully and placed it in his shirt pocket. "Governor Sylvester said he had cancer. He said he met you this afternoon. Found out you were a clinical psychologist and asked you to come back this evening to help him deal with his depression. Later this afternoon, he decided instead to take his life. He said he was leaving the letter so we wouldn't think you were involved. It's really a shame, isn't it?"

"Yes, it is," Finley agreed.

"He meant so much to this town, and yet no one knew he had cancer. Maybe we could have helped him."

"Maybe he had it for a long time and just didn't want to tell anyone," Finley said.

"I suppose, but it's a shame. Will you be around for a few days in case we need anything from you?"

"Yes, I'm staying in the hotel."

Finley and the policeman walked through the lobby and out onto the front steps of the bank building.

"You know, there just aren't too many men like John J. Sylvester," the policeman said somewhat nostalgically. He locked the door and turned off the light above the portico. "He was a most honorable gentleman."

"Indeed he was," Finley agreed.

When he walked back to the hotel, the lights were dimmed and there was no one in the lobby except for the desk clerk, who was snoring on his cot behind the counter. Finley slipped quietly past and walked up the stairs to his room. He sat down on the bed and pulled out Sylvester's other letter, the one he had handed Finley before he killed himself.

As he read and reread the letter, Finley tried to place Sylvester's story in the context of the other information he had managed to gather about Judd McCarthy's disappearance. Still he was puzzled. It was early morning before he finally fell asleep.

In the street below Finley's room, Benny folded his awning pole and stepped into the pool hall. He fell asleep on one of the dusty slate tables, his arm draped over the pole like a man cuddling up to his wife. Farther down the street, Harmon lay dead drunk across the front counter of his newspaper office. He snored face up and dreamed of the novel he was planning to write someday, if he could ever get past the first paragraph.

Elsewhere, Marsha Williams stepped out from behind the DX station and looked at the dark prairie on both ends of Main Street. It was her birthday and she had been unable to sleep because old memories kept haunting her dreams. So she got up and walked out into the darkness.

As a young girl, she had often gotten up at night to walk down to Main Street. She liked to stand in the middle of the street and look up at the distant stars that hovered high in the sky above the sleeping town. And she liked to smell the freshly cut hay and straw as it drifted in from the prairie. Most of all, she liked to sit on the curb and dream about the fake Greek pillars and arches that adorned the front walls of John J. Sylvester's bank. They made her think of faraway places and wild exotic loves and romances, and all the other exciting things she had never experienced.

But sometimes her dreams were not strong enough to take her away from the small prairie town and the sight of the abandoned buildings on Main Street. This was one of those nights. She sat for a long time, until she felt the cold, late-night breezes against her cheeks. Then she pulled her shawl tightly around her shoulders and walked home.

She would have to tell John Sylvester the next time she saw him that the green light above his doorway had burned out and would have to be replaced.

As Martha Williams disappeared behind the corner of the DX station, someone else stepped out of the shadows across the street from the bank building. He had been standing there for hours, waiting for the street to clear so he could step out and see if the buildings were as he had remembered them.

He had watched the ambulance pull up to the bank building, and he had seen the attendants carry the sheet-draped stretcher down the short flight of stairs to Main Street. Later, from his hiding place, he had overheard bits and pieces of the conversation between the policeman and the tall man in the brown beret. From their conversation, he learned that John J. Sylvester had died earlier that evening. He was disappointed because he knew that Sylvester was involved in some way in what had happened to him in the thicket on October 12, 1926. Now Sylvester had taken those secrets with him to the grave. He would still find out what had happened to him, but it would be more difficult.

With bare, bloody feet, he padded slowly out to the middle of Main Street. Once again the pain shot up into his ankles and calves as he walked across the asphalt. He ignored the pain. He had known greater pain before—much greater pain.

Main Street was almost as he had remembered it. Some of the buildings were older and he did not recognize the names on many of the signs. Still, the brick and stone structures looked very much as they had on the day they had completed construction on the county building.

He felt the cool evening breezes penetrate the thin hospital uniform as he walked down the street to the county building and stood beneath the shadow of the eagle.

Everything had been so right then. It had felt so good to be alive as he stood on a ledge and guided the eagle to the top of the building. After the eagle was secured to the side, he had waved his cap to the cheering mob of construction workers in the street below. They had laughed and roared back their approval. Even John J. Sylvester had stepped out of his bank to participate in the celebration. Sylvester had smiled up at him, but he had never trusted Sylvester and he refused to smile back.

As he looked at the eagle, the breeze continued to penetrate the hospital uniform. He needed different clothes, and he needed a shave.

He could not search for Kate looking like this. Even if he should find her, she would never recognize him. It had been so long since he had seen his Lady Kate, and he did not want to disappoint her.

He padded quietly back toward the bank building, peering into the display windows of the stores along the way. In the rear of one store, he saw piles of men's work clothing neatly folded on top of several tables. He put his shoulder to the door and pushed hard. The lock snapped easily.

He shut the door behind him and looked back out into the street to make certain no one had seen him. Then he retreated into the shadows in the rear of the building.

Boots, shirts, hats, pants—everything he needed was arranged across display tables. He tore off the hospital uniform and put on a new shirt, pants, and a pair of boots. He stuffed the uniform inside the shirt. Then he slid a wood panel off a glass display case and pulled out a long hunting knife. He began hacking at his beard with the sharp blade.

He would reset the lock on the door, and he would bury the hospital uniform in the fields outside of town. Then he would find someplace out in the country and sleep during the day . . .

Suddenly he heard a sound outside the store. He lowered the knife and retreated further into the shadows.

As he looked in that direction, a bearded face appeared in the display window. Slowly, the eyes glanced upwards at the tattered canvas awning that ran the length of the storefront. The figure raised a long pole and the awning groaned out over the sidewalk.

Benny? He had seen him walk into the pool hall earlier that evening, but he did not recognize him. Benny was only a teenager, walking the streets with his awning pole, when he had last seen him. He remembered that some of the locals had teased Benny mercilessly. They fed him rotten fruit and taught him to make grotesque faces at strangers. But it was Fred Hanley who had played the cruelest joke of all on Benny. When Benny did what Fred Hanley told him to do, the girl screamed hysterically. Then she went home to tell her brothers. They came back and beat Benny until he was unconscious. After that they laid him out on the road, pulled down his trousers, and stomped on him with their heavy boots until the blood poured out onto the dirt.

He remembered how he had found Benny that way, moaning incoherently and clutching his groin with both hands to stop the blood from flowing out of his wounds. He had carried Benny up the hill, but the doctor just shook his head and sewed what was left of him back together. Benny never spoke to anyone ever again. He just patrolled the streets of Danvers, cranking the awnings out over the sidewalks, and then cranking them back up again. His mind was gone, and with it went the laughter and the trust.

He remembered how he had confronted the Farwell brothers. He had planned to make them pay for what they had done to Benny. They begged and pleaded with him and told him it was Fred Hanley's fault, and he let them go because he knew what they were telling him was the truth.

He was filled with rage at what Fred Hanley had done to Benny, and what Hanley had done to him as well. It had to have been him. Who else? Hanley had hated him ever since Benny was nearly killed, and he, Judd McCarthy, had stormed into the company offices and threatened to do to Hanley what the Farwell brothers had done to Benny.

"You touch me, Mac, and I'll have your job or your life," Hanley had said as he backed against the wall and hissed at him like a rat fighting for its life.

"Ain't no threat ya can make'll keep me from callin' ya a son of a bitch," he had fired back at Hanley.

"I been called worse," Hanley blurted out. "Besides, weren't my fault the Farwells thought so highly of their sister's honor. It got outta hand, I admit, but it weren't my fault."

He had glared at Hanley as he fought the urge to throw him against the wall and batter him into submission.

"Look, Mac, I know ya got a sweetheart. And I know ya got plans. But ya ain't goin' nowhere unless ya got a job. An' I'll see

*that ya never work again, leastways not anywhere along the Little
Sioux line. Not unless you get out of this office right now."*

*The thought of Kate caused him to lower his hands. He had
promised her he would never fight again. He glared at Hanley,
then turned and walked out of the office. He heard the laughter
behind him as he walked back to town. Months later, he thought he
heard the laughter again, from somewhere in the darkness.*

*It was years ago. But the name Fred Hanley brought back the
rage that had burned in his soul . . .*

Joel tucked the hunting knife into the top of his boots. He
chose a floppy black hat from the back counter, placed it on his
head, and walked toward the front door of the store. His new
clothes and boots fit him poorly, but at least they were warmer
than the hospital uniform and they offered some disguise. He
closed the door behind him and reset the lock. Across the street,
he heard the metal awnings creaking in the night air. He glanced
over at Benny, then slipped into the shadows of an alley and
walked to the edge of town.

He remembered that Fred Hanley owned a home two blocks
away from the library, next to a small apple orchard. Hanley hated
to sleep in the construction tents, and he had bought a home in
town, which he planned to sell after the water reclamation project
was completed.

The home was pretty much as he remembered it, although the
apple trees were much taller. He crept up to a side window and
peered into the living room. A single light glowed in the darkness
of the house. Next to the light, someone was sitting with his back
turned toward the window.

He felt the anger build as he walked around to the rear of the
house. He stepped onto a screen-enclosed porch and turned the
doorknob. When the door would not open, he stepped back, plant-
ed the sole of his boot against it, and pushed hard. The shattered
door exploded into a kitchen. As he stomped across the linoleum
floor, a figure rose quickly out of a chair in the living room.

"So, Fred Hanley, ya still be alive," Joel muttered as he paused
in the doorway leading into the room.

"Who . . .?" a voice whispered from the shadows.

"You know who I be, Fred Hanley," Joel bellowed as he stormed
into the living room.

Joel grabbed the man by the throat and lifted him into the air.
"Take a good look, Fred Hanley. Ya thought ya were through with
me, now didn't ya?"

An incomprehensible gurgle escaped from the man's throat as he dangled in the air and fought to breathe. Nearby, a grandfather clock chimed.

Joel held the man closer to the light.

What had Fred Hanley looked like? Was this him? He couldn't remember!

He set the man back down.

"Who . . . are you?" the man whispered weakly as he massaged his throat.

"I be the man whose life you took, Fred Hanley," Joel muttered angrily. He grasped the shirt of the quivering figure.

"I'm not Fred Hanley," the man blurted out.

"Who be ya, then?" Joel twisted the man's shirt and bent him closer to the light.

"I'm his son."

Joel studied the man's face.

It was not Fred Hanley. This man was taller, and the lines on his face were softer, gentler.

"Where's your father?" Joel asked, letting go of the man's shirt.

"Dead."

"Dead?" Joel exploded, grabbing the shirt again.

"He died over twenty years ago," the man replied, still massaging his throat.

Joel studied the face in front of him. Panic gleamed in the man's eyes.

"How did he die?"

"Old age . . . He moved to the East Coast . . . died in the thirties."

He had come this far only to find that Fred Hanley was already dead.

"Who are you?" the man asked, stepping back. He glanced nervously around the room. "I've seen you before."

There was no revenge to be gained on a dead man!

"You're Judd McCarthy, aren't you?" the man asked from the shadows. "But how can that be?"

"How do you know who I am?" Joel demanded.

"My father showed me a picture of you. When I was a boy."

"Did he tell you what happened to me?"

"No," the man admitted. "But I know he had something to do with your disappearance."

"What did he tell you?"

"Nothing. My father could be a very evil man. But it can't be you. You would have to be . . . seventy years old."

He had made a mistake. The answer was not to be found in this house. He would have to go elsewhere.

"Sorry," Joel whispered awkwardly. "I thought you were . . ."

"What happened to you?" the man inquired. "Where have you been?"

"I'm not Judd McCarthy. I don't know who . . ."

Joel turned and walked toward the kitchen door. He saw a paring knife gleaming on the drain board. He deftly picked it up and slipped it into his jacket pocket. The hunting knife was still tucked into his boot. The stars were glowing brightly as he stomped outside into the night air.

He would follow the river north to Carson . . . and walk the Little Sioux line until he found the thicket where it had all begun . . . Then he would know . . . And he would find Kate . . . and maybe, at last, he would be free of the nightmare . . .

At the edge of town, he broke into a brisk trot as he ran across the fields toward the river. The boots rubbed painfully against his feet as he tried to outrun the stars that were aligning themselves in strange patterns and pursuing him across the darkness of space.

CHAPTER TWELVE

Sylvester's letter was long, puzzling, provocative, and it raised almost as many questions as it answered. More than anything else, it reinforced what Sylvester had said before he committed suicide. If he was telling the truth, he was indeed ignorant of much that was going on behind the scenes of the Hanley Brothers Construction Company and the Little Sioux Water Reclamation Project. Either that, or Sylvester was making one last, desperate attempt to protect his honor and reputation.

In the morning, Finley read the letter again. He laid it on the table next to the front window of his room. As he read Sylvester's highly ornate prose, he paused frequently to look out at the abandoned businesses on Main Street—and he began to understand Sylvester's agony:

My dear Mr. Finley,

Now that you have had the opportunity to savor the significance of our last conversation, you will undoubtedly have arrived at some interesting conclusions concerning the life and career of John J. Sylvester. I trust that your instincts will enable you to winnow away the chaff to find the grain of truth hidden therein. I then trust in your compassion to decide whether the truth or the lie would be the more appropriate way of presenting John J. Sylvester to his small constituency. I myself have expended enough effort in search of human acceptance. I now seek a higher stamp of approval, if such is possible.

No doubt, you will also think I am still hiding some of the facts to protect my tarnished reputation. I can only give you my word that I am telling you everything I know about the disappearance of Judd McCarthy. If I have not your trust, please at least grant me your indulgence. Very few souls find it expedient to tell lies on their deathbeds, which, as one philosopher has written so eloquently, "is the only truly reliable confessional."

I hear from some of those in our fair town that you suspect there is a connection between McCarthy and Katharine Sumners. I think that is not too likely. McCarthy was a semiliterate, itinerant laborer. Katharine was a young woman of class and social distinction, albeit she was somewhat reluctant to accept the obvious advantages of her birthright. All of which is to say that she had no designs on greatness, but rather was shy and timid and undemanding of life. I knew her well, but not intimately, for almost one year, although it would be fair to say it was more her mother's design than anything Katharine felt for me. Agnes Sumners wanted her daughter to be the wife of a banker, but Katharine was not charmed, certainly not in awe of the mystique that surrounded John J. Sylvester. So we parted, if "parting" is an appropriate term for two people who were never truly together. After the spring of 1926, I was never to see Katharine again. As you know, she died in a fire in Chicago and her remains were returned to our town for burial.

So you see, I think you must search elsewhere for the key that will unlock the great mystery surrounding the disappearance of Judd McCarthy. I would suggest you begin with a scene that I am about to describe to you. I do not understand its significance myself, but it has weighed heavily on my conscience and has been the source of many sleepless nights and long evening walks.

I knew of the plot to get rid of McCarthy, of course, but I knew nothing of its implementation. The Hanley brothers never trusted me with the details of their many schemes, for I was considered "unreliable." Perhaps they recognized an ethical dimension in John J. Sylvester that was surpassed only by his ambition. I suppose it could be said that my ambition placed a crown on its head and proclaimed my shackled virtues slaves to the throne. Nonetheless, I had it in my power to terminate their schemes at any time, simply by telling McCarthy of the designs on his life. The fact that I failed to act in this manner was my own undoing.

What little I know of the details of McCarthy's sudden disappearance, I learned during a late evening conversation with Fred Hanley. I was alone in my office on the evening of October 12, 1926, when there was a loud knock on the front door. When I walked into the lobby and opened the door, Fred stepped into the room. The smell of liquor was heavy on his breath, and he carried a bottle of whiskey with him. He was breathing heavily, like a man who had just run a long distance. There was a maniacal grin on his face as he reeled past me into my office. When I joined him, he was raising the bottle to his lips like a man toasting a victory.

"We did it!" he said loudly, thumping the bottle down hard on my desk and laughing like an insane man.

"Did what?" I asked.

He looked at me with a fierce glow of hatred and revenge in his eyes. "We got rid of that bastard!"

"McCarthy?" I asked.

"Yes, we got rid of him for good," Fred said as he drank deeply from the bottle. "He knew too much, that no-good Irish bastard. He suspected what we were doing with the league. Can you imagine? It was only a matter of time before he went to the authorities. But he won't be going anywhere now."

At that point, he laughed hysterically, almost bending over in his chair.

"What did you do to him?" I asked.

"Nothing. I didn't have to do nothing! Oh, maybe I lent a little assistance, but I didn't have to do nothing except move a little dirt around." He laughed again, then grew deathly serious. "There was someone who despised McCarthy even more than we did. Someone who wanted him dead a long time ago."

"Who?" I asked.

"Mr. John J. Sylvester," he said sarcastically, "the great tin god of this dumpy small town, there are some things you should never know and that is one of them. Let us just say McCarthy is out of our way for good, and we can now split the real payroll and leave this godforsaken bump on the prairie."

Fred was very pleased with himself that evening. He sat in my office and drank, while he ridiculed my reputation and spoke of McCarthy in the most vindictive terms imaginable. Then he said something strange. I still do not know what credence to place on it. Perhaps it was merely the ramblings of a drunken mind.

"Mr. John J. Sylvester," he said, again with considerable sarcasm. "Do you remember that Irish woman who came through here in the 1890s?"

"What Irish woman?" I asked. "I was a boy then."

"She spit in my face, that slut," he growled. "Tonight I got even with her through her bastard son." He laughed loudly again and drank to his revenge, whatever form it had taken. "No one would ever guess who was his father," he said, looking up at me with the eyes of a madman.

He would say nothing more.

Before he left that evening, Fred unwrapped a money belt from around his waist. He placed several stacks of currency on my desk. It was my share of the real payroll. He laughed as my fingers trembled above the stacks of money. Then he lurched toward the front door. Still laughing, he disappeared into the darkness outside.

Mr. Finley, I stared at that money for a long time before I finally picked it up and put it in the safe. To this day, I wish I had had the courage to leave it on the desk and go to the authorities with what I knew about McCarthy's disappearance. The next thirty years of my life would have been infinitely less agonizing if I had done that one simple thing. But I did not, and so you have found me today, an old man carrying the burden of his guilt in a town that worships his image, but knows nothing of his true character. It is an intolerable contradiction, a charade of virtue that conceals the most hideous of crimes.

Mr. Finley, I must take my leave of you now. I wish you success in your pursuit of Judd McCarthy and those who took his life. I think if you find the Irish woman Fred Hanley talked about that night in my office, you will have the answers to the many questions you have been asking the people in our small town.

As for the reputation of John J. Sylvester, you will have to decide for yourself whether justice would be better served by printing this letter or having it destroyed.

Sincerely yours,
John J. Sylvester

The desk clerk spotted Finley as soon as he walked down the stairs and entered the hotel lobby.

"Dr. Finley," he yelled. "I have something for you." He held out a small piece of notepaper. "A message. It came for you yesterday morning. I must have been asleep and didn't hear you come in last night."

Finley read the note quickly. "Are you sure it was the security division that called?"

"That's what I wrote down, now didn't I? The security division of the Farmington State Mental Hospital. That's who called. Said it was about one of your patients and it was important."

"Thanks."

"You're welcome. Oh, and someone else called too. Someone by the name of Susan. I forgot all about that one until just now. Must've been my turn to deal and I forgot to write it down."

"Thanks," Finley said again.

Finley stepped into the phone booth and made the call.

"Security Division, Farmington State Mental Hospital," a husky male voice responded.

"This is Dr. Ned Finley. I have a message here to call you."

"Yes, Dr. Finley," the voice continued. "There's a problem with a patient of yours, Joel Hampton. He's been missing for almost two days now."

"He escaped?" Finley asked.

"We think so. At first we thought maybe he was hiding somewhere in the hospital, but we've checked everywhere. Now we're pretty sure he has escaped."

"How'd he get out? Wasn't he in restraints?" Finley was almost yelling into the telephone.

"Somehow he worked himself loose. We still don't know how he got out of the building. 'Course security's pretty lax on the first floor. Shouldn't have had him there in the first place. By the way, who authorized that transfer?"

"I did," Finley admitted, trying to calm down.

"There's going to be an investigation, I'm sure. Police in five counties are looking for him. Several newspapers have published descriptions. Guess you know he tried to kill a couple of people before he was committed, and that's got people around here plenty frightened."

"Look, if they find him, get ahold of me right away. I don't want someone shooting him because of inflammatory newspaper articles."

There was a short pause at the other end of the line. "Dr. Finley," the male voice continued, "they will, of course, try to take him peacefully. But if he offers resistance, or if lives are endangered, they'll do what has to be done."

"Even if that means killing him," Finley asked bitterly.

"Yes, but we don't think it'll come to that. We think we know which direction he's headed. Probably try to do something to his wife and child. Guess he tried it before. But we've got the roads to Kenyon under surveillance, so they're safe. Which reminds me, his wife wants you to call her."

Finley hung up the phone and immediately called Susan.

"Susan, this is Dr. Finley—"

"Dr. Finley," she interrupted him excitedly. "Joel—"

"Yes, I know. He escaped." Finley tried to sound as calm as possible. "Are you and Aggy okay?"

"Yes, but they think he might be coming this way."

"I don't want the two of you to take any chances, but I don't think Joel's coming back there."

"Why do you say that?"

"Because I believe your husband is now totally trapped in Judd McCarthy's world. If he's going anywhere, it'll be back to Carver County."

"Why?"

"To find out what happened to him in 1926."

There was a pause at the other end. "What do we do in the meantime?" Susan asked.

"Could you join me up here? I need to talk to you in person about some things. I also need the photograph of the farmhouse and the envelope it came in. I think I left them with you the last time we met."

There was another pause. "Shouldn't we be out looking for him?" Susan asked.

"No, the best thing we can do is try to unravel the puzzle that is the life and disappearance of Judd McCarthy. If we can do that, we'll find your husband because I'm convinced he'll be looking for the same thing. We just want to be there first, waiting for him."

"What if the police find him first?"

"I honestly don't think they're looking in the right place. They're looking for Joel. They should be looking for McCarthy. He'll be here in Carver County very shortly, if he isn't already."

"Dr. Finley?"

"Yes, Susan?"

"I love Joel," she said with deep emotion. "I want you to know that. If anything happens to him, my life won't be worth living. I'm trying to harden myself for the inevitable, if it comes to that. But, please, just do everything you can to bring him back to me—as Joel Hampton, not Judd McCarthy."

"I'll do my best, Susan."

Finley parked his car outside the Peace Lutheran Cemetery and walked through the wrought iron gate. A large green tent had been set up near the statue of the Union soldier. Next to the tent, a pile of black soil was spread out across the grass. As Finley approached the area, he saw that metal chairs had been arranged in neat rows inside the tent, and a green tarp had been stretched across a newly dug grave.

He walked past the tent and over to the Sumnerses' family plot. Some dead leaves had already accumulated over the three gravestones of Oscar, Agnes, and Katharine Sumners. Finley brushed them away with his foot and moved his eyes across the inscriptions on the stones. Then he looked up and shook his head dejectedly.

Finley turned to leave, but as he stepped back from the gravestones, his foot came down hard on something buried below the dead vegetation next to the grave of Oscar Sumners. He tapped it gently with the toe of his shoe. Then he dropped to his knees and scraped away the matted vegetation, uncovering another gravestone that had sunk deeply into the soil. He had to scratch off the fungus and black mold that covered the letters on the granite block. The gravestone, obviously forgotten by the caretakers, yielded the inscription, "Maynard Sumners, December 3, 1870–April 17, 1895."

Finley studied the inscription and then walked back to his car. As he drove out of the cemetery and down the foothill, he met a caravan of cars and pickup trucks. They were following a large black hearse that turned into the road leading to the cemetery. The caravan looked like a procession of small insects led by a large black beetle.

Finley parked on the gravel shoulder and stepped out to watch the funeral procession for John J. Sylvester wind slowly into the cemetery. At the top of the hill, the hearse climbed over a ridge and disappeared from sight. The other cars and trucks followed closely behind until they too disappeared over the ridge, leaving the hill empty except for the bales of hay that were scattered on both sides of the cemetery road.

Finley leaned against his car and pondered the enigmatic character he had met only a few days earlier. Sylvester was so sincere in his letter that Finley was almost convinced the former governor was telling the truth about his role in McCarthy's disappearance. But Finley knew too much about Sylvester and the others who were involved in the water reclamation project to trust that any of them was innocent. Sylvester seemed more like an aging actor who reshaped and reinvented himself whenever a new audience crossed his path. Or maybe he was a seasoned con artist who sized up his victims with considerable skill and gave them exactly what they wanted to hear to gain their trust before he defrauded them.

Or perhaps Sylvester *was* the real thing—an honorable man who made one great, tragic mistake, and he was doing everything in his power to cover it up so it would not destroy his legacy among the people who idolized him.

Finley was not sure which John J. Sylvester was the real one. But as he heard the soft murmur of a eulogy in the cemetery, he realized it wasn't *who* Sylvester was that mattered. It was *what* he meant to the people of Danvers.

As he looked at the small town in the distance, Finley pulled Sylvester's letter out of his pocket. He tore it into tiny pieces, threw them into the wind, and watched the last words of John J. Sylvester disappear over the prairie.

Susan's blue Chevrolet was parked in front of the general store when Finley arrived back in Danvers. She was sitting at a small table in the window of the store, drinking a cup of coffee. Finley gestured for her to wait for him. Then he walked across the street to the county building.

The county recorder was talking to a middle-aged farmer at the front desk as Finley entered the office. When the county recorder was finished with the farmer, he looked over at Finley. "What da ya need today?" he asked.

"I would like to see a death certificate," Finley said as he walked over to where the county recorder was standing.

"Who ya lookin' for this time?"

"The name is Maynard Sumners. He died on April 17, 1895."

"Just a minute," he said, disappearing into the vault in the back of the room. He returned shortly with an ancient, brown volume. "What was that date again?" he asked as he flopped the volume down on the counter.

"April 17, 1895."

"Here it is," the county recorder said as he ran his index finger along the lines of the death certificate.

"What does it say?" Finley asked anxiously.

"'Maynard Sumners, born on December 3, 1870, in London, England . . . and, let's see . . . died April 17, 1895, in Carver County . . . unmarried, brother of Oscar Sumners."

"How did he die?"

"He drowned in the Little Sioux River," the county recorder said, reading from the book. "It says here that it was a possible suicide."

"Suicide?"

"Yup, 'possible suicide.' That's what it says here. Date of death is an approximation. Apparently they found the body wrapped around a tree farther downstream. River almost dragged him into the Mississippi. Little Sioux River's mighty powerful that time of year."

"Can I read that myself?"

"Sure can." The county recorder spun the volume around on top of the counter.

Finley read carefully through the death certificate. "Why do you suppose they call it a possible suicide?"

"Hard to say. People around here know enough not to fool around on the riverbanks in the spring. Guess they figured he should have known better. Either that or he meant to be out there. In which case he was probably fixin' to kill himself."

Finley nodded and walked quickly out of the office. Susan was still sitting in the window of the general store when he crossed Main Street. As he stepped into the store, a bell jangled above the door. Packages of cereal, canned foods, and other grocery items were displayed on wooden shelves and tables scattered around the room. A bald, middle-aged clerk in a white apron was filling an order for an elderly woman at the front counter. Finley walked past the brass cash register and over to where Susan was sitting.

"Any word on Joel yet?" he asked.

"No," Susan said dejectedly. "They're still looking for him."

"Where's Aggy?"

"With my mother. I don't know how to explain all this to her. She keeps asking questions about her daddy."

Finley poured a cup of coffee from a metal pot on a heater next to the table. "I know who Maynard is," he said as he sat down. "He's Katharine Sumners's uncle, Oscar's brother. He drowned in the Little Sioux River on April 17, 1895. A possible suicide. He's buried next to his brother in the Peace Lutheran Cemetery just outside of town."

"Wasn't Maureen McCarthy committed to Farmington around that time?" Susan asked.

Finley nodded. "Three days earlier."

"And he's the brother of one of the men who signed to have her committed," Susan said. "It can't be coincidence."

"I know."

"What does it all add up to?"

"I'm not sure, but I have my suspicions. I'll let you know more about them later. Did you bring the envelope and the photograph?"

"Yes," Susan said, opening her purse and handing the envelope to Finley.

They sat in silence for a time, staring out at Main Street.

"You said you had some other things to tell me," Susan said. "Have you found out anything more about Judd McCarthy and how he might be connected to my husband?"

"Yes." Finley removed his beret and ran his fingers through his hair. "I've found out why he disappeared. Part of the reason anyhow."

"What happened to him?"

"He was set up. He was carrying a phony payroll when he disappeared. He worked for the Hanley Brothers Construction Company. They were involved in a clever scam called the Little Sioux Water Reclamation Project. Along with John J. Sylvester, a local banker, they bilked the people of this town out of their savings and then set McCarthy up so they could divide the real payroll among themselves. In fact, I'm pretty sure that's why Joel attacked Jim Morris. There's a slight physical resemblance between Morris and Sylvester."

"How do you know all this?"

"I had a talk with Sylvester."

"He's still alive?" Susan asked, surprised.

"He was. He killed himself right after I talked to him."

"Why?"

"He was afraid the people here would find out about his past. It was important to Sylvester that they believed in him. He gave them dreams and they worshipped him for it."

"How did they kill McCarthy?"

"Apparently they didn't kill him."

"You just said they set him up."

"They did, but someone else killed him. Sylvester said he didn't know who it was. His partner told him someone else despised McCarthy. Someone that Sylvester didn't even suspect."

"Who?"

"That, I think, must have something to do with Maureen McCarthy. Sylvester left me a letter before he died. He quoted his partner, Fred Hanley, apparently a man much older than Sylvester, as making some statements about an Irish woman who lived in Danvers in the 1890s. It has to be her. Hanley hated her. I don't know why. Maybe it was just his nature. Sylvester described him as a sick, vindictive man who would apparently go to any extremes to get his way or to gain revenge."

"What is the connection between her and Judd McCarthy?" Susan asked, struggling to comprehend what Finley was telling her.

"I think she was his mother."

"You're sure?"

"No, I'm not sure."

"Who was the father?"

"I don't know. Maybe Maynard Sumners."

Susan paused briefly to consider everything Finley had just told her. "That still doesn't explain why my husband is taking on the personality of someone who lived in Carver County in the 1920s."

"No, it doesn't. But I have my suspicions."

"What are they?"

Finley looked out the window at Benny, who was rolling up one of the green awnings. "Susan, I know this sounds bizarre, but during my sessions with Joel, I sensed that Judd McCarthy meant to do something when he got back to Danvers. Something so important to him that his spirit leaped across time and is working on your husband to complete whatever it was he left undone. I know that sounds crazy, but I believe that's what we're dealing with here."

Susan looked strangely at Finley. She spoke nervously. "What is he trying to do?"

"I don't have the slightest idea. Sylvester said everyone involved in the plot against McCarthy is dead, but it could still be revenge."

"It would explain why Joel is so violent."

"Yes."

"So you think McCarthy's spirit is trying to turn my husband into a killer to get revenge on those who were responsible for his death?" A note of confused anger crept into Susan's voice.

"It's possible," Finley admitted. "I know it sounds outrageous, but I can't think of any other explanation for what's happening to your husband."

Susan struggled to control her emotions. "Dr. Finley, do you know how hard it is to remain calm and rational about this whole thing when all I want to do is scream at someone and demand that they give my husband back to me?"

"I know," Finley said reassuringly. "Maybe on the way back home you should do just that. Open the car window and scream as loud as you can. It might help."

"It wouldn't be so bad if we had a lousy marriage," Susan said somewhat bitterly. "But we were truly happy together. That's a very hard thing to come by."

Her voice trailed off into a soft, incomprehensible whisper.

"I know," Finley comforted her. "I know."

Lost in thought, he drank coffee and stared out the window long after Susan had left. The store was quiet until a red-haired teenage boy burst through the front door. The boy tore off a brown topcoat as he walked behind the counter.

"Where ya been?" the clerk asked.

"I was at Mr. Sylvester's funeral," the boy responded as he placed the coat on a metal hanger and tied a white apron around his waist. "Got later'n I thought."

"I just couldn't get away," the clerk said. "Wanted to, but just been too busy. Listen, you better get workin' on those orders. Seems like just about everyone in Carver County wants a delivery today."

"Where are the lists?" the boy asked.

Suddenly, the shrill notes of "Amazing Grace" poured mournfully out of the fire siren, drowning out the conversation in the store.

><><><

After burying the hospital uniform in a field outside of Danvers, he had walked the rest of that night. Occasionally, a lonely farm dog barked, and the plaintive lament drifted across the brisk October night. The barking reminded him of the dog he had suffocated. He hadn't meant to kill the poor animal, and he felt terrible about what had happened.

In the distance, he could see some twinkling farm lights etched against the horizon. He passed other farms that were dark and abandoned.

So much had changed. Graham, Olson, Johnson, Tobin, Mosley—he remembered the names of the families that had once lived in those farmhouses. Somehow, he felt they were still there, staring at him from the gables in the thick clusters of trees. He alone had been spared. Why? He did not know. He only knew he had to go back to a time that once was . . .

He stayed to the fields, avoiding the denser clusters of trees where people might still be living. When he reached the Little Sioux River, he walked a few miles north along the riverbank. Then he stopped to unlace the stiff leather boots he had stolen from the store in Danvers. He sat on a dead log next to the river and let the cool waters gently massage his bloody feet. He leaned back on the log and watched the stars roam freely in the sky.

It had been like this with Kate. They had sat on the riverbank at night and watched the stars. She had held his hand and stroked his forearm while they talked and made plans. He had to get back to her.

He tried to put on one of the boots, but it would not fit. His feet were so cut and bruised and infected that once they were released from the boots, they had swollen to twice their normal size. They throbbed and the pain shot up into his legs.

He was angry with himself for having taken off the boots. He could have handled the pain, and he would have been in Carson later that night. Now he would have to find a place to hide, while he waited for his feet to heal.

He thought about walking barefoot along the riverbank until morning. But he knew at some point his feet would fail him. Besides, after having waited so long, what was another day or two? He could wait.

He picked up the boots and limped barefoot toward one of the clusters of trees he had passed earlier. The farmhouse in the middle of the trees was deserted and covered with large, dead weeds that grew several feet high next to tilting, ancient sheds and barns. The moonlight sent elongated shadows of the buildings across the yard.

He entered one of the sheds and walked to the back wall where he collapsed on a pile of straw. Throughout the night, he listened to an owl somewhere in the darkness, far beyond the deserted farmyard. Far beyond the moon and the stars, or so it seemed . . .

In the morning, if it was safe, he would soak his swollen feet in the river. Then the next night, or the night thereafter, he would continue up the river, keeping always to the riverbank, for they would be looking for him. Now that he had come this far, he could not fail.

Farther north, he would walk across the fields to Carson. He would start out as he had thirty-three years earlier, walking south along the Little Sioux Railroad toward the outskirts of Danvers— and Kate.

Only this time he would make it. This time he would not fail.

When Finley awoke, the first thing he saw was a large black spider spinning a web across the smoke-stained ceiling of his room. The spider had managed to attach several filaments to a crack in the ceiling, but it seemed unable to expand the web in any direction. It crawled frantically back and forth across the ceiling. Then it returned to the center of the web and remained motionless, gazing into the crack. It was still doing that when Finley sat up in bed.

While he was eating breakfast, Finley made a decision to spend the day in the newspaper office. He hoped that perhaps something in the earlier editions of the *Danvers Sun* might provide the clue he needed. He was at a dead end. He had no logical course to follow now that he had moved this far into the complex reasons behind McCarthy's disappearance. He decided to trust his intuition, and it told him to look in the old newspapers. If Joel showed up in Carver County, Finley wanted to know where he might be heading. The papers might help him find that place.

The steady beat of a typewriter's keys clacked out of the back room as Finley walked into the *Danvers Sun*. As he approached the counter, the steady rhythm of the typewriter continued uninterrupted. He decided that Harmon was probably hard at work on the next issue, so he did not interrupt him. Instead, he opened the basement door and walked down the stairs. He pulled on a long string in the center of the ceiling, and the room was quickly bathed in light.

Finley walked over to the stack of newspapers he had sorted through earlier. He placed the papers on top of a table and began reading through them. Occasionally, he would stand to pace around the room as he tried to think of any question he hadn't asked himself, anything at all he might have overlooked. Then he would sit down again and read through more of the newspapers.

He began reading aloud. "'Nina Jensen was an afternoon dinner guest of Florence Hagen' . . . 'Mr. and Mrs. Stanley Walsh were overnight guests at the Ed Messner home' . . . 'The Herbert Swensen family returned from a two-week fishing trip in Canada.'" Finley was both amused and surprised that so much trivial information had made it into the newspaper. "Every time someone opens their front door, it gets into the *Danvers Sun,*" he said with mock sarcasm.

He stood and began pacing again. "Maybe that's it?" he speculated. "If Katharine McCarthy is really Katharine Sumners, and if she left this area shortly after Judd McCarthy disappeared, then her mother would have had to put that news in the paper. Especially if she wanted to avoid any gossip about the real reasons for her daughter's decision to leave."

Finley returned to his work with a renewed vigor and enthusiasm. Much later he pointed excitedly at the small print and read a passage out loud. "This is it! 'Katharine Sumners left last Sunday morning for an extended vacation with her uncle and aunt, Mr. and Mrs. Christopher Walker of Chicago, Illinois'!"

Finley looked up. In the window well on the other side of the basement, the salamander that had struggled mightily against the pane lay dead beneath a pile of damp leaves. Although the body had curled over and fallen to the base of the frame, one claw remained flattened against the glass, as though even in death the salamander was still fighting for its freedom.

"This is it!" Finley repeated emphatically. He quickly stood and walked up the flight of stairs. The rhythmic beat of the typewriter keys still filled the newspaper office as he stepped out of the basement and into the sunlight pouring in through the front window.

He walked across the street to the general store. The bell above the front door jangled loudly as he stepped inside and approached the counter.

"You deliver groceries here, don't you?" Finley asked the bald clerk.

"Yup. Only store in town that does."

"You deliver to Gina Walker, then?"

"Every Wednesday. She leaves a list for us on her mailbox on Tuesday. We pick it up and deliver the next day. Leave everything on the porch as she requested."

"Could I—"

"Even the big supermarkets in the cities can't make that claim," the clerk continued.

"Could I see the last grocery list she gave you?" Finley asked.

"Why?" the clerk asked suspiciously.

"She asked me to stop by," Finley lied. "She thinks you sent her some things she didn't order."

"Who are you?"

"I'm a relative, just visiting."

"I double-check everything. But, sure, just a minute." The clerk disappeared into the back room and reappeared a few seconds later. He handed a list to Finley. "Here it is."'

"Mind if I sit down over there and look this over?" Finley asked, gesturing toward the table next to the front window.

"Suit yourself," the clerk shrugged as he started packing canned goods into a cardboard box.

Finley sat down and reached into his pocket to pull out the envelope Susan had given him the previous day. He laid it on the table and placed the grocery list next to it. He moved his eyes slowly back and forth between the two items. Then he stood and walked over to the counter.

"Thanks," Finley said, handing the list to the clerk.

"Everything in order?"

"Yes, Gina ordered all of these things. She must have forgotten."

"Well, you tell her to bring anything back if she don't need it. Don't need no receipt either."

"Thanks," Finley said.

"You know," the clerk said, testing his memory, "I didn't know Miss Walker had any relatives. She always seems to be pretty much alone out there."

"Oh, she has other relatives," Finley said. "Some that she hasn't seen in a long time!"

CHAPTER THIRTEEN

Finley turned his Studebaker into the weed-infested road leading to the old Sumnerses' farm. At the end of the road, he parked beside the lath fence that surrounded the house. Through the open window of the car, he could hear the windmill. On the other side of the house, the tornado-damaged silo rose ominously above the autumn foliage.

Finley studied the gray walls and gables of the farmhouse. Then he walked up the stone pathway to the porch. He knocked on the door, waited, and knocked again.

When Gina Walker answered, she had the same distant look in her eyes, and she seemed even more confused than before. Finley remembered seeing that look in the eyes of patients who had retreated into their own private worlds and retained only a tenuous connection to reality.

"Yes?" she inquired.

"Katharine Sumners," Finley replied boldly, testing his suspicions, "I think we have something to discuss."

"What do you mean?" she asked without emotion.

"Ms. Sumners, I know who you are. There is no need to lie to me."

"Who are you?" she asked quietly.

"My name is Ned Finley. I'm a clinical psychologist at Farmington."

"What do you want from me?"

"I need some information about someone you knew when you still called yourself Katharine Sumners. Your secret is safe with me."

She looked more directly into Finley's eyes, then opened the door wider. "Come in, please." She turned her back on him, shuffled down the parlor, and disappeared into one of the side rooms.

As Finley's eyes adjusted to the semidarkness of the parlor, he saw that the interior of the house had been preserved in the styles popular much earlier in the century. The wallpaper, furniture, and curtains were seemingly untouched by time, just as the badly weathered, gray exterior of the house was a monument to the passage of time and the changes created by the seasonal cycles.

By the time Finley entered the living room, his eyes had adjusted to the lighting, and he could see that the woman who called herself Gina Walker was dressed in the styles of the 1920s and 1930s. She was sitting in a rocking chair on a patterned tapestry rug. Behind her, an ancient gramophone had been placed on a walnut parlor table.

From what he could see of the house's interior, Finley surmised that his earlier impressions of her were accurate. She had created a life where time and the modern world almost ceased to exist.

Finley sat down on a small couch on the edge of the rug. Next to him, on a tea table, he noticed a framed newspaper photograph of two huge, perspiring men smiling broadly and shaking hands. He recognized the smaller of the two as Judd McCarthy. The larger man he assumed was Farmer Tobin.

"How did you find out about me?" Katharine Sumners asked as she rocked back and forth.

"I was only guessing," Finley replied, "until I read in the *Danvers Sun* that you vacationed in 1926 with Mr. and Mrs. Christopher Walker. I knew it had to be more than coincidence that you had the same last name as Katharine Sumners's uncle and aunt. Then I checked the handwriting on a grocery list you wrote last week. It matched the handwriting on an envelope you had addressed many years ago."

"Why am I important to you? I'm only an old woman, living in a house full of memories."

"You aren't important to me. But you might be important to someone else. Someone we both know."

"I don't understand."

"Ms. Sumners—"

"I haven't been called by that name in a long time," she said, interrupting him. "I had almost forgotten what it sounded like."

"Then you *are* Katharine Sumners?" Finley said as though to reassure himself that his conclusions were correct.

"Yes, but it's been more than thirty years," she sighed. "I never thought I would ever hear that name again."

"If you are her, then tell me, who is buried in the grave next to your mother and father?"

"I don't know."

"I don't understand."

"I left the Walker home and moved into a boarding house in Chicago. There were other girls there. Most of them had no one they could turn to for help."

She paused to collect her thoughts.

"Then what happened?" Finley asked gently.

"One day I decided to destroy Katharine Sumners. I put every piece of identification I had on a bureau and walked out the front door. Two days later the boarding house burned to the ground. It said in the newspapers that everyone was killed."

"So another girl probably picked up your identification cards, and her body was sent back here for burial."

"I suppose. I go out there every once in a while to put flowers on the grave. The poor thing. She was probably just a young girl who had no one to turn to when she got into trouble."

"Trouble?"

"Most of the girls who lived there were unwed mothers from poor families. Some of them had no families."

"So your mother and everyone else in this area thought you had died in that fire?"

"Yes."

Finley glanced at the framed newspaper photograph on the tea table.

"Before Katharine Sumners died, what part did a gold locket play in her life?" he asked cautiously, remembering the song Joel had sung while under hypnosis.

"What do you know about that?"

"Please, you tell me."

Katharine stood and walked out of the room, disappearing into a rear hallway. When she returned, she was holding something tenderly in her hands. She placed a gold pocket watch with a long chain on the couch next to Finley.

"We took a trip to Carson together, several weeks before he disappeared. I admired a locket in one of the store windows, and he promised to buy it for me when he had the money. I, in turn, said I would buy him a new watch. That old watch of his made so much noise, and he tied it to his trousers with a piece of baling twine."

She avoided mentioning McCarthy's name, as though there was still too much pain in the memory.

"Who was *he*?" Finley asked.

Katharine ignored the question and walked over to the gramophone. She wound the crank and what sounded like an instrumental version of an old Irish ballad poured out of the black horn.

"Do you see the eagle engraved on the back of the watch?" she asked as she sat down and began slowly rocking back and forth. "He was like an eagle. Always trying to be free. I thought I had changed him, but I guess I didn't."

"Was his name Judd McCarthy?"

"How did you know that?" she asked, surprised.

"I know a great deal about you, but I know very little about him. I need to know more. Who was he?"

"I thought he was the gentlest man I had ever met," she began. "Mother called him an uncultured scoundrel, but he was really the kindest man. Oh, he was a nobody, really, a common laborer, a very powerful man physically. That's a picture of him on the table next to you."

"Yes, I know," Finley responded. "I saw the copy of the *Carson Chronicle* that this came from. Tell me more about him."

"Judd McCarthy came here in 1925, along with many other drifters and construction workers. They built most of the buildings on Danvers's Main Street. Then they came out here to work on the Little Sioux Water Reclamation Project. You could see the men and machinery from that very window right over there . . ."

It was July of 1926. The men who worked for the Hanley Brothers Construction Company were gathered on both sides of an open trench near the Little Sioux Railroad. The workers were surrounded by tents, heavy machinery and equipment, and teams of horses feeding during the midday break.

At the bottom of the trench, a huge, shirtless, dark-haired man was carefully wrapping a rope around his wrists. Judd McCarthy projected a boisterous, lighthearted cheerfulness, and a fierce determination and proud masculinity. The other end of the rope was attached to a small black and white horse that pawed nervously at the mud and rainwater at the bottom of the trench.

"Ain't no man can whip a horse in a tug of war," one of the workers said emphatically as he stared into the trench.

"Five dollars says Mac can do it," another worker challenged.

"You're on," the first man said enthusiastically. *"Might as well get your money out now, 'cause this thing's 'bout good as over."*

At the bottom of the trench, McCarthy finished curling the rope tightly around both forearms. He braced his feet for the initial impact of the horse's charge up the embankment. A small man in a floppy white hat held the horse by the bridle as it continued to paw at the ground. The owner of the horse stood nearby, ready to whip the animal once the signal was given.

"Now remember, Mac," the small man holding the horse said, *"if this horse gets you over the top of the ridge, you lose."*

"Got it. Get with it, Scotty. Turn 'em loose."

The small man let go of the bridle, and the owner of the horse began whipping the animal furiously. As the veins bulged in his neck and arms, McCarthy managed to hold his own while the horse slipped in the muddy trench. Then the horse gained its footing and charged up the side of the embankment while McCarthy, refusing to let go of the rope and yelling incoherent phrases, was dragged belly down through the mud.

At the top of the ridge, the horse again lost its footing. As it slipped backward, McCarthy managed to get to his feet. He braced himself once again at the bottom of the trench. Suddenly, in a state of panic, the horse reared up on its hind legs, lost its balance, and began to fall backward. Seizing the opportunity, McCarthy yanked with all of his strength on the rope, and the horse tumbled down the embankment, splashing into the mud at the bottom of the trench.

"Well, I'll be gawddamned," one of the workers exclaimed as he looked down at the horse lying flat on its back. *"He did it!"*

"Damn it!" another worker muttered angrily as he slapped a wad of bills into a dirty extended hand.

McCarthy and the rest of the construction crew were momentarily stunned by what had just happened. He was a comical sight, standing at the bottom of the trench, his brown eyes peering out from a face completely caked with mud. As he looked up at the many faces peering at him, his eyes focused on a young woman giggling shyly and looking down at him with nervous excitement. It was the first time Katharine Sumners had ever set eyes on Judd McCarthy. She was always to remember him like that, standing at the bottom of the trench, caked with mud and looking up at her like a little boy.

A loud laugh suddenly boomed out of the mud-covered figure staring back at her. It was a laugh that seemed to challenge the *entire universe as it roared from the trench. McCarthy fell back into the mud and allowed his body to sink slowly into the goo as the workers at the top erupted wildly. Before he disappeared beneath the thick mud, McCarthy smiled and waved at Katharine Sumners, who stood giggling at the top of the trench.*

Later, as the bets were being paid, McCarthy climbed up the embankment and began wiping himself off with a large rag. A few feet away, the horse he had pulled into the trench was limping noticeably.

"Goddamn worthless animal!" the owner yelled bitterly. He raised a whip to bring it down across the animal's head. "Cost me two hundred bucks, will ya!"

McCarthy stepped quickly between the horse and its owner. He brought his huge hand down across the owner's forearm, stopping the whip in midair. "The horse didn't make the bet, mister. You did," McCarthy said in a menacing tone.

"This is none of your business," the owner replied defiantly, trying to extract his arm from McCarthy's powerful grip.

"You ain't beatin' this horse!" McCarthy issued an even sterner warning.

With his free hand, the owner reached into his coat pocket and pulled out a small revolver He pointed it at McCarthy's stomach.

"This horse is my property. You'd do well to stay out of this."

As McCarthy stepped back, the owner again raised the whip over the horse's head.

"What's the horse worth ta ya?" McCarthy quickly said before the owner could bring the whip down across the animal's head.

"Two hundred bucks," he replied tersely.

"Give me the money, Scotty," McCarthy said to the small man with the floppy hat.

"You can't, Mac. Not on a lame horse, for Christ's sake."

"Give it to me!"

"Christ's sake, Mac," Scotty said as he handed McCarthy the money, "every time we get something, you just lose it in a card game or give it away."

"Here's your two hundred dollars, mister," McCarthy said, handing the wad of bills to the owner. "But I don't want no creases in me horse's forehead."

As the man stuffed the wad of bills into his pocket, McCarthy's right arm snaked out and tore the pistol out of his hand. He picked up the owner by his belt and pitched him into the trench, where he did a belly flop and slid across the mud.

"Any man who beats a horse is no better'n a lizard," McCarthy yelled. *"Slide around in there for a while."*

Almost as an afterthought, McCarthy pitched the revolver into the trench, where it sank into the mud and disappeared. He walked back to the lame animal and patted it on the neck. Under his gentle caress, the horse began to calm down.

"There, ole buddy, we know I didn't beat ya," he spoke softly into the horse's ear. *"Ya slipped or I'd still be followin' ya 'cross the prairie."*

As he stroked the horse's head, McCarthy saw Katharine standing nearby. *"Now, ole buddy, who'd ya suppose that pretty lady might be?"*

"Katharine," she whispered shyly.

"Ah, Kate it is. Such a pretty name for such a pretty lady. Now what's someone like you doin' out here 'mong these hooligans?" he asked, pretending to admonish her.

"I live right over there," she said shyly, pointing at a farmhouse in the distance.

"Well, here's a present for me Lady Kate," McCarthy said, handing her the horse's reins. *"An' let me help ya get him home."*

As the construction machinery howled and screeched, and work commenced on the water reclamation project, Judd McCarthy and Katharine Sumners walked toward the farmhouse. The horse limped along behind them, its reins held loosely in Katharine's tiny hands.

McCarthy and Katharine were together almost every day from July to October of 1926. With her mother visiting relatives in the East, Katharine had the run of the family farm for the first time in her life. This was Agnes Sumners's first vacation since her husband's death in 1920, and she stayed back East until early fall. Her absence gave Katharine the freedom to do things she never had the courage to do in her mother's presence, things as insignificant as walking over to the construction site to watch the workers build the huge culvert at the bottom of the trench.

Under the ruling thumb of Agnes Sumners, who had kept her daughter a virtual prisoner in the family home through her teens and early twenties, Katharine had never really grown up. Instead, she retained a charm and innocence that gave her a childlike *appeal, at the same time that it made her extremely vulnerable and naive about men.*

McCarthy recognized this in her, and he made a pledge to himself not to violate or harm that innocence in any way, for she was too much like the birds and animals of the prairie with whom he felt a deep kinship. He was more accustomed to the hard-drinking women who frequented the taverns throughout the Midwest, but he had long since tired of their company and the pleasures they had to offer. He grew to cherish and love the twenty-seven-year-old child that was Katharine Sumners, at the same time that he taught her to grow as a woman without taking her to the pinnacle of love and intimacy. With every other woman in his life, he had progressed well beyond that point after several beers and one or two Irish ballads. But Lady Kate was special to him, and he meant to keep it that way.

By August of 1926, Katharine knew she was deeply in love with McCarthy. He would come over after the day's work had ceased on the construction site, and they would sit on the porch and talk while the gramophone played in the house.

"What do you know about the stars?" she asked him one night as they sat on the porch.

McCarthy looked up at the stars glowing brightly in the night sky. "Nuthin', Kate. Only that they're up there. And they're free." As he spoke, a flock of Canadian geese flew across the moon in V-formation.

"Some people think the stars aren't up there at all," Katharine continued. "Some scientists say they're only explosions, and all we're seeing is the light."

"Don't make no difference, does it?"

"Why do you say that?"

"It don't matter if somethin' is or isn't, just so long as you believe it is."

"I don't understand."

"It's thinkin' somethin' is or thinkin' ya can do somethin' that's important. Nothin's impossible when ya believe in it. Ain't no prison can hold ya then. Those stars, even if they're not in the sky, they're still beautiful. No one's told them 'bout it yet. They still believe in themselves. Long as they keep on shinin', what difference does it make what some scientist says about them bein' up there or not?"

Katharine looked off into the distance at the little clusters of farm lights on the horizon. "How long do you plan to keep drifting, Judd?"

"Why do you ask?"

"The world's changing. You can't just muscle your way through it forever. You've got to set down some roots, have some goals. You can't drift all your life."

"I don't know no other way."

"I'll teach you," she said, "if you'll let me."

He turned to kiss her gently on the cheek. "I'll try, Kate. But I ain't no prize, girl."

"You don't have to be a prize. I'll only demand one thing from you, Judd McCarthy."

"What's that?"

"You have to stop calling me Kate. It reminds me of the kind of name you'd give a mule."

"I'll try, Kate, but it'll take some gettin' used to," he laughed.

"There's a whole different world out there, isn't there, Judd?" she said, turning and looking into the distance. "A whole new world of things to experience, people to know."

"It ain't quite as pretty as it looks from here," he said. "But, if you'll let me, I'll protect you from the bad parts."

"Is that a promise?"

"That's a promise."

"I guess we decided something important tonight, didn't we?"

"Yes, Kate, we sure did."

"There you go again," she said, laughing and grabbing his huge hand in her two smaller ones.

McCarthy sneaked back into the construction camp late that night. He didn't tell the other members of the work crew that he was seeing Katharine because he knew he had a reputation with women, and he didn't want them to make crude jokes about his Lady Kate.

In the morning, he slipped out of the camp shortly after daybreak and made his way back to the Sumnerses' farm. It was a Saturday and Katharine had planned a picnic for the two of them down by the river. The picnic basket was on the front porch when he walked up to the house. Katharine was sitting in a swing that hung from a huge oak tree. She was very gently pushing herself back and forth, when he sneaked up behind her and began pushing her higher. An early frost had turned the leaves into various shades of reds and yellows, and her golden hair sparkled as the sunlight sifted through the branches and illuminated the individual strands. She laughed and leaned backward as he propelled her higher and higher into the blue sky.

Suddenly he pushed her too hard, and she fell out of the swing and landed in a heap. She lay motionless as he rushed over and knelt beside her.

"Kate, are ya all right?" he asked, a note of panic in his voice.

"I think so," she said, sitting up slowly.

"God, I'm sorry, girl," he said. He picked her up gently and carried her over to the softer grass beneath the oak tree. "Sometimes I don't know me own strength."

"I'm all right, Judd. Really, I'm all right," she insisted.

"I'm mighty sorry," he said, kissing her tenderly.

She returned his kiss passionately as they lay back on the grass. She would always remember the leaves rustling as the child that was Katharine Sumners became a woman under the oak tree, while the rope swing swayed in the autumn breeze and the windmill whispered to the sky.

Afterward, McCarthy was remorseful. He had crossed a barrier he had promised himself he would never cross. "I'm awful sorry, Kate," he whispered.

"There's no need to be sorry, Judd. We've already made an important decision, now haven't we?" she said, stroking the back of his neck.

"We sure have, Kate," he said softly and reassuringly as he held her close. "We sure have."

When Agnes Sumners returned from the East, she was furious to learn that her daughter had been seeing a common laborer during her absence. She insisted that Katharine stop seeing McCarthy immediately. Katharine, who was terrified of her mother, put up a brief struggle, then acquiesced—for a few days. But her love for McCarthy was too strong, and soon she was stealing forbidden hours with him.

It was during one of their meetings on the riverbank that they made plans to leave the area.

"Mother will never accept you, Judd," Katharine said. "It's no use. She has dreams of her daughter becoming the wife of a banker or governor."

"Is that what you want, Kate?"

"No. I don't even like going to small parties. How would I fit in with that kind of life? I'm . . ."

"You're what, Kate?"

"I'm kind of a misfit, I guess. Not too many men ever paid attention to me before you. I'm not really as pretty as you think I am."

"I don't want to hear that kind of talk, girl. You stop that nonsense."

"I'm . . . it's just . . ."

"What is it, Kate?"

"I'm twenty-seven years old, and I never truly knew a man until a couple of months ago when I met you. And that's all I want. There's nothing else that could make me happy now."

"That settles it then, girl," he said emphatically.

"What do you mean?"

"I get paid this Saturday. Three months' wages. It's not a lot. But it's enough to get us a start."

"What about Mother?"

"Ya can't live for your mother all your life. Someday you gotta make a choice. It might as well be now."

Katharine watched the river flow past the riverbank where they were sitting. "Where will we go?"

"They're buildin' a dam just south of here. Down by the Mississippi. They'll need help. We'll get married, save some money, and buy a place. Maybe over in the Dakotas. Land's still cheap there."

Katharine considered the offer carefully. "I'll go with you," she said firmly.

"Next Saturday I have ta go to Carson for Fred Hanley. I'll collect my wages and meet you right here, just before sundown."

"Just one thing, Judd . . ."

"Yes, I know. I'll learn ta call ya Katharine. It just takes some gettin' used to, that's all."

"No, just be here next Saturday." She kissed him lightly on the cheek, then stood and ran in the direction of her home.

Katharine was to see McCarthy only one more time before he disappeared. On the morning of October 12, 1926, he stood on the tracks of the Little Sioux Railroad and waved to her as she watched him from one of the gables of her home. He did an awkward dance step *for her benefit on the railroad trestles, then smiled broadly and disappeared in the direction of Carson.*

Later that day, she waited for him by the riverbank until long after the sun had set. When it became apparent that he was not coming back for her, she sadly picked up her white bonnet from the pile of dead leaves and walked across the fields to her home. Her mother greeted her at the front door.

"You're late! Where have you been all day, Katharine?" Agnes Sumners demanded.

"Down by the river," Katharine said, brushing past and entering the parlor.

"You were meeting Judd McCarthy, weren't you?" Agnes asked sternly.

"Yes."

"I thought I told you not to see him anymore."

"Mother, I'm twenty-seven years old. I have a right to live my life the way I choose!" Katharine yelled.

"He didn't come back to get you, did he?" Agnes asked coldly.

"No." The earlier firmness in Katharine's voice changed to fear, and she began to cry softly.

"And you're in trouble, aren't you?"

"Yes," she answered tearfully.

"Go upstairs, Katharine. We'll talk about this in the morning."

She slept fitfully that night. Once she woke to what she thought was the sound of horses neighing and what sounded like men talking in the yard below. Another time she thought she heard Mc-Carthy calling to her from somewhere in the darkness. Each time she woke, she only heard the rustling of the leaves as the evening breezes blew steadily through the trees outside her window.

In the morning, a black Ford coupe was waiting outside the gate of the farmhouse. As Katharine walked down the pathway, she looked briefly in the direction of the Little Sioux Railroad where she had last seen McCarthy. Then she climbed into the car and shut the door behind her. The Ford coupe chugged down the dirt road, turned east at the entrance to the Sumnerses' home, and quickly disappeared behind a small hill . . .

>≪≪≪≪

The elderly Katharine Sumners continued to rock back and forth on the tapestry rug as she finished telling her story. Finley sat across from her on the couch. The gramophone had long since quit playing.

"It must have been a sad trip for him," she said quietly. "He could have gone through life wrestling men like Tobin, but the world was changing all around him. I think he wanted to change with it, but he was a free spirit and needed room. They think he fled into the Dakotas."

"Yes, I know," Finley said. "I read the newspaper account of his disappearance."

"When he didn't return that evening, Mother insisted that I go back east. Judd McCarthy was the only man I had ever known. This farm was my only home. When I left, I gave up my entire world."

"Then you had a baby boy and signed the adoption papers as Katharine McCarthy. And after your mother died, you came back here to live?"

"How did you know it was a boy?" she asked, startled.

"I will tell you everything I know. First, tell me, did anything unusual happen the night you were planning to leave with McCarthy?"

"No, not that I remember. Mother was very angry. She knew I was going to have a baby. I think she knew long before that night."

"Did anything else happen?"

"No. I already told you I thought I heard horses neighing and men talking outside my window. But it must have been a dream. Please, tell me, what do you know about the baby?"

"Ms. Sumners, there is someone who needs you very much!"

It was late evening when Finley arrived back in Danvers. The hotel lobby was dark except for the light that glowed above the back counter and the lights that filtered in through the windows.

He passed the gleaming blue eyes of John J. Sylvester that stared out at him from the gold-leafed frame on the eastern wall. In the back of the lobby, Finley paused to study the smiling face of Judd McCarthy. Then he walked toward the stairs.

"Just a minute, Mr. Finley," the clerk said. He reached beneath the counter and pulled out a package. The edges were folded over and tied neatly together with twine. "Marsha Williams dropped this off for you earlier today."

"What is it?"

"Don't know. She wrote a note for you. It's on the back."

Finley turned the package over and pulled a tiny white envelope out from between the strands of twine. He opened it and stepped closer to the overhead light to read the note, which was penned in small, dainty letters across unlined paper:

Dear Mr. Finley,

    I was going through some things in the basement when I found this. The grandchildren of Frank and Helga Graham donated many books to the library several years ago. This was among them. Since you had asked earlier about Maureen McCarthy, I thought you might want to read this.

Marsha

P.S. Please return this when you have finished with it.

Finley struggled with the tight knots on the package as he climbed the two flights of stairs to his room. Finally, he pulled out his pocketknife and cut the twine. He unfolded the brown wrapping paper and pulled out a small book bound with green velvet. A tiny strap with a brass clasp at the end dangled beneath the book. A small brass lock was firmly set on the green velvet cover.

Finley turned the volume over in his hands as he walked through the darkened hallway toward his room. Once inside, he switched on the light and opened the book. The handwritten title, "The Diary of Maureen McCarthy," leaped out at him as he closed the door. He sat down in a chair next to the front window and started reading.

July 20, 1893

Today I arrived at the home of Frank and Helga Graham. I will work for them until I save enough money to go north, where there are better jobs and more opportunities.

I have come a long way to this strange land. I am already homesick for Ireland, but my mind is set. I will not return.

As I traveled from New York to Danvers, I was often overwhelmed by the many moods of America. It is a powerful land, one that is savage and gentle at the same time. But it is now my home, and from this day on I will speak nothing but good things about my new country.

The Grahams are very stern, uncompromising people. I hope I shall be accepted here . . .

><><><

He had rested for one entire day and part of the evening. Most of the time, he remained in the shed that was buried in the weeds and foliage of the abandoned farmyard. Periodically, he would hobble down to the river to soak his swollen feet in the cool water. He had watched the blood pour out of his wounds and flow away with the river, and he had felt the swelling subside.

Toward nightfall, he forced the leather boots over his feet. He laced the boots tightly and hobbled back to the riverbank. At first the pain was almost unbearable, but he dared not take the boots off. He had to get to Carson. As he walked along the riverbank, his feet became numb and he lost all feeling in them.

He followed the river north for several miles, then headed east across the fields toward Carson. He wanted to see the old railroad town at night to determine if it was as he had remembered it. Then he would find a place to hide. In midafternoon, at precisely the time that he had started back to Danvers on October 12, 1926, he would walk back to the railroad embankment and begin the long journey home.

There were very few lights glowing along the streets of the old railroad town. He remembered the rumors that the Little Sioux line planned to pull out of Carson in the 1920s. He knew that must have been what happened. The once teeming city was almost a ghost town.

He stood in the shadows and watched the few lights flicker weakly on Main Street. The street itself was badly in need of repair. Large holes had opened up in the dirt surface, and barriers were set up on several side streets. A large wooden sign hung from wires anchored into two buildings on opposite sides of the street. The name "Carson" was painted across the sign in faded white letters.

As he glanced at the sign, he remembered something else. He crossed the street, stepped over one of the barriers, and walked toward the old railroad yard. As he approached the depot, he could not keep his eyes off the stars. They seemed to be beckoning to him from beyond the darkness of space, telling him it was long past time for him to leave.

But he could not leave. Not yet!

He walked over to the western side of the depot, where another light shone on the wall just below the gable. He glanced down at a thin layer of straw spread lightly over a flat open area of dirt and rocks.

He had wrestled Tobin right there. Tobin had sweated and grunted and cursed as he rolled through the dirt and the rocks and straw.

The thought brought a smile to his lips, and he looked again at the stars.

What had happened to Tobin? What had happened to all of them?

"What are you doing back here?" a male voice suddenly demanded from behind him. As Joel turned around, a state trooper stepped out of the shadows next to the depot. "Who are you?"

"Judd McCarthy."

"Who?" the trooper asked suspiciously. The moonlight gleamed off the polished black barrel of his service revolver as he pointed it at Joel.

Joel did not move as the trooper cautiously walked over to where he was standing.

"What's your business back here?" the trooper demanded, stopping a few feet away.

Joel remained silent.

Suddenly, an owl hooted from above one of the depot gables, and the trooper glanced reflexively in that direction. As he did so, Joel's right arm snaked out and twisted the man's wrist, causing the revolver to fall into the straw.

"Why is it ya be sneakin' 'round behind me back?" Joel demanded angrily. He picked up the trooper by the shirt and slammed him against the depot wall.

"Who are you?" the trooper inquired meekly as his shoes beat harmlessly against the wood siding. Even in the darkness, Joel's eyes glowed with a fierce, almost insane inner fire. "Are you the escapee from Farmington?"

Joel tightened his grip on the man's shirt. He was reaching for the knife in his pocket when he heard voices on the other side of the depot. He listened carefully. Then he loosened his grip on the trooper's shirt, allowing the terrified man to slip slowly to the ground.

"Help! I'm back here!" the trooper yelled as he scrambled up a slight incline and disappeared around the corner of the depot.

Joel stared at a piece of the trooper's shirt he was still holding. The voices grew nearer and more threatening. He reached down into the straw and extracted the revolver.

He had carried a revolver with him the day he journeyed from Carson to Danvers. It was much heavier than this one. But if he had carried a weapon, why had he been unable to protect himself?

As Joel thrust the gun into the waistband of his trousers, two more troopers appeared around the corner. Joel heard several muffled threats and two sharp warning shots as he leaped into a thicket. He scrambled down an embankment. Behind him, the shouts and warnings grew more distant as he disappeared into the prairie.

CHAPTER FOURTEEN

Early the next morning, Finley made a hurried trip to Farmington. He knew Schlepler had honored many police requests to visit crime scenes to solve murders or locate missing persons. He hoped to persuade the retired psychic to accompany him to the Sumnerses' farm so together they could visit some of the places where McCarthy was last seen before he disappeared. Finley also hoped his old friend might help him find Joel and rid the young man of the terrible demon that was gnawing at his soul and threatening his life.

Maureen McCarthy's diary and his conversation with Katharine Sumners had provided most of the remaining pieces to the elaborate puzzle. There were only a few questions that Finley still could not answer. He didn't know what had happened to Maureen after her escape from Farmington. He also didn't know how Judd McCarthy had been killed, and why his powerful spirit lingered on in Joel more than three decades later.

As he walked through Farmington's gates, Finley spotted Schlepler standing next to some dead vines on one of the granite walls. Schlepler's hands were thrust into his coat pockets, and he wore an oversized, wrinkled gray hat that came down over the top of his ears. Below the brim, his sad eyes gazed out at the many vines and tendrils that clung to the wall.

"You were right, Aurther," Finley said as he approached. "Your flowers were dying."

"No," Schlepler replied, "they are only becoming a part of the vine. All along this wall, wherever the flowers have died, they have left a notch in the tendrils. In the spring, out of these notches will grow other stems and flowers, and out of those still other stems and flowers. On it goes, year after year, decade after decade, century after century, until the vines and flowers will cover this entire wall. They build on one another. Of course, it won't happen in my lifetime or yours. But it will happen."

"I've figured out most of the Hampton case," Finley said. "But I still need your help."

"You don't know what happened to Maureen McCarthy, do you?"

"No," Finley admitted.

"It's not important that you know anything more about her, Ned."

"Why do you say that?"

"The puzzle you are trying to solve has some pieces that do not fit. It would be inhuman to pretend otherwise."

"What are you trying to say?"

"She is one of those people who disappear into the human race and is never heard from again. It is what was meant to be. Neither you nor I can change it."

"Are you saying I should forget about her?"

"She was wrongly judged and suffered for it," Schlepler said solemnly. "But her soul is free. Your concern must be for the young man who wanders alone out there, searching for something he does not understand." Schlepler gestured toward the front gate and the fields beyond. "He harbors a soul that has yet to be freed from this world."

"That's why I need your help. I want you to go with me to the Sumnerses' farm."

"You do not need me, Ned," Schlepler said. "You need only to return there yourself. Your answer will be waiting for you."

"Aurther, please!" Finley pleaded.

"It will be waiting for you," Schlepler repeated. He gestured toward the mental institution. "Susan is waiting for you in the lobby. Take her with you. You need *her* help, not mine."

Finley watched Schlepler shuffle away, and then he walked over to the hospital. Susan rushed out the front door and met him at the bottom of the staircase.

"They've found Joel!" she gasped.

"Where?" Finley demanded.

"Someone reported seeing him in Danvers two nights ago. And last night a state trooper found him wandering through the streets of Carson."

"Did they capture him?"

Susan shook her head. "No, he got away before they could make an arrest. They're looking for him north of Carson. They think he fled in that direction."

"He'll be coming south, along the Little Sioux line," Finley said emphatically. He grabbed Susan's arm and rushed her toward the gate. "We have to get back to the Sumnerses' farm."

"Wait! I couldn't find a babysitter for Aggy," Susan said as she tried to match Finley's long strides. "One of the orderlies took her over to a park while I talked to security."

"We'll pick her up on the way," Finley said as they rushed through the gate. "I also have some things to tell you. I think I've figured out most of what happened on October 12th in 1926, and what it all has to do with Joel."

The day was almost as he remembered it. Signs of late autumn were all around him. The stubble of recently harvested wheat fields poked out of the parched earth alongside the railroad embankment, and dead leaves drifted across the countryside. Hen pheasants clucked contentedly in the brush, while an occasional rooster pheasant emitted a shrill mating call.

And he was walking on the Little Sioux line, moving south toward Danvers and Kate.

The sky was a different color than he remembered. It had been blue—bright blue. Now, as he looked to the west, the sun attempted to break through a gray overcast sky, but it was quickly covered by a layer of clouds.

The leather boots he had stolen crunched through the dry weeds that covered the crossties and rusty tracks. His eyes moved constantly across the landscape, searching for any movement in the brush.

As he walked, he thought about the song. He had sung it many times before, but the words were only a distant memory. He hummed the tune as he surveyed the terrain. The song brought a smile to his lips, and he knew it had once made him happy.

Why couldn't he remember the words?

Ahead of him, in the marsh, the crickets began to chirp, and frogs leaped off fallen logs and splashed into the shallow slough. On the edge of the slough, dead reeds swayed as the breezes arched the vegetation gracefully toward the earth.

Something happened to him in there. He thought someone was hiding in the thick brush, and he threw a rock into the marsh. Then he reached cautiously into the reeds with his huge, callused hands.

In the dried vegetation, a rooster pheasant lay dying. He placed his hand on the bird and felt a convulsive movement in the animal's chest as it shuddered and died. It saddened him, and he buried the pheasant in the soil alongside the embankment. Then he stood and continued walking.

As he stepped out of the marsh, the gray haze parted, revealing the sun as it moved steadily toward the western horizon. He watched the sun cast shadows across the fields. In the distance, the Little Sioux River curled around the small town and continued on its course toward the Mississippi.

Off to the side of the embankment was where it happened. A sudden gust of wind blew through the trees, sending dead leaves tumbling into the prairie. Someone waved to him from the edge of the thicket. As she stepped out from the shadows, he recognized who it was and he walked over to her.

"So, at last we meet, Mr. McCarthy," she said to him. She smiled strangely and gestured for him to join her. "Do you know who I am?"

"Yes, ma'am," he said politely. "You be Kate's mother."

"Yes, I certainly am." She introduced herself by holding out one tiny, limp hand. He had felt uncomfortable shaking it. "I understand you are about to become my son-in-law," she said. He could not tell if she was being sarcastic, or if she was simply trying to make him comfortable. Something about the way she said it was not right.

"Yes, ma'am."

"Do you think that I disapprove of your marriage to my daughter?"

"That be what Kate says, yes."

Agnes Sumners sighed deeply, and again the peculiar smile spread across her lips. "Mr. McCarthy, I do not disapprove of you marrying my daughter. What I disapprove of is the fact that you feel you must sneak around behind my back to do it. I know that you are on your way to meet Katharine, and I know you are planning to run away together. That is Katharine's decision, of course. But if I am not to be a part of your wedding plans, could you at least give Katharine something from me, so she will know I approve? Then the two of you can decide whether to go ahead with your plans, or whether you would prefer to be married right here in Danvers. With my blessing."

He studied her sharp, piercing green eyes to determine if she was telling him the truth, or if she was disguising her true feelings for some other reason.

"Don't you trust me, Mr. McCarthy?" she asked, almost teasing him.

"Yes, ma'am, I trust you. Do you want me to get Kate? She's waiting for me . . ."

"No, like I said, Katharine can make up her own mind once you bring her something from me. I have a family heirloom I want you to give to her, a silver plate that has been used in the weddings on my late husband's side of the family for more than a century. When Katharine sees it, she will know my true feelings. Then the two of you can decide how you would like to be married."

"Yes, Mrs. Sumners. I'll bring it to her."

"Very good, Mr. McCarthy. Please, come this way with me. The plate is back at the house."

They had walked out of the thicket. In the distance, the gables of the farmhouse rose out of the prairie. As they walked across the fields, he felt the fading sun against the back of his neck. He knew Katharine would be happy that her mother approved of the marriage.

"I will only keep you for a minute," Agnes Sumners said as they walked up to the farmhouse. "Please, come this way."

Finley directed the Studebaker toward the church steeple, grain elevator, and water tower in the distance. Aggy sat in the backseat, watching the countryside roll by the rear window. Susan sat in the passenger seat.

Finley had been strangely quiet for the first few miles of the trip to Danvers, and Susan had thought it best not to interrupt his thoughts.

"Susan, I talked to Katharine Sumners," he suddenly said.

"She's alive?" Susan asked, surprised.

"Yes."

"I thought you said she was killed in a fire in Chicago."

"That was another young woman. Katharine, for many reasons at that point in her life, wanted everyone in Danvers to think she had died in the fire in Chicago."

"Why?"

"She was pregnant with Joel at the time."

"Are you certain she's Joel's mother?"

"Yes. Joel is the son of Katharine Sumners and Judd McCarthy. She signed the name Katharine McCarthy to the adoption certificate even though she wasn't married."

"What was she able to tell you?"

"She was pregnant with McCarthy's son when he disappeared somewhere between Carson and Danvers. She was waiting for him down by the river. They were planning to leave together, but someone got in the way of their plans."

"Sylvester and the Hanley brothers?"

"No, it was someone else. Someone who despised McCarthy even more than the Hanley brothers."

"Who was that?"

"That part of the puzzle goes back to the 1890s," Finley said. "Marsha Williams, a museum curator and archivist in Danvers, found the diary Maureen McCarthy kept during her first two years in this country. She gave it to me. It answers a lot of questions."

"Was she Judd McCarthy's mother, as you suspected?" Susan asked.

"Yes. She came to this country to tend house for Frank and Helga Graham. She planned for it to be a temporary job, only until she could save enough money to move farther north. She came here full of hope and idealism, but she found something quite unexpected when she arrived. Most of the people in Carver County were not like her. She was an independent young woman, a free spirit who loved to drink with the men in the saloons. She was also Irish in a predominantly Scandinavian and British county. The social elite of Danvers looked on her with scorn, especially when many of their husbands became enthralled with this charming Irish girl. Later their scorn turned to anger and, finally, hatred when people in the community began to whisper about her pregnancy. They believed that any errant husband could have been the father. They trumped up a case against her and had her committed to Farmington."

"Who *was* the father?" Susan asked.

"Let me fit in some of the smaller pieces of the puzzle, then I will insert the final piece. Maureen McCarthy was hated by two groups of people in the county. The very proper, stern-faced men and women whose portraits now hang in the Danvers library thought she had the morals of a prostitute. Then, of course, men like Fred Hanley hated her because she would have nothing to do with them. Apparently Hanley tried in every way to coerce her into a relationship, but she was a shrewd judge of character. She hated him and spit in his face. Hanley threatened to kill her, but she laughed at him. On the surface, she might have appeared to be promiscuous, but the reality is that she knew only one man."

"Maynard?"

"No," Finley said, shaking his head. "Maynard allowed himself to become the object of the community's contempt and accusations. After all, he was a single man, and it was better that he be the father of her child than a married man with a family. In the process, she fell in love with Maynard, even though she was carrying another man's child."

"Is that why he killed himself?" Susan asked.

"Maynard befriended her during the early months of her pregnancy. But his compassion for her brought the wrath of the community down on him. He knew who the real father was, but he never revealed his name. He was protecting someone very close to him, and he undoubtedly loved Maureen. When the community succeeded in getting her committed to Farmington on some trumped-up moral charges, Maynard became extremely depressed. He went to the one man who should have stood beside her, but that man refused to get involved. Feeling totally powerless to help, and knowing the living nightmare she would experience at Farmington, Maynard ended up committing suicide. When the ice was breaking on the river, he threw himself off a bridge. They found his body wrapped around a tree miles downstream."

Finley drove the Studebaker through Danvers's Main Street. Within seconds, the car sped out into the countryside northwest of town.

"Who *was* the father of her child if it wasn't Maynard?" Susan asked.

"Judd McCarthy's father was Oscar Sumners," Finley said, glancing over at Susan.

"My God!" she blurted out. "Are you sure?"

"Yes. Maureen describes the relationship in her diary. It was one she came to regret after she met Maynard. And, of course, Oscar was a married man."

"That would make Judd and Katharine brother and sister!" Susan exclaimed in disbelief.

"Half brother and sister," Finley corrected her.

"Did either of them know that?"

"No. They were innocent victims of fate. I doubt that Maureen ever told her son anything about his past. And, of course, Oscar and Agnes Sumners wanted to forget the whole thing. They didn't want to taint the family tree by acknowledging an illegitimate son. So obviously they never told their daughter she had a half-brother. It was just pure coincidence that McCarthy drifted back into the lives of the Sumnerses."

"Did you tell Katharine that McCarthy was her half-brother?"

"No."

"Why?"

"I didn't know about it then. Even so, she's lived too long with those dreams," Finley said. "It would serve no purpose to take them away from her now."

Susan struggled to make some sense of everything he was telling her. "What does all of this have to do with McCarthy's disappearance?" she asked.

"Sylvester and the Hanleys wanted McCarthy out of the way for obvious reasons. Somehow Fred Hanley knew McCarthy was the illegitimate son of Oscar Sumners and Maureen McCarthy. How he found out, I do not know. Hanley seemed to have ways of finding out what he needed to know about people, things he would then use to his own advantage. Whatever the case, he told Agnes that McCarthy was the child her husband had fathered with Maureen. Agnes Sumners was none too stable anyhow. When she heard this and was told that McCarthy was coming back from Carson alone to get her daughter, who was pregnant, she found a way to get rid of him. In fact, I think that's why your husband threatened to take your daughter's life. It was the name Aggy that provoked him. He associated it with Agnes Sumners. A simple nickname concocted by the children in your neighborhood is what almost cost your daughter her life."

Susan had been so involved in their conversation that she had forgotten that Aggy was sitting in the back of the car. She glanced at her daughter, who was seemingly oblivious to what was taking place in the front seat. Aggy smiled innocently at her mother and looked back out the window.

"If Joel and Aggy are the products of an incestuous relationship, what does that mean?" Susan stammered, turning again to face Finley.

"It was an accidentally incestuous relationship," Finley said. "McCarthy and Katharine did not know they were half brother and sister. There was no moral issue involved."

"Still, aren't there many physical and psychological consequences?"

"Yes, there can be a Jekyll–Hyde effect. Virtues and vices, strengths and weaknesses can all be accentuated. Great talents and also mental defects have accompanied incestuous births."

"And madness?"

"Yes," Finley replied reluctantly.

"Is that Joel's problem?"

"I don't know, but I think it's much more than that."

Susan glanced again at Aggy. "What about the second generation?" Susan asked. "How will Aggy be affected by all of this?"

"I don't think anyone knows how the second generation is
affected by an incestuous relationship in the family tree. Theo-
retically, the effects should be nullified by the second and third
generations, but that's no guarantee. It bears watching in your
daughter." Finley turned sharply onto the road leading to the
Sumnerses' farmhouse. "We're almost there," he announced.
"Katharine should be expecting us."

"You said Agnes Sumners was responsible for McCarthy's
disappearance," Susan said, her eyes fixed on the Victorian farmhouse. "What did she do to him?"

"That's what we plan to find out," Finley said.

The dust from the driveway billowed out from underneath the
Studebaker as it came to a halt next to the lath fence.

"Dr. Finley, look, that's Joel over there!" Susan screamed as
she pointed out the car window.

Joel had just emerged from behind some tall brush near the
windmill. He walked over to the fence and paused to stare at the
gables of the farmhouse.

"Come on!" Finley said. "Grab your daughter. Let's get over
there!"

"Is it safe?" Susan asked as she reached into the back for
Aggy.

"Yes. He's not thinking about us. He's thinking about things
that happened a long time ago."

Finley helped Susan and Aggy out of the car.

"What's wrong with Daddy?" Aggy asked softly. "He looks
funny."

"Shh," Susan said, quieting the little girl.

Joel looked puzzled and dazed as he moved his eyes across
the farmyard. A slight breeze blew, rustling the dead leaves that
littered the lawn and causing the windmill to creak. Joel studied
the silo, the swing dangling by one rope from the oak tree, and

the sun-bleached wagon, shorn of one wheel and weathering in dying, waist-high vegetation.

The trees were in fuller foliage then. Red and yellow leaves dancing in the trees and tumbling out into the fields, while the windmill whistled a much gayer song. Underneath the leaves, the girl in the white linen dress soared higher and higher into a blue sky as he pushed her from behind with his great strength. The sunlight sparkled off her golden hair and her laughter rang out beneath the huge oak tree . . .

Joel heard the sound of the gramophone coming from the farmhouse, and he looked in that direction. Katharine Sumners was sitting on a porch swing that squeaked on its chains as she pushed herself back and forth in slow, delicate movements. She looked weary and sad, and seemed not to notice her visitors.

As Joel walked up to the porch, he grew increasingly excited. He approached the swing with unrestrained joy, then leaned over to look closely into Katharine's eyes.

"Kate, me lass," he teased, "why so sad? Would ya take a penny fur yur thoughts now, girl?" He reached into his pants pocket as though to extract a coin, all the time continuing to tease her with his eyes.

"Who are you?" she asked, completely bewildered.

"Come now, lass. I got a present for ya. But first I gotta see me Lady Kate smile."

Katharine reached slowly out to touch him, but Joel leaped playfully out of the way and did an awkward dance step on the porch.

"Judd, is it really you?" she asked softly.

"Who'd ya think it was, lass? That little pup down the road yur mother wants ya ta marry? Yes, Kate, it's Judd McCarthy himself, bigger 'n' meaner'n anyone else in the county. That is, till he met you."

Katharine glanced at Finley, her eyes imploring him to advise her on how she should respond to the strange figure in front of her. Sensing her confusion, Finley nodded gently, urging her to interact with Joel as though McCarthy himself was standing on her porch after a thirty-three-year absence.

"You'd better learn to call me Katharine, Judd," she said to Joel, playing his game, though a little reluctantly. "You know how I hate the name Kate."

"Sorry, Kate, I keep forgettin'. But I'll get it right one of these days." He leaned over, still teasing her. "I gotta present for ya. Ya want ta see it?"

"Did you? You went to Carson, now didn't you? Where'd you get that kind of money, Judd?"

"Wrestlin'," he proclaimed proudly, rising again to his full height. "I beat Tobin, Kate. Fair 'n' square. Had 'em on his back in five minutes. There's no Norwegian alive can whip Judd McCarthy."

"You told me you'd stop that foolishness," Katharine admonished him gently.

"I said *after* we were married," he corrected her. "Now you take this and wear it for me."

"Will nothing ever tame you?" she asked, shaking her head in mock disgust.

As Joel searched in his pants pockets, he became more frantic, and his mood changed from joviality to confusion and finally anger.

"It's not here! Where did . . . where did I put it?"

"Judd, please . . ."

Suddenly Joel leaped off the porch and ran to the corner of the house. He looked wildly in all directions.

Something was not right. When he had walked up to the farmhouse with Agnes Sumners, he expected her to go right up to the porch. Instead, she took him around to the back of the house.

"Mr. McCarthy, I hope I will not shock you when I say I know Katharine is pregnant with your child," she said as they walked around the corner of the house. "I think it is very noble of you to marry her when you could very easily have said to yourself that it was just another easy conquest."

"Kate never told me about that," he said. The statement surprised him. "'Course it don't make no difference, but she never told me. It's just all the more reason for us to get married."

"She never told me, either. But we mothers have a way of knowing about those things." Agnes stopped and looked at him with her sharp green eyes. "Maybe Katharine was afraid to tell you for fear you'd leave her?"

"It would never cross me mind to leave Kate."

"As I said, that is a very noble gesture, Mr. McCarthy." She headed toward an embankment behind the house. "Now, I've had this silver tray in storage for years, and I just didn't want to go

down there by myself to get it. The rats, you know. I'm terrified of them . . ."

Joel pointed emphatically at something behind the house. "It's back there!" he yelled angrily.

He drew the state trooper's revolver out of the waistband of his trousers, raised it to shoulder height, and turned slowly. He pointed it menacingly at Finley, Aggy, and the two women who were gathered in front of the house. Then, as though venting his rage on the old Victorian structure, he fired six shots into the gable above the porch. He continued squeezing the trigger long after the last shell had been spent, until the monotonous clicking of the firing pin seemed to pull him out of his trance. As he lowered the gun, the look on his face changed from anger and bitterness to a confused sadness. Tears filled his eyes and he stared at the revolver as though contemplating some deep, impenetrable mystery.

Suddenly he reared back and threw the revolver into the field. Almost in the same motion, he bent over and extracted a rusty iron fence post from out of the leaves that covered the yard. Grasping it in his right hand, he ran around to the back of the house.

As Joel disappeared, Finley approached Katharine. "What's back there?" he demanded.

"Nothing . . . Just . . . an old cellar," she stammered.

"I don't know why my husband didn't bury this cellar and be done with it," Agnes said as she led him over to a large wooden door protruding from the embankment. "But he always said we needed the storage space. And, of course, it is protection against tornados. Now, Mr. McCarthy, if you will just lift this door for me."

The door creaked on its hinges as he lifted it off its concrete foundation and watched it flop open against the ground. Several concrete steps led down to a second, much larger door at the bottom. Three large pieces of lumber stretched across the door, fitting snugly into huge metal clamps bolted into the walls of the staircase.

"My husband had this reinforced several years ago," she said as she inserted a key into one of the two large padlocks. "We have some valuable pieces of silver down here . . ."

Finley grasped Katharine by both shoulders and looked into her eyes. "Were the men working back by the cellar the morning you left to have the baby?"

She searched carefully into her memories. "No. But mother must have had it buried sometime before I left. She said it was a haven for rats. It was only in the last year or two that the rains washed away the dirt . . ."

"Let's get back there!" Finley said, grasping her firmly by the hand and pulling her out of the porch swing.

"Dr. Finley, what is it?" Susan pleaded as he led the two women and Aggy around to the back of the house.

"We need to get back there," Finley repeated, ignoring the question.

As they approached the half-buried cellar, Joel was beating on the heavy wooden door with the fence post. Then he forced the post behind the rusty lock and tore it off.

"Joel, what are you doing?" Susan pleaded as he dropped to his knees and tore madly at the dirt blocking the entrance to the cellar.

"Leave him alone," Finley said firmly, restraining her.

When the dirt was removed from the bottom of the door, Joel grabbed it with both hands, ripped it from its rusty hinges, and plunged into the cellar. There was a loud crash as the second door collapsed. Then there was a hollow echo from somewhere in the darkness, and finally a deep, overwhelming silence.

The second cellar door creaked open slowly. He immediately heard the soft padding feet scurrying across the floor.

"As you can see," Agnes Sumners said, "it has certainly become a haven for rats."

"Yes, ma'am," he replied. "Do you have a lantern?"

"No, but I can tell you where the tray is. It's in a large box, way over there in the back corner. Can you see it?"

"No, ma'am."

"If you'll just go over there, I'm sure you'll find it. I wouldn't ask you to, but I know it'll mean so much to Katharine. Just bring the box out here and we can go back outside and look through it."

He walked into the darkness, brushing aside the cobwebs as he felt his way cautiously across the floor to the other side of the cellar. He could feel nothing against the far wall except the cold concrete.

"There's nothing over here except an old bench and some jars, Mrs. Sumners," he said as he groped around in the darkness.

"Oh, I think that's where you are wrong, Mr. McCarthy," he heard her say. The tone in her voice had changed completely. She seemed almost to be mocking his efforts to find the box she had instructed him to find. "You're in there, now aren't you? And so are the rats!"

THE SEARCH FOR JUDD McCARTHY

"What?" he asked as he turned to face her. Her body was sil-houetted against the sunlight outside the partially open cellar door. She turned slightly, and as the light illuminated her face, a strange, evil smile spread across her lips as she looked back at him.

"You didn't really think I would let you marry my daughter, did you?" she asked scornfully.

"What do you mean?"

He heard the hinges squeak as the door started to close.

"Katharine is too good for you. You belong in here—with all the other rats."

"Why?" he yelled as she closed the door, blocking out the sun-light. He suddenly realized that he had been set up. He made a lunge toward the door, but it was too late. She had lured him too far into the cellar. He heard the pieces of lumber fall into their slots.

"Why?" she replied, taunting him from the other side of the door. Then he heard an insane, muffled laugh. "Because she's your sister, Mr. McCarthy!"

"So she lured him in here," Finley said softly, staring into the cellar.

"What do you mean?" Susan said, not comprehending. "Dr. Finley—"

"Katharine," Finley said, turning to face the older woman, "your mother tricked Judd into this cellar the day you were to meet him by the river."

"What are you trying to say?" she whispered, unwilling or un-able to comprehend what Finley was telling her.

"Your mother lured him in here," Finley explained. "She must have made up some excuse. Probably told him she would accept the marriage, then asked him to get something for her out of the cellar. He probably sensed something was wrong, but he wanted to make peace with your mother. And he went in here anyhow, most likely against his better judgment."

"Oh, my God!" Katharine exclaimed.

"Then she locked the doors and Fred Hanley buried the cellar. Even with all of his strength, Judd couldn't break down that door and dig through six feet of solid earth."

Finley turned away from the two women and walked down the concrete steps. From the light filtering through the doorway, he surveyed the contents of the cellar. A broken bench, smashed crates, the butt handle of a knife, and a .45-caliber revolver lit-tered the floor. Unable to free himself from his prison, McCarthy had vented his rage on the contents of the cellar, destroying almost everything before he died.

Joel lay prostrate on the floor. He did not move. He did not even appear to be breathing. Nearby, a large human skeleton was half buried in the wreckage next to a canvas bag. The bag's contents, worthless pieces of paper cut to the size of currency, were scattered over the floor.

But it did not end there. It was days later. Maybe weeks. Maybe even months. It did not matter. Surrounded by the impenetrable darkness, time ceased to exist. Except as measured by his failing strength, his dying will.

At first he lashed out frantically, until the blade of the hunting knife shattered. When that failed, he fired the revolver into the darkness. He watched the orange flames spit out of the barrel as the muffled gunshots echoed harmlessly around him. Still it did not end.

And each time he fell, the rats would scurry over to sniff at his mildewed clothing. Bolder they became with the passage of time, until he would lash out with the butt end of the knife, sending them scurrying away. But always they came back. Relentlessly. And he grew weaker.

Sometime, near the end, he heard the scream. Loud and shrill, it echoed in the darkness. First in anger, then in agony. Growing weaker as his strength deserted him. When it too failed, he again heard the rats' tiny feet moving ceaselessly, relentlessly.

When the end came, he was lying face down. The rats sensed that he had lost his strength, his will to fight. He heard them padding softly across the ground to where he lay. They sniffed at his clothing and brushed against his cheek. Then a sharp pain tore through his arm like a thousand needles penetrating his flesh. But he was too weak to care. He lay there, enduring the pain until it turned into a moist numbness.

As the life poured out of his body, he was filled with rage at the horror of how he had been duped. And even as he yielded to the darkness, his soul held firm against the night and refused to accept what had been left undone.

It was then that he thought of the locket. He reached for his pocket to see if it was still there. But the numbness had spread over his entire body, and his arm would not move . . .

"He tore this place apart trying to get out of here," Finley observed. He knelt down to examine the fake paper money on the floor. Suddenly, Joel blinked twice and stared at the doorway. Katharine, Susan, and Aggy were silhouetted against the rays of sunlight that entered the dark cellar for the first time in more than three decades. Susan held her daughter close to her chest.

Joel raised himself slowly to one knee, stood, and walked awkwardly toward the doorway. Blinking repeatedly against the sunlight, he stepped out of the cellar and turned to face the women.

At first he did not seem to recognize them. Susan fearfully clutched her daughter, not knowing what he would do next. Then Joel slowly reached his hand out to her.

"Susan, Aggy," he whispered, gently pulling them close to him.

They stood together, locked in an embrace, until Susan gestured toward Katharine and said in a voice filled with deep emotion, "Joel, this is your mother, Katharine."

Seemingly confused, Joel turned slowly toward Katharine Sumners. He reached out his hand as the fading sunlight burst between them. She also reached out to him. As they were about to touch, Joel paused, his hand a few inches above hers, and he dropped the locket he had found on the cellar floor into her palm. The chain dangled from his hand to hers, connecting the two of them as sunlight sparkled off the golden links.

Behind them, Finley stepped out of the darkness of the cellar. He paused when he heard a faint, almost mournful sound somewhere in the distance. As he glanced overhead, a lone bull goose, delayed in its departure from the north, spread its magnificent white wings against the sky and echoed a lonely mating call at the departing sun as it flew southward—following, or so it seemed, the course of the Little Sioux River to where it bent into the Mississippi, and from there into the Great Sea beyond . . .

The things that are meant to be—will be. The spirit confined in this cell refused to die in his own lifetime, but rather lived on into the next generation to place a locket in the hand of his Lady Kate.

THE END

ABOUT THE AUTHOR

DENNIS M. CLAUSEN grew up in west central Minnesota. There, he gained a close, intimate knowledge of the small towns and the lives they harbored. They provide the inspiration for *The Search for Judd McCarthy*, which was a best-selling paperback original when first published under a different title in 1982. Clausen is also the author of *Prairie Son* (1999), an award-winning book of creative nonfiction. This work recreates his father's struggles as an adopted child to survive the Great Depression in a farm home where he was treated more as a worker than a son. In addition to his creative work, Clausen has authored textbooks, including *Screenwriting and Literature* (2009), which explores the relationships between writing screenplays and writing novels. For over thirty years, he has been teaching literature and screenwriting courses at the University of San Diego and has written editorials and columns for various newspapers. He enjoys writing stories that combine and transcend traditional literary genres. He has several works in progress, including a novel, *The Sins of Rachel Sims*, which is a sequel to *The Search for Judd McCarthy*.